GIRLS LIKE GIRLS

A NOVEL

HAYLEY KIYOKO

WEDNESDAY BOOKS
NEW YORK

This is a work of fiction. All of the names, characters, organizations, places, and events portrayed in this work are either products of the author's imagination or used fictitiously.

Published in the United States by Wednesday Books, an imprint of St. Martin's Publishing Group.

For information, address St. Martin's Publishing Group, 120 Broadway, New York, NY 10271.

www.wednesdaybooks.com

Designed by Devan Norman
Illustrations by Rhys Davies

The Library of Congress Cataloging-in-Publication Data has cataloged the hardcover edition as follows:

Names: Kiyoko, Hayley, author.
Title: Girls like girls : a novel / Hayley Kiyoko.
Description: First edition. | New York : Wednesday Books, 2023. |
Identifiers: LCCN 2023002001 | ISBN 9781250817631 (hardcover) | ISBN 9781250817648 (ebook)
Subjects: CYAC: Moving, Household—Fiction. | LGBTQ+ people—Fiction. | Grief—Fiction. | Interpersonal relations—Fiction. | LCGFT: Novels.
Classification: LCC PZ7.1.K6326 Gi 2023 | DDC [Fic]—dc23
LC record available at https://lccn.loc.gov/2023002001

ISBN 978-1-250-47074-4 (movie tie-in edition)

Our books may be purchased in bulk for specialty retail/wholesale, literacy, corporate/premium, educational, and subscription box use. Please contact MacmillanSpecialMarkets@macmillan.com.

Wednesday Books Movie Tie-In Edition: 2026

10 9 8 7 6 5 4 3 2 1

This is dedicated to anyone who has ever felt hopeless
and didn't believe they could have a happy ending.
You are worthy.

Please note that this book contains themes
about and nongraphic references to suicide

ONE

Do you want to know a secret?

I mean, when has the answer to that question ever been no? Even if you're sure it's gonna lead to something like doom, there's still a part of you that needs to answer yes, right? A part that wants to *know* more than anything else.

I know all about secrets. The good ones: Christmas presents and ditching class, hidden boxes of Funfetti mix for birthday cakes. And the hard secrets—the ones that gnaw until they work their way free of you like a scream. The bad ones that are less secret, more lie: *I'm fine, Coley* (she wasn't). *I'll call my therapist* (she didn't). *I'll be here after school* (liar, liar, liar).

Once upon a time, I thought I had a handle on it. A juggling act: Mom's secrets and mine, never the two should meet. But it all came crashing down.

And now I have no mom and a dad who barely has a hold on the meaning of that word, and there are way too many things simmering under my skin. Secrets that are more like truths when you winnow them down:

I'm not like other girls.

And no, not in that bullshit way guys use to try to compliment you. Please—give me some credit here.

You watch the movies, you hear enough songs, you read the love stories, and they all tell you how it's *supposed* to go:

Girl is double-braided, freckled sweetness. Light-up sneakers and torn jeans as she plays and skips and twirls on the city sidewalk. Girl is unbothered. There's no gnawing question. There's no *What if you're . . .*

So Girl grows up. Girl gets the boy next door tripping over his feet, or the football player missing his throws, or the quiet geek proving his worth (while getting hot during a makeover montage; let's be real). And then Girl marches off, arm in arm with her guy, happily ever after. The road's so well-worn there's probably a trench in the middle of it. It's the road you're supposed to choose. The one everyone expects you to travel.

But you, the girl not like other girls . . . you look down that road, and it's not shiny and bright. The thought of it doesn't make you feel any of the ways ever described in story or song. And those people, they're not all lying—which means there's a secret you're keeping even from yourself. That feeling you can't—and now maybe won't—name.

You push it down. You ignore it like it's a plant that'll shrivel away. But you're the thing that's shrinking.

And one day you learn: it's not that you're not like other girls.

It's just that you've never met a girl like you.

And then, you do. You meet *her*.

And suddenly the songs make sense.

TWO

LJ User: SonyatSunrisex0Ox [Public Entry]

Date: June 8, 2006

[**Mood:** blah]

[**Music:** "SOS"–Rihanna]

Bored. Bored. Bored.

Nothing ever changes in this town. Except I think it's getting hotter. Maybe that Al Gore movie is right.

I've been reduced to talking about the weather, sweeties. Someone save me from this terrible fate! Tell me there's a party or a plan or something happening tomorrow. I am in desperate need of distraction.

xoox

Sonya

Comments:

TOnofTrentOnnn:

I can distract you anytime.

SonyatSunrisex0Ox:

Ew, Trenton. That's not what I was talking about.

SJbabayy:
Lol, Trenton, do you ever think of anything else?

SJbabayy:
Want to hit that club tomorrow? Alex was saying he knew a guy who could sneak us in.

SonyatSunrisex00x:
Yes! Call Alex!

MadeYouBrooke23:
Didn't Trenton tell you? I told him to when we were at the piercing studio. It's Lake Day, baby! But I have to wait for my mom to go to work cause she's still mad I got my belly button pierced.

SJBabayy:
Wait. You got your belly button done and you didn't ask ME to come with?

SJBabayy:
Why was Trenton with you?

SonyatSunrisex00x:
Yeah, Brooke. Why was Trenton with you?

MadeYouBrooke23:
He offered me a ride cause I couldn't borrow my mom's car since she's all anti-piercing. Remember? I told you about this! Weirdos.

SonyatSunrisex00x:
Whatever. Call when you get to the lake, I guess.

THREE

So here's the thing: I'm not supposed to be here. Not like I've ever felt like I'm supposed to be anywhere. I'm never white enough. Never Asian enough. Never . . . enough.

But here I am in Bumfuck Nowhere, Oregon. There are more trees than people around.

I miss the sounds of *life*, you know? People on the streets. Sirens. Honking and talking and the lights and the buzz that come with a bunch of homes crammed into a tiny space.

But here, it's quiet and spread out, and crickets chirp—like, actually *chirp*. The shadows the trees cast everywhere make it all even greener, until you're so soaked in the palette you might as well be a leprechaun.

I'm not supposed to be here, yet I am. Flung into the middle of the Oregon wilderness with my not-so-long-lost-just-deadbeat father. But I guess some things force some deadbeats to rise to the occasion—the occasion here being there was no one else left.

Mom was gone. And that felt so real and so fake at the same time.

I didn't want to move here. I told him as much. Once

I realized who he was—which took a full ten seconds after I opened the door and stared at this frayed man, with gray in his hair, trying to place him.

I guess he *was* lost in a way. Lost inside fuzzy memories that don't go past three years old. It's kind of hard to remember that distant a memory.

And now I don't just get to remember. I get to live with it. With *him*. In the land of green and silence and no public transportation.

It's, as they say, fucked.

I know I should be glad Curtis didn't abandon me completely. He could've let me go into the system. I think I'm supposed to be glad he didn't.

Pretty low bar, if you ask me. But that's kind of my life lately. All I've got is crumbs, and I keep scrambling for them because there's nothing else.

Curtis doesn't know how to be a dad. And even if he does figure it out, I certainly don't know how to have a father, and I learned the hard way that the only person you can need without getting hurt is yourself. So I think we're pretty much screwed, both of us secretly counting down until I'm eighteen and I can get out and he can be rid of me.

Such a low bar. Is this what Mom wanted for me? God . . . who am I kidding?

She wasn't thinking about me. I have to tell myself that she *wasn't* thinking about me. That if she had been—if my name or eyes or smile or any part of me had broken through the fog that'd settled over her—she wouldn't have done it.

The thought of me would've stopped her. (Because

I wasn't there to stop her.) Told you I was scrambling for crumbs.

I'm awake before my alarm, so I turn it off and pull the covers back over my head, even though it's already hot at nine in the morning. I hear Curtis in the kitchen, rustling around getting ready to leave for work as I hide in my blankets. He's restless. *A restless soul.* She used to call him that, the times I got her to talk about him, when I was younger and interested. When I was younger and thought *Maybe he'll come back.*

She'd smile when she said it, but it was a strange mix of bitter and sweet. Like she could never figure out which way to feel about him. I wonder if she ever did. Figure it out.

Was there clarity at the end?

Regret?

Did *anything* break through the gray-thick fog that had cloaked her and our apartment and our lives for those months before . . . ?

I can't think about it. If I do, then I'll think about that day and the weeks before, and that will lead to the months when I was telling myself it was okay, but I knew it wasn't. And it'll all circle into: *Why weren't you better, Coley? Why weren't you faster? Why didn't you realize how bad it was?*

There's no good or easy answer to any of the questions, so I'm just gonna keep running from them, thank you very much.

Curtis leaves for work, and now that the house is empty and there's no risk of awkward breakfast time, I fling myself free of the blankets. I've been here for over a week, but my boxes are barely unpacked. If I unpack, then it's permanent.

But it's not like I'm deluding myself. I know I'm stuck here. I'm just delaying the unpacking a little. Even though it's inevitable. That's why there's that whole saying about people denying the inevitable. It's a human condition or something.

I'm acting perfectly normal.

He's left coffee in the maker. I stare at it for a second, wondering if it's a peace offering. He bitched at me the second morning I got here when he caught me drinking it. Like it was gonna stunt my growth or something. Like he should have a say in what I put in my body, after all these years of ignoring me.

If it's a peace offering, it makes me even madder than if he just forgot. I know I'm supposed to be *grateful* . . . and I think there's a part of him that's kind of confused I'm not. There's that low bar I was talking about again. An ant could hop over it.

On the fridge, there's a note and a twenty-dollar bill tucked under a plastic grape magnet: MOVERS FOUND YOUR BIKE. GO MAKE FRIENDS.

I pocket the twenty and trash the note. I try not to think about the countless notes I have tucked away in a tin somewhere in those boxes I haven't unpacked. My mom liked scribbling stuff down for the fridge. Quotes and song lyrics and jokes and affirmations. Sometimes, when she was low, I could track when she was pulling out of it because she'd start filling the fridge door again. But it hadn't been a sure science.

Not the last time.

GO MAKE FRIENDS. He writes that like it's easy. Like I have

anything in common with anyone out there. Maybe if some other girl out there is delaying some inevitable shit, I guess. But that's not exactly something you can ask someone when meeting them. That'd just be weird.

I think about staying home all day, in defiance of his note. But Curtis's still enough of a wild card that I don't know how he'd react. He hasn't yelled at me or anything. But you never know. All I've got is some stories of him fifteen years ago and the knowledge that I was easy for him to let go of.

And staying in this house with its swamp cooler and no real AC is like being in hell. So I grab my bike and ride off. Maybe I'll stay out too late. It's not like he can say he's worried. Or that I have a curfew.

I'm pretty sure it didn't even occur to him to give me one. Amateur.

The neighborhood Curtis lives in is frayed at the edges, but it's trying not to look it. Kinda like him. The houses are old and as neat as you can keep them when you can't really afford to. In the tiny, mowed yards, the grass is patchy, like even the earth knows it's no use. It's given up.

"Howdy!"

It's such a weird greeting, I just stare at the lady before I zip past her.

"Yeah!" I call back, tossing it over my shoulder like a dumbass. But really, who says *Howdy*? Is this what I can expect? That would *suck*. School's gonna suck. I've got the summer's reprieve, but it's not like Curtis's gonna let me ditch senior year.

I get out of the neighborhood and cross the big stone bridge that has no bike lane or sidewalk, so the truck behind me thinks it's helpful to honk every few seconds even though I'm going as fast as I can. The dude eventually just pulls ahead of me, but not before flipping me the bird. Nice show of small-town friendliness.

As I bike across the railroad tracks, I think about trying to hop a train. Letting it carry me off to the unknown.

It's something my mom would've done back in the day, I bet. Ride the rails or whatever they call it—there's probably a cooler term. She was fearless, my mom. Totally the type to hop a train and leave everything she knew behind.

We'd always been a team, she and I. But it turned out we were playing a game I didn't understand, and we both ended up losing. All I ever seem to do is lose things.

Finally, I get a glimpse of civilization instead of just a bunch of scrubby houses and trees. It's so hot, the horizon shimmers as I spot the strip mall, making it look almost magical instead of just the source of some AC. Sweat trickles down my back as I pedal into the parking lot. There's a Chinese place, a tanning salon called Sunkissed, with a creepy kissy-face sun logo . . . and *there*, an arcade, with a big sign: WE HAVE AC. A few stores are boarded up next door, and there are some guys skateboarding over the speed bump. I guess you take your concrete where you can get it out here in the land of trees and two-lane roads.

I swing my leg off my bike, wheeling it toward the post near the arcade—the perfect spot to chain it up. Do you even chain your bike up in Oregon? Do people not steal here? No. Of course not. People steal everywhere.

Screech! The sound of car wheels coming too fast and too

close rakes through me, and I jerk back so fast I go down, elbows scraping into the pavement, my bike clattering over me, pedal cramming into thigh as a minivan careens toward me.

My life doesn't flash in front of my eyes. It's just *Ow* and then *Shit!* and then . . .

Nothing.

My eyes are screwed shut. I don't realize it until I don't feel the impact. I have to force them open, my face and body squinched, ready for the crash.

"Holy crap!"

"Oh my God—*Trenton!*" a girl's voice says.

"What! *What?!* She came out of nowhere!"

"You're an idiot!" she snaps and I can't help but dazedly agree: Trenton *is* an idiot.

I push up off my scraped elbows, wincing, and when I take in the driver who almost killed me, he actually *grins* at me like that's gonna charm me. There's another boy in the front seat, but he's not grinning; he looks as shell-shocked as I feel.

"Trent! I can't believe you," the girl shouts out a window, and then the door slides open and she steps out. Striped shirt, cropped high and effortless. Some girls can just *wear* clothes, you know? She's a stretch of tan skin and long legs. Dark hair, brushing down her shoulders. She tucks it behind her ears as she hurries toward me. I track the movement, snagging on the color of her nails, that funny color between purple and blue: periwinkle.

I'm more breathless now than I was on the ground, when I was sure I was gonna get smushed.

Her dark eyes—bottomless, endless, fearless eyes—meet

mine, and it's like almost getting hit all over. A cataclysm to the senses.

I can't zoom out. I can't get perspective.

She is the only thing I can see.

FOUR

"Are you, um, good?" the girl asks.

She's the kind of pretty that's undeniable. With some girls, it's a toss-up. Don't think I'm being a jerk here. I definitely fall into the "some girls" category. More cute than anything, you know? It's just how it is. I'm a realist.

But this girl—she's beautiful. Head-turning, I-lost-my-train-of-thought-mid-sentence beautiful.

She's looking right at me, and I have to snap out of it and answer, but I'm frozen. The asshat driver is standing there, laughing like the fact that my bike's on the ground is the funniest thing in the world.

"Hello?" The girl waves a hand in front of my face impatiently.

I scowl at her. "Yeah. I'm good."

She casts a glance over her shoulder at the tall boy, flapping her hand at him in a kind of quieting motion, but when she turns back, she's kind of smiling at his antics.

I huff and grab my bike, stalking off to chain it up. Back to reality, because this day has been shitty so far. I mean, I guess the asshole could've *actually* run me over instead of almost.

I'm killing it with the low bars today.

"You came out of nowhere!" the boy calls as I storm off toward the arcade, and I hate that my cheeks burn, and I fight off the urge to flip him off. Instead, I chain my bike against one of the steel poles and duck inside, trying to ignore my stomach. When that doesn't work, I tell myself it's jumping because of my near-death experience.

Adrenaline makes you feel all sorts of things. I just need to cool off.

Which is going to be hard, because the "AC" the arcade bragged about outside on the sign is a rickety fan that doesn't even oscillate. Great; just great. I'd be cooler at home.

It's still a breeze, though. I'll take anything at this point before the ride back.

The rest of the arcade is dimly lit but glowing from the games—three bulky rows of machines. There are Foosball tables and air hockey behind them, and a tiny food area to my right with chipped Formica tables crammed inside. I plant myself right in front of the fan and close my eyes, trying to find some kind of calm.

"Dude, that guy at the club was about to stroke out," crows a voice to my right. "He couldn't keep up! And SJ! Bam! Down she goes." He laughs loudly.

I try to ignore it.

"You've gotta stop pulling this shit, Trenton," someone scolds. The other boy. "You almost gave me an asthma attack."

One of my eyes cracks open.

"What if SJ got hurt?"

That's *her* voice. How do I know it already, after just a few words spoken?

"Didn't see you stopping for SJ, Sonya," Trenton sneers.

The fan's barely doing anything in the cooling department, so I flap the hem of my shirt back and forth, trying to encourage the airflow. God, it's hot.

"Hey."

The moron who can't drive has talked enough now that I recognize his voice, too. So I don't turn around.

"Hey, come on, hottie."

I'd say he's like a dog with a bone, but a dog actually obeys orders. Boys like that? They don't.

"Leave her alone," says the other guy.

"I'm just being friendly! Come on, come over here."

I look over my shoulder, but I skim over him as the other boy claps his hand over Trenton's mouth and he ducks away. My focus goes to her: Sonya, he called her. She's sitting between the two boys at one of the Formica tables, and when she looks up, I move forward. Trenton lets out a pleased sound, like it's him I'm coming for, but there's a quirk to her mouth that makes me think she knows the truth.

"Did you want something?" I ask Trenton.

But before he can respond, the arcade doors slam open so dramatically, they make the rickety tables rattle. A girl with bangs and bloody scrapes on her knees comes hobbling over. "What the fuck, you guys!?" she spits at the three sitting down before she slumps into the empty chair I'm standing next to. "I can't believe you left me all on my own with that pissed-off bouncer. If my knees get scarred, you're paying for my plastic surgery."

Trenton laughs. "You should chill. Maybe get me a Coke?"

Pigtails swats at Trenton. I almost admire her restraint,

because I would've gone for a punch. "I went down for *you*, asshole! *You* get *me* a Coke. And a pretzel. I deserve carbs."

"I'm sorry, babe," Sonya tells her, slinging a soothing arm around her neck. "The boys made me run. I had no choice."

"You're never on my side," Pigtails grouches at her, and then her gaze rises to me, standing there like a total loser-lurker. The disdain in her eyes makes my cheeks heat up just as they were starting to cool down. "Who's this?" she asks, cuddling closer to Sonya.

"The girl I almost killed," Trenton says, eyes glinting. "Though, if you look at it another way, the girl whose life I saved by hitting my brakes at *just* the right moment. My mom would be so proud."

I don't even bother to answer. I should leave, but I can't seem to make my feet move.

"SJ, did you hear from Brooke about the lake yet?" Sonya asks.

"Not yet." Her gaze flicks to me again. "So, you are . . . ?"

"Coley."

"What's your deal?" SJ asks. "Do you just not talk?"

"I talk," I say.

"You know they say the smartest people are the quiet ones, because they listen," pipes up the other boy. The nice one I automatically like more just because he's not Trenton.

"Oh, great," Trenton sneers. "Another smart girl. Just what we need." He leans forward, his grin pure lech. "I bet you're a good listener, Coley."

"Well, you certainly say a lot of dumb shit, so it's a pretty easy job," I tell him.

"Oh my God," SJ says as Sonya starts laughing with her. The

boys gape. But SJ's attention slides away from me. "Brooke got back to me. We're on the north side of the lake today."

"Awesome," Trenton says, getting to his feet, and it's like he's the king or something, because they're all getting up at his cue. I step back, away from her, as Sonya scoots her chair from the table and stands.

They walk past me like I'm not even there, but as they go out the door, she looks over her shoulder at me one last time, and I can't help it. I follow.

The heat is still oppressive when I walk outside. I bend down to unlock my bike, trying to ignore them grouped down the way as Trenton gets the minivan.

"Hey! Coley!"

I look over my shoulder. She's halfway inside the minivan already, Trenton scowling in the driver's seat.

"We're meeting some friends at the lake," Sonya continues.

"Okay," I say.

She rolls her eyes and then snaps her fingers at me. It's rude and it's pushy.

My stomach drops like I'm on a roller coaster when the snap's followed by: "Well, are you coming with?"

It's like a split screen in my mind, the options: Curtis's house-that-isn't-home or this girl.

Anything's better than Curtis.

"I'm coming," I say.

FIVE

Sonya plucks the keys out of the ignition. "Alex, you move up front. I'll ride in back with Coley."

She gets out and opens up the back, waving me over. I go before she starts snapping at me again, because I'm not sure I'm supposed to like the leaping thing it makes my stomach do. *Bossy.* Is that what she is?

I would've given that label to SJ before Sonya got all impatient on me. Now I'm wondering: Did I almost get run over by the summer version of the cool kids' table? What am I doing here? I should just tell her I have to go. That's exactly what I'm going to do. As soon as I round the corner of the van, I'm going to say it: "I just remembered, I've gotta be somewhere." Play it cool and just . . . bike off before this gets messier. No one wants me here but her.

Why is that the thing that roots my feet to the ground when she smiles at me?

"There's lots of room," she says, bending down and grabbing the spokes, and it's like I'm looking to memorize her, every detail absorbing into me. Those periwinkle nails of hers, not quite purple, not quite blue: a question mark of a color for a question mark of a girl.

"Careful," I warn her as the wheel spins forward.

"I got it." She lifts the front of my yellow bike and I grab the rear wheel, hefting it in.

"Hurry up!" Trenton calls from the front.

"I could've biked," I tell her as she shuts the back.

She laughs. "Have you been to the lake?"

I shake my head. "I just moved here."

"Well, that explains why I've never seen you before," she says. "Anyway, lake's like a half hour by bike. It's way too hot for that shit. Come on."

Sonya clambers into the back bench seat and I follow, the stale smell of weed and corn chips hitting my nose. SJ's sitting in the middle captain's chair, with the boys in the front, and she turns back to talk to us as we buckle up.

"So, Coley, did you just move here?"

Sonya waves her off airily. "That's old news. Coley's already filled me in."

SJ rolls her eyes. "I was just asking a question! Where did you live before?"

"San Diego."

"A real city." Sonya sighs enviously.

"It's not like it's L.A. or New York," SJ scoffs.

"It's definitely not," I say, and she blinks at me, thrown that I've agreed with her.

"Do you miss it?" Sonya asks.

The canned answer is *no.* The truth is so much more complicated.

"This is definitely different," is what I finally say. But it's like she can read in between the lines, because she scoots a little closer and pats me on my leg. My entire mouth goes dry at the touch.

"We'll make you feel at home in no time," she says. "You're lucky you found us."

"Lucky I almost got run over?" I ask dryly.

"Hey! I'm doing you a favor, transporting you and your dirty bike in my van," Trenton calls from the front. My stomach turns a little; I hadn't realized he could hear us all the way in the back. My eyes flick up, and there he is, watching me in the rearview mirror. He has kaleidoscope eyes—not in the Beatles sense, but in the way that they seem knowing, but then with a small shift they're sly and shiny bright with a fever that can boil over.

"Just ignore him, please, I beg of you," Alex tells me, clasping his hands together.

"I should dump you all on the side of the road," Trenton mutters.

"Ditch me again, and I'll make sure you're roadkill," SJ shoots back.

I have to duck my head so I don't cough, I'm choking so hard on laughter. The SJs of the world are definitely not fans of girls like me, and this SJ wasn't giving me any reason to think differently, but sometimes bitchy humor is universal.

"You tell him, SJ." Sonya leans back in the seat, stretching her arms. Her fingers drape over the back of my seat, periwinkle nails standing out stark against the fading maroon plush.

"Don't you start on that girl-power rah-rah shit, Sonya," Trenton says as he pulls into a parking lot surrounded by, you guessed it, more pine trees. Is there any other kind of tree in this town?

She doesn't answer. Her fingers drum against the seat, little crescendos of annoyance. As the boys get out, I wonder if her tongue hurts from biting her words back so hard.

"Come on, Sonya, we need to find Brooke," SJ urges as we pile out of the van.

"Go ahead," I tell her when she hesitates, and SJ lets out a frustrated huff. "I just need to lock up my bike."

SJ laughs. "No one's gonna steal that piece of crap."

"SJ." Sonya shakes her head.

"Oh my God," SJ says disgustedly. I focus hard on the pavement. "Come on. Your *friends* are waiting, Sonya."

She grabs Sonya's hand and tugs her toward the path through the trees. I turn back to the minivan and pop the back open, pulling out my bike. It doesn't matter if she's looking back at me. It doesn't.

I chain my bike to one of the light poles, then head through the trees after them. Everything's darker under the canopy of the pines, until the path spills out into a clearing.

My eyes snag on her instantly, even though she's already down by the bank. Far away from me, but I would've found her even if she was across the lake. She laughs at something SJ says, her head tilting back, and the sun shines on her like it's an eighties movie about camp or something.

She fits here, with boys roughhousing in the water, girls in bikinis sunbathing on towels spread across the rocky shore, a bonfire crackling, Igloos full of sweating beer cans set on one of the picnic tables.

I don't fit here. At all. Oh my God, why did I come here? She didn't even wait for me. I should just go.

"Hey, Coley!"

Shit. I look to the right. Alex waves me over from his seat on top of the table near the coolers. At least he's got an open Altoid tin of rolling papers and weed balanced on his knee. Maybe I can handle this if I'm stoned.

I can't run now, so I join him. Alex doesn't have the frat-bro sheen that Trenton does, and I wonder where he fits in all this. Every friend group is like a see-saw: there's always someone reaching out to balance everyone. When I sit down next to Alex and he smiles, affable and handsome—he's got to have girls cooing over his dark hair—I wonder if he's the one who steadies everything.

I try not to glance over my shoulder too obviously. Just a quick look. But Sonya's not even facing our way. She's kicking a striped ball at one of her friends—probably the Brooke that they'd mentioned at the arcade. It's like I don't even exist.

"I was wondering if you got lost in the woods," Alex says.

"The path was pretty clear," I say, turning a little on the picnic table, so I don't have to look over my shoulder at the waterline. At her.

"Just make sure you stay alert. There are bears out here." His eyes twinkle as he teases me, letting me in on the joke. So I play along.

"Oh yeah, I fought off three of them on the walk here. With my bare hands."

He laughs at the bad pun.

Out of the corner of my eye, I watch Sonya kick the beach ball into the water, stripping off her shirt as she bounds into the water, the white wake of her splash shining against the red of her bikini. My stomach dips as she disappears under the water, shimmering like a mermaid when she surfaces, and then I *have* to look away, because if I don't, I'm going to go as scarlet as her bathing suit.

"Are you living in town?" Alex asks.

"Yeah."

"Then no bear violence will befall you. You gotta be a little more careful in the boonies; my ex has to lock up her trash."

"Not gonna lie, that sounds kind of terrifying. Rats and cockroaches were my main wildlife nemeses in San Diego."

"Wait until you see the forest centipedes."

"Ew!" I shiver at the thought. "All those little legs creep me out."

"I totally agree." He taps the ground herb from the tin into the folded paper, rolling it shut with easy, practiced movements. He holds it out to me. "I feel like I owe you one of these, considering we almost ran you over."

"I absolutely agree with that logic," I say, taking the joint and tucking it in my pocket. "Thanks."

"Sure. Let me know if you need to be hooked up. Just herb, though. I don't mess with anything else."

"Cool. I'm not into anything else."

"Straight edge, huh?"

It makes me laugh. There's something relaxing about him.

Out of the corner of my eye, Sonya wrings water out of her hair at the edge of the lake, chatting with SJ, laughing at something she says, gesturing wildly in response as the other girl dissolves into giggles. Sonya slings an arm around SJ's neck, pressing an exaggerated kiss against the top of her head and then pulling back to fake swoon, SJ catching her before she falls back into the water.

What a drama queen.

I want to know everything about her.

"I really hope we didn't scare you too much in the parking lot," Alex says earnestly. "Trenton is . . ."

I swear to God, saying his name summons him, because he comes bounding forward, three other boys trailing after. Trenton shakes his soaking-wet hair toward Alex like he's a dog. Water flies everywhere, and Alex yelps, throwing himself bodily over his setup.

"What the hell, Trenton! My papers!"

Trenton just laughs.

"You swimming?" Trenton jerks his still-wet head toward the lake.

"Nope," I say, the "p" popping a little, hoping he'll take the hint.

He doesn't. At all. "What's wrong?" he asks. "Can't get wet?"

My stomach drops horribly at the innuendo.

"Jesus Christ, Trenton," Alex snarls.

But Trenton just snickers. "Don't worry, I can help with that."

Before I can even think about snapping at him, he ducks down and just *goes* for me. He's got at least a foot of height on me and scoops me up like I'm a bag of flour, slinging me over his shoulder.

Goddammit, I *hate* guys like him. Guys think it's funny to pick you up whenever they want. They think it's hilarious when you twist and turn and try to get free; they think it's an excuse to grab at the parts of you they're not supposed to.

Fucking guys. You're not supposed to grab *any* part of someone unless they want it. It's not that hard to understand.

"Could you put me down? I'm not wearing a suit," I say, aiming for calm, because this is the kind of guy who laughed instead of freaked over almost running me over. He wants me to be pissed. And I am. But I'm fighting to not give in to his bullshit.

My hair swings back and forth as Trenton jogs toward the beach, laughing hysterically, his grip on me tight. Blood rushes into my face, and I seriously consider pantsing him then and there in revenge. But he's already splashing into the water, and the ends of my hair drag in it, and there aren't *really* biting fish, right? I just made that up in my head. This is Oregon. Not Australia where everything wants to kill you.

He swings around, spinning in the water, and black spots dance along my vision—the sudden blood rush to my head combined with the spinning making me so dizzy it's hard to fight. I flail, trying to get upright, and the shift of my weight makes him stumble and then spin, the two of us tumbling awkwardly into the water with a crash. The water's murky and not like being in a pool at all, but the wet shock of it is enough to banish the dizziness. By the time I struggle to my feet, I pretty much hate everything, especially when I see Sonya ankle-deep in the water, her hair slicked back from her face, staring at me, and the most absurd thought strikes me as our eyes meet and her eyebrows draw together: *Were you coming out here to get me?*

"What the fuck's wrong with you?" Trenton demands, getting right in my face, blocking Sonya from my vision. He splashes water at me with his big, meaty hands. "I was just playing! I wasn't going to throw you in!"

I finally give in and flip him off. He doesn't deserve another word. None of them do. I slosh out of the water and stalk right past everyone staring at me, toward my bike. Fuck all of this and all of them. Fuck Curtis and his "go make friends" bullshit. What friends? Why would I want to be friends with these people, except that "*they live here*"?

What a horrible reason to be friends: proximity.

This is never going to be home. And now I'm gonna get a ton of grief at school because I didn't giggle when a guy carried and tossed me into the water caveman-style.

"Hey, wait!"

I keep going, even though it's her voice. I can see her out of the corner of my eye as I head across the parking lot. She's pulling her striped shirt back on over her bikini top but doesn't stop to button it up, and I try to focus on the way the red ties of her suit are knotted around her neck instead of on anywhere else.

"Are you okay?"

I get to my bike, and my hands grip the handles. Every time I move, my shoes squish with water and what I hope is just mud and not that gross algae.

"Trenton can be an asshole sometimes," she says, with an embarrassed little grin that makes my stomach turn. "But I swear, he's a good guy. I've known him forever."

"I'm *sure* he's a good guy," I say, and the sarcasm drips off my words faster than the water from my hair.

"Hey." She frowns at me, her eyebrows scrunching into a V. "Don't be mad at me," she says. "I came all the way out here to make sure you were okay."

"All the way out here. As in, up the path and across the parking lot to the road?"

That little V gets deeper. A part of me wants to push. To see how deep that frown of hers can get, because she looks like the kind of girl who isn't built for it, and when she does, it's more cute than angry. There's no gravity to it.

But this day—I'm done with it. My hair's dripping down my back, and thank God I pulled on a gray tank top this morning instead of a white one, or Trenton probably would've insisted that I stay.

"Look, I don't know you or your friends. I don't know anyone here. And then you just—" I close my mouth. God, I'm so tired. Wet and tired and *done.* "What he did was fucked up. And not stopping it—it's just fucked."

She rolls her eyes. "You came with us to the lake."

"You asked me to come!" I snap. "I don't know you people. I'm starting to wonder if I want to. That guy's an ass."

Her face smooths out suddenly. No more frown. "Look, I don't know what happened back there with you and Trenton, but *I* didn't do anything but come out here to see if you were okay."

"Why didn't you try to stop him?"

Her frown's back, and then off her face in a second, like a glitch in a video. It happens so fast I almost think I've imagined it, but then she says, softer this time, "I didn't know how—"

She's like gasoline on a fire that's already burned for months. "So you just go along with whatever he wants?"

"What? I do *not!*" she says, overlapping me.

"—as long as you get to be a part of it. Always gotta be the center of attention, even when your *good guy*'s acting like trash."

"Wow," she says. "Harsh. And untrue."

"Then what was that out there?" I fling my arm toward the lake, staring her down. She'd asked me out here, talked to me the whole ride, and then bounced off like I wasn't cool enough to hold her interest. It shouldn't hurt so much, so fast. But it does.

"I—" She's not fighting the frown anymore. I've either pissed her off or stumped her. I'm not sure which, but I'm not sure I care at this point.

"I don't have energy for people who make excuses," I say, going for bravado and hating how it comes out a little weak, and then I stalk off. I think at least I look kind of badass, but my heart's hammering and then it feels like it skips right out of my chest when she yells:

"Who the fuck do you think you are?"

She's following me. It's a feeling I've never had before, because when a guy follows you, it's scary, not thrilling. But this is . . .

It's like I can count every beat of blood in my veins.

"You don't have any right to judge me," she rages behind me as I keep walking, dizzy with the heat of her words, unable to run from her because then she'd *know*.

Know *what*, Coley? *I* don't even know.

"I mean, what the fuck? Who do you think you are? You're just some . . . mean, grumpy *bitch!*" On the last word, she grabs my shoulder and whirls me around.

It's like all the heat's gone to my face and is about to pour out of my eyes in tears. I can't run or breathe, and really all I *can* do is bury my face in my hands, which is *humiliating*.

"Hey." Her voice changes again, going soft like it was before. "Hey, are you okay?"

How many times has she asked me that today? Have I ever answered her honestly?

Her arms come around me before I can think of any consequences, and suddenly everything is *warm*. Not hot. Warm. Like sinking into a bath that's the perfect temperature.

"I'm so sorry I said that," Sonya says, right into my ear, and I didn't even know a person could *shiver* like this. It's down my spine and my legs, swirling around the tops of my feet. Since when do the tops of my feet have any sensation unless I've dropped something on them?

"That's not—it's not about what you said . . . it's just—" I run out of words as her hands tighten around my waist.

"Can we start over?" she asks, again right in my ear, and I think this is how I'm going to die. Just shiver into pieces right here on the road. But then she pulls back, and we're close enough now for me to really see her eyes, brown tinged golden in the light spilling down the road. She steps away from me, and later I'm going to think about the way her fingers linger on the outside of my elbows for hours. She smiles, cocking her head. "You have to let me redeem myself. I'm just—stupid. Honestly. I make terrible choices. Ask anyone."

"I'm good," I say. "And you're not."

"Not what?"

"You're not stupid. You may play it really well. But that's what smart girls do when they want to get away with shit. And you seem to get away with a lot of shit."

Her smile turns up on the right side more than the left at my words. It edges into something that's not sweet, but real. "Does that make *you* a smart girl, Coley?"

"I thought we covered that in the arcade," I shoot back. "Even Good Guy Trenton thinks I'm smart. Much to his woe."

She lets out a breath that has to be a laugh, but she doesn't want it to be. I feel a little thrill: I'm keeping her on her toes.

"You're so serious," she says, even though I just made a joke. But it was calling her on her shit.

I'm starting to see no one does that.

"Serious, huh?"

"Very intense," she says, sticking her lower lip out in a mock pout, adding to her scowl in an imitation of me.

I raise an eyebrow.

"It's not a bad thing!" she says hastily. "It's different. Everyone around here . . . it's just . . . everyone knows everyone, you know?"

"I don't, actually."

"Oh. Huh," she says, like the idea is strange to her. "Really not helping me here."

"Didn't realize I was supposed to be."

She laughs. "Ugh! I wanna make *you* laugh."

"You could start by being funny."

She gasps, flinging her arms against her chest like I've wounded her. "*You* could start by chilling out!"

And it finally makes me laugh, because this girl is the opposite of chilled out.

"Ha! See! My dramatics are good for something."

"I wasn't laughing at your whole swooning act," I tell her, laughing again.

"Then why?"

I smirk and let the silence hang. She's fascinating in her impatience, practically vibrating from it, from being denied anything.

You are used to getting your way, I think as she bites her lip, and then I'm not thinking anything for a whole second, because of that soft indentation she worries there, and then:

"No. Seriously! Tell me!" She dashes in front of me when I push my bike forward.

"You really can't stand silence, can you?" I ask her. "Even when someone's saying goodbye to you."

"And here I was, trying to cheer you up," Sonya pouts.

"I think you're more scared of me not liking you than you are concerned about my happiness level," I tell her. "Which is funny because I never said I *didn't* like you. I just told the truth about your boy toy."

"He's not my—" The outrage comes hot and quick with her, the way she sucks in her breath and blows all the words out in a rush.

"Whatever," I cut her off. Partly because I can't bear to hear an explanation. You only protect a boy like Trenton if you've made the mistake of making out with him a lot. My fingers curl around my bike handles at the thought. "I really should get going. I live all the way over on Cliff's Edge Drive. Curtis—I mean, my dad—he'll be waiting."

I know she caught my slipup, because her head tilts like she's filing away the information for later. "Ugh, fine, you can go, I guess," she says, like she has any say in it. What a princess. "But you have to give me your number so we can hang out again."

I dig in my soggy pocket for my flip phone, holding it out as it drips between us on the asphalt. "My phone's kinda dead now."

She winces. "What about a pen?"

"A pen?"

"Yeah. You know, a writing implement? What those in ancient times used to write with, before cell phones and computers?"

"Does it look like I have a pen?" I gesture to my wet clothes.

"Honestly, Coley, I'm not used to doing all the work like you're making me do," she sighs, but she plucks a pen out of the back pocket of her shorts, like she slipped it there just for this moment.

"Arm!"

"What?"

She rolls her eyes and then she grabs my arm; her fingertips wrap around my wrist like it's not something monumental. But it is, isn't it? Her touch is a jolt that has made everything inside me buzz alive, like spring has come and I've been hibernating in a denial cave with a grief boulder blocking the entrance.

She presses the Sharpie against my arm, and my skin prickles as she writes her AIM screen name and number, carefully and so slow; my hand is just an inch away from the soft-looking stretch of her stomach where her shirt flaps open, and if she doesn't let go, I'll turn bright red.

"There we go! Call me from your house. We'll be all old-fashioned."

I look down at the numbers, trying to breathe around this twist in my chest and understand it at the same time.

"You could've just given me it on paper." Is that my voice? Is it that hoarse? Is this what she's done to me, with just a few big smiles and a handful of minutes bickering and some ink scrawled on my arm like it was my heart?

She tilts her head back when she laughs this time. "Dahhl-linnggg, it's called *romance*!" she trills, and that *word*, it swirls around in my head as she blows me an exaggerated kiss and skips off, back toward the lake.

I make my way down the road, a happy fizz inside me. But the idea of going home and facing Curtis and all my boxes and reminders of a life that got left behind flattens that fizz.

"Hey, Coley," she shouts from down the road.

It's like sunshine pouring down on me. Like she knew I needed one more boost. One more excuse to turn toward her.

"You forget something?"

She shakes her head, bouncing on her heels. "Promise you'll call?"

I wrap my hand around the numbers, precious slashes

against my skin. That happy fizz is back, and it's like it'll never leave, it's so strong inside me.

"Promise!" I shout back.

My promise echoes in the trees. And only when the last echo fades does she turn and walk away.

SIX

LJ User: SonyatSunrisex0Ox [Private Entry]

Date: June 9, 2006

[**Mood:** curious]
[**Music:** "Portions for Foxes"–Rilo Kiley]

Nothing ever changes in small towns. Until it does. Even a little ripple feels like a wave when it happens.

Today I met a girl.

Today, I almost ran over a girl. Well, Trenton almost did. I would've just been an accessory if he'd actually done it and pulled a hit-and-run.

God, Trenton is totally the kind of guy to pull a hit-and-run, isn't he?

He isn't getting the message about the whole breakup thing. He spent the entire afternoon trying to untie my bikini.

He always has to get his way. It'd probably just be easier to give in for the summer or something. But then we always fight. I'm so over fighting.

Brooke says I'm lucky, and SJ says I'm better off than most of the girls in school.

But God, is it supposed to be this hard?

Coley. Is it short for Nicole? She doesn't look like a Nicole. She looks like a Coley should look. Like, no nonsense, to-the-point, kind of sharp at the edges. She looks like if you touch her, you might pull away bleeding. Ripped jeans and a choker that's like a slash of lace against her throat. Ugh. Jealous. The last time I wore a choker, my mom told me it made my neck look fat. I should've told her I didn't care, but I just took it off.

This girl wears a choker and it's like a dare. *Grab me. Try it.*

She's kind of lucky Trenton almost ran her over. Otherwise I wouldn't know about her and she'd probably end up with no one cool to hang out with once school starts. I'm saving her from having to eat lunch with the rejects. Or worse—eat lunch all alone.

And she's just . . .

She's not boring.

—Sonya

SEVEN

When I squish, sodden, into the house, I'm hoping to avoid Curtis. But my luck's run out: he's home early from work and in the living room.

He's gray-streaked worry, tightly wound, and it makes me nervous because I haven't figured out what kind of guy he is yet.

For most of my life, Curtis was a guy in a leather jacket in a black-and-white photo—the only one my mom kept of him to show me—dark and remotely cool, like a man from an ad or something. A cigarette dangled from his smiling lips as he gazed at the camera like he loved whoever was behind it.

He was frozen in my memory in black-and-white in that cool vintage leather jacket. An idea, more than a person. And now he's a person to me, and maybe now I'm a person to him; we're not possibilities to each other anymore, and it *sucks.* I don't know what to do with it. I don't think I can love him. I don't know *how.* I don't know him.

He rises from the couch, taking me in. My hair's still sopping and my shoes are going to take a day to dry out.

"What happened to you?" he asks in concern.

"I took a dip in the lake," I say, walking past the row of guitars hanging in the hallway, me squelching with each step.

"Wait a second!" he protests, following me. "Coley, are you okay?"

I turn around, trying not to feel humiliated and failing miserably. "I did what you told me. I made some friends. Now I really need to clean up, okay?"

Before he can sputter an answer, I duck into the bathroom and close the door loud enough to make a statement. At least he won't bother me in here.

I turn on the shower, the steam from the water slowly filling the room as I peel out of my wet boots and socks, and then slowly peel off my jeans. Wet jean chafing is an experience I wouldn't wish on my worst enemy. Well. Maybe Trenton. If he's experiencing the same chafing issue as me, then there is some justice in the world. But I don't have a lot of faith in that, unfortunately.

I peel off my tank top, and that's when I see it, standing there in my bra and underwear in a bathroom that's so clearly a dude's bathroom. The smear of ink on my arm.

"Oh no. No. No!" I stare at my arm, the phone number and screen name Sonya scribbled on it bleeding ink down my skin. My arm must've brushed against my wet clothes as I walked.

"Fuck!" I angle my arm to the light, trying to make out the blurred numbers. But it's just black ink ghosting to gray across my skin.

I sit down on the edge of the tub, the knot in my stomach tightening unbearably.

"Fuck," I say again, just to say it, because if I don't, I think I might cry.

And that's so stupid, right? I can make friends when school starts in August. Or I can just stay a loner. I don't need . . .

I don't need anything. Or anyone.

Not anymore.

I don't.

When I wake up the next morning, the first thing I see is the notebook still on my stomach. Four pages full of scribbled-down numbers and possible screen names, trying to remember what Sonya wrote on my arm.

So yeah, I didn't give up after I accidentally smeared it all up. Pitiful, right?

I just . . .

I dunno.

It was like forgetting for a second. That everything isn't shit. Talking to her, I mean.

And I don't want to forget everything. I don't want to forget my mom.

Some things you have to forget so you can keep going. Otherwise they haunt you. I never understood it before—maybe if I had, I could've helped my mom more—but I do now. I understand the thoughts you can't run away from, and I'm trying to learn how to live with them, but it's so hard.

Everything has been so hard since that day.

"Coley?"

I jump at the knock on my door, the notebook in my hand falling into the mess of blankets as Curtis opens the door and peers inside.

"You up?"

"Obviously," I say, gesturing to my awake self. He can't tell, can he? He can't tell I was about to crumble right here, wrapped in the comforter my mom bought me when I was thirteen. He doesn't know me well enough to see the signs. He never bothered to try to know me.

"I made coffee, if you want some."

I frown at him. "I thought it was gonna stunt my growth."

"Guess you're done growing, like you said," he says with a shrug, and then leaves. I crawl out of bed and change, listening to him rustle around the kitchen. When the clock ticks past nine and he still doesn't leave for work, I realize he must have the day off.

My need for caffeine outweighs my need to be left alone, so I go into the kitchen and pour myself a cup. He leans against the counter, sipping his own.

"What are you planning on doing today?" he asks.

"Um."

"Because we could . . ."

Oh no. Not the dreaded *we*. There is no *we*. There's him and there's me—that's it.

"I was actually going to unpack," I cut him off. Anything to keep him from finishing whatever *we* plan he has.

"I can help you?" he suggests.

The idea of him going through my things sends a flash of cold through me. I shake my head. "No! No, it's okay. I'll do it. I'll just—" I look around the kitchen, landing on the bag of chips on the counter. I grab them. "I just need sustenance. You know. Keep my energy up."

Before he can respond, I hustle out of the kitchen, coffee

in one hand, salt-and-vinegar chips in the other. I don't even like this flavor; what the hell am I thinking? But now I'm stuck, doing what I said I was going to do. I should've told him I was going out or something—not like there's anywhere to go or anything to do. There might've been if I hadn't screwed up Sonya's number. My stomach drops every time I think about it, no matter how many times I tell myself it doesn't matter.

I close myself up in my room and shut the curtains so it feels even more like a little cave. Sunlight streaming in through the windows seems wrong as I unpack a life I'll never get back.

The first box I grab is heavy, so it's gotta be my books. I don't know why I brought my old textbooks. Maybe it was because the idea of throwing anything out as I tossed my life into fifteen boxes was too hard. Now it seems stupid. Why would I need my old history book?

Pushing the textbooks to the side, I set the stack of paperback mysteries on top of my dresser. There are some cinder blocks in the backyard. If I scrounge up some planks or something, I could make a little bookcase for them. I don't want to ask Curtis for anything if I don't have to. I need to remember he's not that guy, you know? He only showed up when the worst happened, and that's what I need to expect: to get anything only at the worst moments.

I grab the second, much-lighter box from the stack taking up half of my room and pull the tape off. I'd actually labeled this one—CLOTHES—scrawled on one side.

I've been living in the clothes I'd tossed in my suitcase, so it's kind of nice to see the rest of my stuff. The miniature bunny wearing a pink kimono my grandmother gave me.

My favorite pair of black Converse, my gray Henley that's three sizes too big and softer than anything, and all my tank tops, which is good because it's just as hot as Southern California up here—and a little muggy to boot. I pull out a few sleep shirts, and that's when I see it, tucked between a pair of pajamas and a hoodie: a jean jacket, classic Levi's, the material worn to ragged soft perfection by a woman who loved hard and lived hard in it.

That's what she always told me. *You've gotta love hard and live hard, Coley.*

I pull the jacket toward me, pressing the material against my cheek. Rose oil—faint, but there—fills my senses, and my eyes burn as I sit on the floor, holding it against me like I held her on the floor of the apartment, trying to hold it all in.

Some things you need to forget to keep going. But I don't know how to do that without forgetting her, too.

Breathing around the burn in my throat and eyes, I unclench my fingers around the jacket and pull it on. I have to fold up the cuffs on the arms—Mom was a lot taller than me—but when I'm done, the jacket holds me like an embrace.

I lean against my dresser, wrapped up in memories, knowing the rose smell will fade someday, but the ache of losing her never will. I want to be a girl who rises to the occasion, who lives out her mother's motto . . . the one she couldn't embody.

But how can you love hard and live hard when the hurt is all you feel?

EIGHT

LJ User: SonyatSunrisex0Ox [Public Entry]

Date: June 10, 2006

[**Mood:** devilish]

[**Music:** "It's My Life"–No Doubt]

Babysitting the little sister today. Mom's idea of punishment after I came home late from @MadeyouBrooke23's lake bash. Worth it!

Also: Corrupting my little sis into a mini-me instead of a mini-Mom seems like a worthwhile use of my time.

What do you bet we have the ingredients for s'mores in the cupboards? Let's hope I don't let Emma burn the house down making them!

xoox
Sonya

Comments:

SJbabayy:

You're a terror, babe. I love it.

SonyatSunrisex0Ox:
My mom would agree with you.

SJbabayy:
You're HER terror, though.

SonyatSunrisex0Ox:
Lol. Can you remind her of that when she's mad I got an A and not an A+?

SJbabayy:
Your grades are great! I'd kill to get an A in Anderson's class. I barely scraped by with a C.

SonyatSunrisex0Ox:
Great is not perfect, as Mom likes to remind me.

SJbabayy:
Sigh. Yeah. <3

LJ User: SonyatSunrisex0Ox [Private Entry]

Date: June 10, 2006

[**Mood:** annoyed]
[**Music:** "Escape"—Enrique Iglesias]

So, it's not like I waited all day and night for Coley to IM me or anything. I'm not pitiful or something. But I left my away message on to be nice and like welcoming-to-town and stuff. But nothing. Not even a message on the machine.

Who does she think she is, ignoring me?

Maybe she's not. Maybe she just forgot.

Ugh. I'm not forgettable. I am, like, the opposite of that.

Right?

Do I not even get a chance, here, with her? I'm a good friend when you let me!

It's just . . . like . . . what the fuck?

I mean, I'm the one who knows what street she lives on. I could probably go down there and find which yard her bike's in.

But that might be way too try-hard. If she really is ignoring me, then that would be downright humiliating.

So not doing that.

But . . .

What if she just forgot?

Cuz she looked like she needed a friend. It wasn't just because she was dripping wet and kind of pitiful at that point.

She grabbed me back like no one had hugged her in I don't know how long, and that's just . . . Fuck, what's that like? My mom's not a huge hugger, but I get Emma snuggles and stuff.

I think Coley might need me. You know, as a friend. And I'm a good friend. SJ would totally say I was a good friend if I asked her. Brooke . . . well, Brooke has her own issues. Mainly the whole being in love with my ex-boyfriend thing. But whatever.

I'll just go over to Cliff's Edge Drive tomorrow. It'll be fine.

—Sonya

NINE

It's like I can't escape him. Curtis's there *again* the next morning, bustling around the house like he owns it. Which I know he does! I know! But I didn't realize he spent so much *time* in it. Does he have work? I'm not even really clear at what he does, but surely he has to go somewhere to do it, right?

I unpacked everything yesterday, so now I don't even have that as an excuse to avoid him. That was such a terrible idea; I should've saved half of it for today, just in case.

I thought I'd have the house more to myself, like I had the apartment with Mom to myself in the good days, when she was working and seeing friends and even sometimes dating. The rarer the good days got, the more she stayed in her room. On the bad days, it was like the floor was made of eggshells that I tiptoed on, desperate to never make a crack. The littlest things could shatter her. But I guess that's it, isn't it? Those things, they didn't seem little to her. Not at all.

I wish I had known that. I wish I had known better.

But I didn't. And now I'm here with Curtis, and the floor feels like eggshells again. Same feeling, different parent. It makes me wonder: Is it me?

I need coffee, so I shuffle into the kitchen to get it. As I pass by the living room, he looks up from the couch.

"I could make you some breakfast," he offers when he sees the coffee cup in my hand.

Having had several of his dinners, I don't think breakfast is going to be his secret skill. "Coffee is fine," I assure him. "I've never eaten a lot in the morning."

"Huh. Maybe you got that from me."

I choke on the coffee, I'm so surprised. "Um. Sure."

"You want to see what I'm doing?" he asks, motioning me forward. There are a bunch of plastic boxes with dividers set on the coffee table. As I draw closer, I can see that there are gemstones inside one of them, finished jewelry in the other.

"What's this?"

"My work."

"You made these?" I lean forward, curious despite myself. He makes *jewelry*? But he doesn't even wear any. I don't know him well or at all, but I can tell you right now, Curtis is not the turquoise-bracelet sort of guy.

"I picked up jewelry making to pay the bills while I made music. Stumbled into it when a buddy of mine got a good deal on some stones. Taught myself the basics, honed my skills through the years. My early pieces were crude as hell." He laughs at the thought, and when he does it, my heart twists, because it's the first time I've seen him smile . . . and it's exactly like mine.

Everyone's always told me I look more like my mom—same eyes and high cheekbones, small nose, and thick, straight hair. But Curtis's smile is staring me in the face. It's *my* smile, and it's like he's stolen it from me, this thing I thought was mine alone.

"They're pretty," I say faintly, even though I can barely see them. *This* is what he was doing all these years, instead of being my father? Shining up pretty stones and melting silver like a blacksmith or something? He could've been doing this from anywhere. He could've stayed in San Diego, even if he didn't want to stay with Mom.

But instead, this place—Bumfuck Nowhere, Oregon—and a bunch of minerals were more important?

"You can touch them," he says, so encouragingly that I do it just to make him happy, even though I feel numb. "I've got a studio smithy set up in the garage now. I could teach you."

I grab the closest necklace, a smooth pendant I have to flip over, the chain filtering through my fingers with the faintest tickle. My stomach drops like I'm diving off a roof into a pool I know is too shallow.

"That's a design I've been doing since the beginning," he explains as I trace a finger over the intricate leaf pattern etched into silver encasing the tiger's-eye.

My fingers know the bumps and grooves of the leaves already. I could draw them with my eyes closed. Mom wore a tiger's-eye pendant just like this when I was younger. I used to hold it when she rocked me to sleep, a talisman to keep the monsters at bay. At some point in my childhood, she stopped wearing it—I guess we both thought the monsters were gone for good. The next time I saw it, it was in the bag of personal effects the coroner gave me. She'd been wearing it when she . . .

I drop the pendant. It clatters to the ground.

"Whoops," Curtis says, bending down to grab it.

I jump up. "I have to go."

"Coley—"

But I'm running down the hall, desperate to get into my room before he stops me. I slam the door shut, wishing I had a lock. He doesn't follow me, though. Thank God he doesn't follow me.

Her jewelry box is right there on my dresser, next to the paperbacks. A little cedar box with a rose carved on top. My hands shake as I push it open, and there it is—the plastic bag they gave me. Inside is my grandmother's topaz ring, Mom's hoop earrings, and the necklace Curtis must have made for her when they were still in love.

I tip them out into my palm, wondering if it means something. It has to, doesn't it? That she chose to wear his necklace that day? It seems like something I should tell Curtis, but I can't even imagine that, so I push the thought down.

The doorbell rings just as I'm shutting the jewelry back in the wooden box, letting it mingle with my tattoo chokers and the tiny white-gold hoops my mom gave me when I was thirteen and she finally let me get my ears pierced.

I throw myself on my bed, ignoring the voices in the living room until I realize whoever Curtis's talking to is a woman. Then I'm too curious to stop myself. If there's some sort of girlfriend situation he hasn't let me in on, I'm gonna be pissed. I have enough to deal with without some stepmother wannabe nosing in on my business like he's been doing. I walk down the hall, the voices growing clearer. When she laughs, I know it's Sonya. Her laugh's already imbedded in my mind like vital knowledge. Like the tiger's-eye pendant and my mother's hands, brushing my hair off my face after a bad dream.

My heart hammers, every bit of my blood rushing as I turn the corner and see her laughing at whatever Curtis's said.

She looks over her shoulder and catches sight of me, her smile widening. "*There* you are," she says, like I was supposed to be there all along. Maybe I was. It certainly feels like it.

"I'll let you two girls hang out," Curtis says.

"Your dad makes gorgeous jewelry," Sonya tells me.

"Nice meeting you, Sonya." Curtis ambles out of the living room. Is the only way to get rid of him to bring friends around? Is this some sort of reverse psychology on his part? Or am I overthinking it? The guy spends all his time working, playing guitar, or making jewelry, so mind games are probably not high on his list. Amethyst, guitar picks, and making sure the long-forgotten kid he got saddled with isn't throwing any fits probably are.

"He's nice," Sonya says.

"Yeah. Um. What are you doing here?"

She looks down, bending and picking up a necklace that has slices of some blue stone strung like icicles on the silver chain. "You didn't message me," she says, not looking up from the necklace nestled in her palm. "You promised."

"I was soaked, Sonya."

She finally looks up at me, frowning.

"My clothes? They were all wet. Because of Trenton. Remember? The ink was all smeared by the time I got home. I couldn't read what you wrote and forgot the numbers."

"Oh," she says, and the silence hangs there as we stare at each other and her cheeks turn red.

She lets out a shaky laugh—not the one I've already got memorized, a different one. I wonder how many there are. How long it would take to learn them all. Weeks? Months? A lifetime?

"Well, *I* keep my promises, unlike you, Miss Coley."

I don't laugh back, I just look at her. "I'll keep that in mind."

She huffs out another shaky laugh. "You're a brat."

"Mm." I may not know a lot about her yet, but I know people give in to her. I'm pretty sure one of the reasons she's in my living room is because I didn't.

Sonya picks at the edge of her striped shirt. "So . . . what do you wanna do?"

I shrug, collapsing on the beige couch. It's ugly but it's comfortable, I'll give Curtis that.

"You're the one that showed up here," I say.

"Because we said we'd hang again. Remember? I keep my promises."

"So?" I throw my arms out wide, encompassing the couch, kicking my feet back for emphasis. The flare in her eyes—it's hilarious. It's like poking a very angry but fluffy kitten. "We're hanging right now, aren't we?"

"Lolling around the house isn't hanging. Not without refreshments," Sonya insists. "Come on." She snaps her fingers at me.

I roll my eyes, getting to my feet. "One of these days, you're gonna snap at the wrong person."

She laughs. "Well, that's certainly not you, so we're cool. Right?"

"Gonna start calling you Snappy," I tease her as we head out of the living room and onto the porch.

"Don't poke the bear, Coley," she warns.

"*Rawr.*" I scrunch my hands up into little claws and paw the air, and her nose wrinkles up when she laughs—that true, unrivaled laughter that I already knew.

"You are such a fucking dork," she says, bending down to get the pink bike that she's got leaning against the tree opposite mine.

"I really think this is a situation where it takes one to know one."

She gasps as I grab my own bike and ride off before she can retort, cackling as she screeches and follows, pedaling furiously. "You don't even know where we're going, Coley!"

"Catch up, then!"

I sail down the street, wind whipping my hair into knots I know I'll regret later, but I don't care then. All I care about is that she's laughing and she's chasing me.

TEN

"The plan's simple," Sonya explains, as we turn the corner onto Oak Street and the 7-Eleven comes into sight on the corner. "They always understaff this store. I'll distract the cashier, you grab the champagne. We'll be in and out. No problem."

"Do you do this a lot?" I ask, opting for casual, but feeling my stomach churn a little. I've never stolen anything. I don't even remember taking candy when I was a kid.

She shrugs. "Fake IDs can be kind of hard in a town where everyone knows everyone."

"Is that why you and your friends were running away from that club the day I met you?"

She smirks. "They got through the bouncer, but the bartender saw right through them. Never taking Alex's word on a 'solid ID' again, let me tell you. SJ's still kind of pissed at me for ditching her."

"I mean, I would be, too."

"Ouch," Sonya pouts. "Mean."

"Getting left behind sucks," I say, and I cringe as soon as I say it. Too much truth.

"Aw, did someone leave you behind?" she asks lightly and almost sarcastically.

When I don't answer—I can't; I won't; not here; probably never—her head tilts and her cheeks flush.

"Shit," she says suddenly, too knowingly. "Who would leave you behind?"

It's so earnest it makes me wonder. . . .

But no. *No.* That'd be crazy.

"So you'll distract the cashier, and I'll grab the booze. Got it. Simple. Easy. Let's do it."

"Coley . . ."

"I'm cool," I say, leaning my bike against the cement pole that holds the 7-Eleven sign. I ignore the worried sound she makes. "You're right. It's not really hanging out without refreshments. Come on."

She catches up with me at the door, leaning forward to grab it and open it for me. Her shoulders square as she sweeps inside, heading right to the cashier as I head to the back.

My palms are damp even though I'm right next to the cool air of the drink fridges. I wipe them hastily on my jeans. If I grab a bottle and it slips, we're done for.

"Can you help me?" I hear Sonya ask the cashier.

"What can I do for you?" he asks.

I edge open the fridge, scanning the wine and beer. Shit. I hadn't asked her what she wanted. What if I choose wrong? Will she laugh at me?

"This is really embarrassing," Sonya says. "But do you carry tampons?" On the last word, she fake-whispers it.

I grab a bottle of champagne, tucking it under my jacket, heading toward the end aisle.

"They're on aisle seven," the cashier tells Sonya, who bats her eyes as she says, "Could you show me where that is?"

Shit. That's my aisle. I reverse course, pretending I desperately need to look at the lighters for a second before putting them back and heading in the opposite direction, away from Sonya and the approaching cashier.

"You're so sweet," she's saying to him, one eye on me.

I turn quickly down aisle five, my focus on Sonya instead of where I'm going, and it's only dumb luck that I don't crash right into the WET FLOOR sign.

The bottle of champagne's tucked under my arm and I keep it tight against my side as I skid to a halt right in front of a girl holding a mop, her headphones plastered over her bleach-blond hair done up in little alien buns all over her head, exposing her dark roots. It should look messy, but it kind of works on her the more you look at it. Her orange name tag says BLAKE on it. She stares at me, chewing her gum; her unfocused eyes make me wonder if she is at least stoned, if not a little faded.

Shit. Why did I let Sonya talk me into this?

"I was just looking for . . ." I look around, reaching mindlessly for something with the only hand I can use. I grab a bag without looking and clutch it to me. "There it is."

"Mmm. Flamin' Hot."

"What?"

"Spicy," Blake says, nodding to the bag I'm holding.

I look down. Cheetos. She's talking about the Cheetos.

"Yeah," I said. "Anyway."

"They're good."

"Yeah," I agree, walking past her and heading back to the cashier, who's returned to his till after helping Sonya. I throw a five-dollar bill down for the chips and rush out without getting my change before anything else goes wrong. For a second, I think I'm gonna be sick, as I head across the parking lot, the adrenaline rush like a roller coaster under me. And then it's nothing but dropping, because she's nowhere to be seen. She's not leaning against the sign or waiting on the sidewalk across the street. She's nowhere to be found.

I turn in a circle and the world spins more than it should. I head toward the 7-Eleven, near the dumpsters. Did she just . . .

Who would leave you behind? "Bwah!"

This time, I almost drop the damn champagne when she jumps out from behind the dumpster, her laughter a full-on cackle as I stumble back.

"Oh my God! The look on your face!" She's slapping her thighs, she's laughing so hard.

"You—" But before I can say anything else, she grabs my hand and I don't have words anymore. All I have is the warmth of her skin against mine, smooth and soft and citrus-scented somehow.

"Come on, slowpoke." She tugs harder and I can't resist. I don't know how and I don't want to. It feels like glowing, following her behind the 7-Eleven, to the lot that fades into grass, and then the shadows of trees are painting my skin as we walk beneath them. The trees are so tall here—and so thick they cool the air around us. It's like stepping into another world as the air chills and then warms again when the trees part to reveal a long wind of train tracks.

"Huh," I say, staring at the tracks. They seem much bigger this close up. When Sonya steps onto the rails, I follow. Walking on them is like trying to balance on a beam.

"They have trains in San Diego," Sonya insists.

"Not in the middle of the trees like this."

"Where else are we gonna put them?" she asks, walking on the rail, raising her arms gracefully like a ballerina as she tiptoes down the metal and spins. Her hair flies out like feathers on a swan unfurling, and I'm caught in the dark line she makes against the blue-gold light.

"So are we gonna ride the rails somewhere?" I ask as she holds out her hand imperiously for the champagne, and I give it to her.

She snorts as she pops the cork, and the champagne spills, fizzy over her fingers. "Shoot," she says, lifting her hand to her mouth and licking it, and the sight of her pink tongue makes me look down, trying to breathe around this press in my chest, a too-big feeling that I don't think I can control.

"Want some?" she asks. "I'll trade you."

I take the bottle, careful to make sure our fingers don't touch this time. I don't think I can handle it. She plucks the bag of Cheetos from me.

I take a swig, hoping it settles the feeling. But it doesn't; it just adds to the hammer that is my heart in my rib cage.

"So your dad seems nice," Sonya says. "Kind of like a creative rocker type. He has *so* many tattoos. My mom would be horrified." She smirks at this last thing, like she wants to horrify her mother just a little.

"I guess." I take another drink.

"You guess he's nice? Or you guess he's the creative rocker type?"

"Both."

She stops, flattening her feet on the rail for balance. "What do you mean?"

"Curtis and I . . . we don't know each other very well."

"Oh," she says. "So he wasn't, like, a two-weekends-a-month-and-half-the-holidays sort, like my dad?"

"No."

"What kind of dad was he?"

I look down, my skin flashing hot with discomfort. "Is this Twenty Questions?"

"I'm just curious. Like . . . this is how people make friends, right? They ask each other questions. They share stuff. I told you about my dad." She takes the champagne and takes a long swig. "Or do you not want to be friends?" she asks after she's done.

I stare at her, wondering what the fuck she's doing.

"What?" she asks, practically wriggling in the face of my silence. "You can't just look at me like that and—"

"And what?" I ask. "Not give you everything you ask for?"

Her mouth twists. "Not to sound, like, conceited or anything, but I can usually tell when people like me. And you . . ."

"Me . . ."

"You're all over the place! And it's making me all over the place! I don't know how to act around you."

"Maybe don't act at all," I suggest. "Just be yourself. Because half of the time, it feels like you're faking something."

"What does *that* mean?"

"I guess I get the feeling you just tell people what you think they want to hear instead of what you actually think."

She laughs nervously, tossing her hair. "You're judging me and you don't even know me."

"How can I know you if you don't let anyone see you?"

Her lips part, her eyes wide at the question. "That's . . ." She can't finish. "Wow, Coley," she says quietly. "I could say the same about you," she challenges finally.

So I decide to give her something real. "Curtis wasn't a two-weekends sort of dad. It's more like a I-haven't-seen-him-since-I-was-three sort of thing with us."

Her eyebrows scrunch together, that little V of sympathy between them. "That's really heavy."

"Yeah," I agree, dreading the next question: Why am I with him if he never wanted anything to do with me before?

But she doesn't ask that. It's almost like she knows it's too much.

"Thanks for telling me," she says, an offering. And then: "My parents split when I was little, too. It sucked at first."

"Just at first?"

"Well, my mom met my stepdad, and he makes her a little more chill. Key words here: *a little*. And they had Emma, my sister. She's eight. Total sweetie. My mom says she won't stay that way if she keeps hero-worshipping me, though."

I frown. "That's kinda mean."

Sonya shrugs. "I'm not very sweet."

"You were sweet to me when I was crying." I flush as soon as it's out of my mouth. *Why, Coley, why would you bring that up?*

"You think so?" Sonya asks curiously. "I kinda made you cry."

I reach out for the Cheetos bag, and this time, our fingers do brush. I let them instead of being careful. Whisper-soft shivers spread through me. Does she feel it too? Am I crazy? I don't think I am.

"It wasn't you," I say. "It was just . . . that whole day." It was more than that: it was this whole year, but I'm not going to get into that. "Unless it's typical for you, first time you meet people, to run them over?" The Cheetos bag crinkles in my grip. "Is that typical for you, first time you meet people?"

"No. You're just really special," she sasses back, and I can't help it, I laugh, and she grins back at me, hip-checking me before spinning away on the rail. My heart thumps so hard, my entire body vibrates like a train's coming.

"Oh shit, what time is it?" Sonya asks, ditching the champagne bottle and pulling her phone out of her pocket.

"Are you late for something?"

"I'm supposed to babysit Emma this afternoon."

"Oh, okay," I say, trying not to feel disappointed. "I can head home on my own."

"No! Come with me!"

I pause. "It's fine—"

"No! Come keep me company. All Emma wants to do lately is watch *The NeverEnding Story* three times a day. I think I have the movie memorized at this point. Save me from such a cruel fate." She clasps her hands together like she's begging me.

I roll my eyes. "Okay," I say. "I'll come."

ELEVEN

When Sonya comes to a stop in front of the house, I try to hide my surprise, but holy fuck, her house is *huge*. It's like the ones they use for exteriors in movies: pristine sprawling lawn, perfect white paint, and a green door with a summer wreath hanging on it.

Sonya casually lets her bike fall on the manicured lawn and strolls up the driveway as I hurry to catch up.

Inside it's even more beautiful, with a big staircase and sprinkled with furniture that's all old wood and antique-y. It's the fancy kind of furniture you don't buy, you inherit. There's even a chandelier in the living room.

"Sonya, is that you?" a woman's voice calls from another room. "Finally! I swear, you're always making me late!" She strolls into the hallway and spots Sonya. "What in the world are you wearing?" She strides forward, her heels clicking against the wood floor. "I buy you so many beautiful clothes, and you wear these ratty—" She stops, her gaze falling on me, hanging behind in the foyer.

"Oh." In just a second, Sonya's mom's face shifts from disappointed to a bright smile. "Who's your friend?"

"This is Coley."

"It's so nice to meet you, Coley. I'm Tracy. What a cute little jacket." She looks me up and down like she means the opposite of what she's saying.

My fingers curl inside the sleeves of my mom's jacket. "Thanks."

"I'll be home late," Tracy tells Sonya. "Your sister's in the den. Money for dinner is on the fridge. Bye, girls."

She grabs her purse and swishes out of the house.

"She's going to some women's thing. Charity or something," Sonya explains, crooking her finger and leading me into the living room. "My stepdad's out of town. Which is why I'm on Emma duty." She bends down in front of a mirrored cabinet that has a fancy crystal decanter and mixers set on top. Sonya pulls the clip out of her hair, poking it into the cabinet lock.

"Are you seriously . . . ?" I don't get to finish my question, because she's got the cabinet open with the ease of a practiced lock picker.

"I'm just full of surprises," Sonya says, grinning at me over her shoulder. She grabs a bottle from the shelf and locks the cabinet back up. "They won't miss this one. It's plum dessert wine that someone gifted them a million years ago."

"If you say so."

"I do," she says, grabbing two glasses from the top of the cabinet. "Come on, let's go check on Emma in the den."

She leads me through the house. Everywhere I look, there's something fancy and breakable that makes me want to tuck my elbows and never, ever bring a backpack inside because I'd accidentally sweep something off a table.

The den is more like a giant media room. The biggest TV I've ever seen on the wall, in the middle of a few plush white couches with all these cozy throw pillows and blankets. A little girl is sitting in front of the TV, wrapped in one of the blankets, watching *The NeverEnding Story*.

"Emma, say hi to my friend Coley," Sonya encourages, sitting down on the couch and pouring the wine. She hands me one of the glasses, and I sit down next to her.

"Hi, Emma."

"Hi!" Emma waves at me before turning back to watch the movie.

"How many times have you watched this today?" Sonya asks.

"Just this once," Emma says.

"Are you lying?"

Her head hangs. "Maybe."

Sonya laughs. "You've gotta get better at it! I could totally tell."

Emma doesn't answer, her attention drawn back to the screen.

"Teaching her your ways, huh?" I ask Sonya.

"Just preparing her for a life with my mom," Sonya says.

I lean back on the couch, clutching the bumpy crystal glass and sampling the wine. It's so sweet I can take only tiny sips, the taste of plum and spice almost overwhelming. I can smell it on the air as I breathe out.

I don't know how to do this. I don't know how to . . . be. Just *be*. Breathe here, next to her, because it's like I'm gonna fly out of my skin every time she moves even a little.

She's not feeling anything I am. She can't be. She's focused on the screen, her hand splayed out on the couch between us like she doesn't even think it's a temptation and a dare and a burning desire.

Her fingers drum against the cream suede of the couch, little *tap-tap-taps* that I fixate on instead of the TV. What would she do if I reached out and stilled her movement? Would she be warm, like she was before at the lake, holding me as if she knew how to already?

I want to find out—so badly my mouth's dry from it. I run my finger along the edge of my tattoo choker, suddenly too tight against my skin, and I remind myself to breathe. I'm being obvious. Can she tell? Oh God, please, let her never find out.

As soon as I think it, she looks at me. She smiles, her chin dipping, devilish as she sips the plum wine, and suddenly, all I can think is *Please, please let her find out.*

Please let her hand brush against mine on the couch.

It does.

Please let her pinkie hook over mine, an unspoken promise, just us two.

She does.

Please let her lean forward, dark spill of hair, eyes sweeping down to our hands like she's slipping into my thoughts.

She whispers, "Let's go up to my room."

The thought of it, soft sheets and sacred space . . . the place where she takes off everything . . . it makes me too aware of every part of my body. She's a chameleon, and I want to see her true colors again, not the act everyone sees. I got a glimpse, so I know I'll recognize her . . . if she shows me.

I follow her up the winding staircase and down the hall, and when she pushes open a door to the right, there's a nervous smile on her face. "Here we are," she says.

I step inside. It's big—like the rest of the house—and I don't know what I expected. Not the canopy bed and ballerina-pink bedspread. Her desk in the corner looks more like her—feathered pom-pom pens and DVDs stacked in a haphazard tower. There's a pair of black dance shoes hanging by their laces on the back of the chair, and notes folded into careful triangles scattered across the desk.

I recognize the notes: they're the kind popular girls traded with each other in my last school, secrets running along each fold of paper. I wouldn't even begin to know how to fold one; is it a prerequisite for being the *it* girl? Are they just born knowing these things? Folded notes perfect for shallow pockets and hair flicks that make your stomach drop and smiles that say *I see you.*

I turn away from the desk and focus on the other wall. There's a shelf set into it reaching all the way up to the ceiling, and it's absolutely full of trophies.

"Ugh," Sonya says, tossing the phone onto the bed. It skitters across the pink bedspread and hits me in the thigh. I can see the text it's still open to:

"Boys are so stupid, right?" Sonya asks me, looking down at the phone. I bite my lip, not knowing what to say. Not knowing the answer, if I should agree or not.

She throws herself on the bed next to me, her hair spreading out on the comforter, strands of it so close I could almost reach out and touch them. I hold back the urge, even though my fingers itch, my mind full of questions: What would it be like to tuck it behind her ear? Would my thumb catch on the bottom of her earring? They're little sparkly studs that I'm sure are real diamonds, now that I've seen her house.

"What do you think of my room, Coley?"

"You're that invested in my opinion, huh?" I lie back next to her on the bed, and I wonder if our arms brush, she'll think it's on purpose.

"Good point. I haven't seen *your* room yet. Maybe you have terrible taste." She can't keep the smirk off her face.

"I have great taste, thank you very much," I say. "But my room was all boxes until yesterday, and now it's just a rickety dresser Curtis bought me and this metal desk that looks like it was made in the 1950s."

"Your dad should be doing more to make you feel welcome," Sonya says, frowning at me, her head turning to meet my eyes, and shit, we're *so* close here on the bed. I shouldn't be lying back like this with her.

"Curtis doesn't know how to 'dad,'" I say. It makes her eyebrows scrunch together, all angry. It's sweet, really. That's the thing about people who've had a good dad or a good stepdad, and it seems like Sonya has both. It's hard for people like that, people who have people to catch them, to imagine life without a net.

"Well, he should *learn* how to dad."

"I don't really want to talk about it," I say, and thankfully she drops it as I continue. "Your room is cool. Very award-heavy, what with your wall o' trophies over there." I push up on my elbows to examine the wall of gold and silver. A lot of the trophies have figures of girls dancing. "So, you're like a ballerina or something?"

"I'm a competitive dancer," Sonya says.

"What's the difference?"

She arches her eyebrow at me like she thinks I'm being sarcastic.

"Seriously!" I say. "I don't know."

"Well, for one, it means I'm there to win. And I do . . . a lot," she says, with no false modesty. "But I'm not a ballerina. I do a lot of different types of dance."

"So you're, like, multifaceted."

She beams. "No one's ever called me that before."

"It sounds harder than just having one focus."

"It is in a way. Some of the girls I danced with when I was younger ended up going into ballet."

"But not you."

She shrugs. "My mom was more into this."

"What about you?"

She laughs. That nervous, uncomfortable burst I've started to come to know. "I like being the best."

"Can I see?"

More eyebrow scrunching. She's cute when she's confused. "You want me to dance?"

"I've never seen any competitive dancing before," I point out, keeping my face straight. "How will I know the difference between competitive and just regular dance if you don't show me?"

Her mouth tilts, skeptical. "You're fucking with me."

I grin. "Maybe a little. But it doesn't mean I don't want to see you do your thing. See how you earned your wall o' trophies."

"You're such a brat," she shoots back, and she sticks her tongue out like a real brat.

"Come on!" I urge, loving needling her. "Show me how to spin!" I raise my arms into a little moon over my head and she dissolves into laughter as I tilt my head back and forth.

"Okay, fine, fine, I'll do one of my old solos. *Just* to appease you."

I clap my hands together. "I win!"

The look she shoots me is all fond exasperation, and it makes me feel like I'm eating melting chocolate, the rush of it thick and too sweet, sticking to every part of me.

"This one solo was actually kind of cool," she continues, shuffling through her CD case, looking for the right song. "I just learned how to do a triple turn, and it was kind of special because I was the first to do that on my team."

"There are *teams*?" I ask, bewildered.

"It's *competitive*, Coley. Who do you think I was winning the trophies against?"

"Right."

She plucks a CD out of the case, slips it into her boom box, and presses PLAY. She kicks at the pile of dirty clothes on the floor, tossing them out of the way of her makeshift dance floor as the music begins to play. Then tinkly piano chords flood the room, and her body stills in front of me, her eyes closing.

"I can't do this if you're judging me," she insists.

"I'm *not* judging you," I tell her. And I'm not—I know shit-all about dance. I couldn't even tell her what a jeté is. All I really want is to see *her.* That's why I'm here. That's why I let her drag me out of my house and into shoplifting and down those railroad tracks and then back here.

She starts to move to the music, her body swaying and dipping as she spins and turns, her leg rising impossibly high. How the hell did she get so bendy? My thighs are screaming just at the sight of her.

Her hair whips across her face, her head swirling as her arms shift up and her leg rises in anticipation of that infamous triple turn. She spins, once, twice—

Bam.

Her elbow slams into the side of her bookcase and the trophies rattle, one of them falling off and crashing to the floor. Sonya grabs her arm, her face screwed up trying to fight it as her cheeks flood with red.

"*Fuck,*" she mutters, her face flaming further.

"Shit! Are you okay?" I leap to my feet, hurrying over to her, and I don't think it through when I reach out and grab her unhurt arm, pulling her out of the way of the still-wobbling trophies.

"I'm fine," she says, in a choked voice that tells me the opposite.

"You were great," I insist.

"Fuck," she mutters again. "My elbow."

"Do you need ice?"

She shakes her head. That red isn't fading on her cheeks, and all I can think is I want to make her feel better. To tease her out of her humiliation.

"Thank you, *competitive dance champion,* for showing me such a *competitive* dance. I can absolutely see the difference between it and normal dancing now."

"Hey! I won for that song!"

It's working.

"I've no doubt you won."

Her smile fights itself. "If you're gonna be that way, *you* dance."

"Me?" I mock-gasp and press a hand against my chest. "But I don't have any trophies or titles to defend! Do they have competitive dance titles? A sash you wear? Are you queen of something?"

She snickers. "If you're gonna make fun, you better be able to back it up."

"Okay," I say, rising to her bait. "Fine. Pick me a song." I shimmy my shoulders at her. "Something sad, achy, and raw."

"So something just like you?"

"Ooh, finally showing your claws, huh?"

She paws the air at me with her periwinkle nails, and I laugh, glowing. Sonya bends down and grabs the CD case, shuffling through it and then grabbing one with a truly wicked smile. "I've got the *perfect* song." She pops it in the boom box and presses PLAY. Imogen Heap's *very* achy vocals fill the room, wrapping around us.

"So," I say, standing in the middle of the room, channeling Sonya. "This is kind of a big deal, 'cause I was the first one on my dance team to lift my arms like this." I fling them dramatically up and give her spirit fingers, waggling furiously, which makes her howl with laughter, clutching her stomach, her entire body writhing with joy. I've never understood triumph until that moment.

"And then when I coined this move at competition . . ." I bring my hands down in exaggerated flaps like a baby bird that hasn't quite learned how to fly yet. "My coaches were actually *weeping* at the swanlike beauty of my choreography."

"Ohmygod, Coley, stopppp! *Icanbarelybreathe!*" she shrieks, laughing even harder.

I fling myself onto the ground, sliding a little on the rug on my knees toward her, pressing my hand to my heart. "You gotta have a big finish."

She claps her hand over her mouth, trying to hold in the hysterical, half-drunk giggles. She hiccups beneath her fingers, swaying a little, and her eyes widen.

"I'llberightback," she says in a rush, lurching through the open door and running out of the room.

Oh shit. I watch her gallop away. Casting a glance at the bottle of plum wine on her dresser, I'm suddenly grateful I'd taken only a few little sips. Rising to my feet, I peek out of Sonya's room to the end of the hall, wondering which direction she went. I take a gamble and go right.

"Sonya?" I call softly, but I don't get an answer.

There are pictures all along the hall, a carefully selected gallery wall that's so perfect it looks like it's out of a magazine. Beautiful black-and-white posed portraits of Sonya's family, and a glamour portrait from the sixties that must be Sonya's grandmother—her winged eyeliner is Elizabeth Taylor–thick. A series of photos of Sonya's mom and her stepdad getting married, followed by maternity photos, followed by baby pictures of Emma and Sonya. The entire family at Disneyland, Sonya's grandmother, now silver-haired but still rocking the eyeliner, next to the family. And finally, something that has me rooted there for a moment: a cluster of Sonya's school photos.

It's a timeline of her, from pigtailed kindergartener to perfect competitive dance champion. The last picture has to be recent; she looks almost exactly the same but her hair's maybe a little longer now. She stares a little off camera, posed against a tree, in clothes that are *so* not her: a white cable-knit sweater and dark denim, her hair held back with a headband, of all things. She's thoughtful and poised but distant. There's no sparkle in her eyes, like earlier when she was fighting her laughter and failing. The moment when she let go, when she let it in—let *me* in . . . I think that girl, *that* was the real her. Or maybe I just hope it.

So why am I the only one who saw it? Sonya is like that card game in which the dealer sets three cards down. Keep your eye on the left one. Queen of hearts. Shuffle. Shuffle. Misdirect. Where is it now?

You always pick wrong. But today I somehow picked right. I saw her.

And she ran.

Where is she?

I turn around, intent on going the other direction, and I almost run into Emma, who's standing there, holding a bag of chips.

"Hi."

Emma just stares at me.

"Did you see where your sister went?"

"She's in the bathroom," Emma says, pointing behind her.

"Thanks." I pause. "Do you need help or anything?"

Emma shakes her head.

"Okay."

I walk past her, heading to where Emma pointed. The door's closed, the light on. I tap lightly on the door.

"Sonya?"

There's silence, and then a faint "Yeah?" floats through the door.

"Are you okay?"

Another pause. "Yeah. I just . . . I'm kind of sick. The champagne and Cheetos combination was not a good idea."

"The wine probably didn't help," I add.

"I never get sick off wine," she insists, muffled and miserable. "I'm just . . . I'm sorry."

"Don't be. It's fine," I assure her. "Do you need anything?"

"No! No!" she says hastily, like she's afraid I'll barge in. "Everything's fine. I can deal. I'll AIM you, okay?"

"Yeah," I say. "Okay."

I bite my lip. Leaving her seems wrong. I've left my jacket in her room, so I go back to get it, and for a second, I stand in her room alone, staring at all those trophies, because if I don't stare at the trophies, I'm going to stare at the bed, and that's just . . .

Not gonna go there, Coley.

I move the bottle of water from her dresser to the little table next to her bed where she can see it. There's a pad of Post-it Notes on the end table, and I grab it, along with a pen from her desk. I scribble down:

As I pass by the bathroom, I almost knock again. But I can hear her retching inside and I don't want to bother her, so all I do is slip the note under the door and go downstairs.

"Bye, Emma," I tell her when I pass by the media room and find her sitting there, watching *The NeverEnding Story* again.

"Bye," she says.

I'm halfway down the street with my bike before I realize that I still have the pad of Post-it Notes clutched in my palm.

I slip it into my pocket, and my hand burns all the way home, as if just touching something of hers heats me from the inside.

TWELVE

"Is that you, Coley?" Curtis calls as I let myself in the house.

"No, it's a burglar, breaking into your house to rob you of your gemstones," I call back.

There's a pause and my stomach drops, wondering if I've pushed too far. And then a low chuckle comes from the living room.

"They're not worth that much," he calls. "But there's left-overs from dinner if you want them. I didn't know when you were coming back."

I sigh, walking down the hall and standing in the doorway of the living room. He's sitting on the couch, watching TV.

"Are you gonna give me a curfew?"

"No," he says, looking horrified. And then: "Should I?" He almost sounds like he's asking both of us, instead of just himself. Or maybe he's asking some spirit of fatherhood he thinks he's going to summon so he can be enlightened. Like, read a book, dude. I know they write them about parenting. There are too many shitty parents for that to not be a booming business.

"I picked up a new phone for you," he says, gesturing to the phone sitting on the coffee table. "Try to make sure this one doesn't go in the lake?"

"Thanks," I say, grabbing it. "I can pay you back—"

"Coley, no," he says, gently, so gently that I kind of hate him for it.

"I should get a job," I protest. "Pull my weight—"

"You're starting a new school in August. That's where your focus should be."

"You don't even know if I'm good at school," I mutter.

"You could sit down and tell me," he offers, scooting over and patting the couch next to him, and for some reason, I draw closer. But when I do, his expression completely changes, his mouth dropping open.

"What?" I ask, looking behind me. Nothing. Is there something on my face?

"That jacket," he says, his voice suddenly choked.

"What?" I say again, clutching it to me.

"Where did you get that?"

I lick my lips. "It was Mom's."

I don't know if I've said that word out loud since I got here. It feels strange in my mouth. Like I've forgotten what it's like to say it half a dozen times a day. Will I forget, someday, what it was like to have a mom at all?

"Yeah, I know," he says, a slow smile breaking across his tired face like sun across busted sidewalk. "She, uh, 'borrowed' it from me years ago. Never gave it back. She always said it looked better on her than me." The smile's so wide now, awash with memories I'm not part of, and I hate him, suddenly, for having so many pieces of her that I will never get now. This was supposed to be *mine*. Mine and hers. A way to hold on to her the way she couldn't hold on to me.

But now I have to share it with him? He's tainted it, and it's like he knows, because he rubs his hand over his stubbled jaw and says, "It looks really good on you."

"I'm not hungry," I say in response, getting up. "I'm really tired. I'm just gonna . . ." I fade off, not even finishing as I hurry to my room. He's not worth it. None of this is worth it. This is just something to endure. Living with him and surviving the next year of high school until I'm eighteen and I can get the fuck out.

And then what? A little voice lurks in my head. Then what? Then I'm alone with no one. No family. No friends. No help. Nothing.

I lie down on my bed, not fighting as tears leak out of the corners of my eyes, my fingers curled in the cuffs of the jacket. No wonder it's so big, if it was his originally.

For better or worse, I'm wrapped up in my family and I hate it instead of love it. Because it's not real. I know whatever Curtis thinks he's trying to build isn't real. I thought Mom and me were real, but now I wonder.

I think about those family portraits on Sonya's walls. How I'll never have that. Don't you have to know what a family feels like to build one? I've been part of a duo. A gruesome twosome, Mom liked to joke. Us against the world. But I can't remember being part of a unit. Two parents and kids and a house and pictures on the walls that chronicle an entire life. All these branches of a family, so it really is like a tree, like a living, breathing thing that makes sure you're never alone.

Sometimes I think that's what killed her. The loneliness. I

know it's not as simple as that. I know it's complicated. That pain is complicated.

But loneliness is gnawing. Like a trapped animal that's unable to do anything but follow instinct. Even when you know better, even when you know yourself and your worth, it can eat away at you, until there's no you left.

I'm scared, sometimes. That I'll lose myself, too.

That I'll never find myself at all.

THIRTEEN

LJ User: SonyatSunrisex00x [Public Entry]

Date: June 13, 2006

[**Mood:** poetic]

[**Music:** "Lover's Spit"—Broken Social Scene]

post-it

little yellow square
secret slipped under the door
drunk on you and me

FOURTEEN

What does it mean?

That's all I can think. Over and over. Skipping in between the few instantly memorized lines of Sonya's poetry.

What does it mean?

It's late. The hush of the house comforts me like nothing else. It's like I can finally relax. Curtis went to bed at least an hour ago. My room's dark, the light shut off, so that if he gets seized with some urge to check on me, he'll think I'm asleep and he'll pass by the door. But I'm not. I'm sitting in front of my computer, the screen the only light, reading her LiveJournal.

I haven't gone back far in her journal entries. Mostly because I keep coming back to that poem. A haiku, I think. I had to google it to make sure, but the rhythm structure—the syllables—match up.

She wrote *poetry* about today. I tuck my legs under my feet, my hand moving from the mouse to the pad of Post-its I'd accidentally taken from her house.

Drunk on you and me. Is she being literal? Or is it just for poetic effect?

Is she just fucking with me?

I jump at the *ding* on my computer. I click over to AIM, not wanting to hope, but . . . oh, but I'm right. It's her.

SonyatSunrisex00x: that water saved my life lol

It's like an ember inside me, too hot to touch for too long, but so tempting in its glow and beauty.

SonyatSunrisex00x: whatcha doing

I bite my lip, my fingers hovering over my keyboard. What to say? Play it cool, right? She's still probably a little buzzed, even with the vomiting.

RollieColey87: thinking about ur triple turn
RollieColey87: im inspired

Once I've started typing, it's almost like I can't stop, the rush of it too much, knowing she's on the other side, waiting . . . for me.

RollieColey87: maybe I'll take up dance. do the whole Julia Stiles in *Save the Last Dance* thing
SonyatSunrisex00x: you're gonna audition for juilliard and fall in love with a cute wannabe doctor?

It's like . . . fuck, it's like a hundred-pound weight off my back. I've forgotten about that—how to talk about things you're into, how to make fun of things—instead of like I've got my fists up all the time. Even though I know Curtis's trying. But I can't help it; he makes me so mad . . . but I'm so tired already.

RollieColey87: definitely gonna nearly miss my juilliard audition for drama reasons. but I think I'd ditch doctor guy in the long run.
SonyatSunrisex00x: not your type?

I almost type this: *More interested in the girl who played his sister.*

But I can't. Even if I don't send it, even typing it is too much. It's like admitting it.

RollieColey87: nah

And then I do type:

RollieColey87: I like dancers.

My hand hovers over the RETURN key and it's like soaring, thinking about the possibilities—about her face, lit by her computer screen, reading my words, like I read hers, that poem that I can't get out of my head. But I'm not brave enough. My fingers shift to the DELETE button instead. It's gone from the screen but not my mind.

SonyatSunrisex00x: not gonna lie, I already have a bruise on my arm
RollieColey87: aw
RollieColey87: poor sonya

I mean it for real, but her response—

SonyatSunrisex00x: so sarcastic
SonyatSunrisex00x: ;)

A deliberate misunderstanding. A game—her and me. A code only we understand. It's like having permission to be honest, and then she'll just pretend it's a joke. Liminal space, between real and fake, between her mask and mine.

It's maybe the bravest thing I've ever done, typing it and sending it, quick before I lose whatever insane nerve I've just summoned.

RollieColey87: if you stop whining now, next time I see you, i'll kiss your fearsome wound better, okay?
SonyatSunrisex00x: gasp!
SonyatSunrisex00x: i am not whining!
SonyatSunrisex00x: bitch

My stomach twists. Was I wrong?

SonyatSunrisex00x: :P

Relief floods me.

SonyatSunrisex00x: tomorrow? you and me?

I don't even know how to breathe or the name of this feeling. All I know is I want to be breathless forever, if it's like this.

RollieColey87: sure

FIFTEEN

LJ User: SonyatSunrisex00x [Private Entry]

Date: June 18, 2006

[**Mood:** thoughtful]

[**Music:** "Pieces of Me"—Ashlee Simpson]

SJ and Brooke have been on my ass—*where are you, come to the lake, we never see you*—but I'm just . . .

I'm over it.

Coley and I went out today. More train-track shit. It's becoming a regular little spot. I kind of love that. No one else has to know.

Her and me, no booze, no barriers, no distractions. We walked along the railroad tracks all the way to the stone bridge. Blue skies and brown hair, that jacket she hasn't stopped wearing since the second day I saw her. She sat down on the edge, dangling her legs like she thought her feet would reach the water. And I had to pull myself up next to her.

Her sneakers knocked against mine, mismatched laces that have to be on purpose.

We played Truth or Dare. A girl's way to while away boredom. She took the bait, thank God. But then . . .

Shit, then it got worse, somehow. Because she looked me dead in the eyes and chose truth.

Who the fuck does that, first time out? Coley, that's who.

I gave her an easy out. Or I thought so. *What's your greatest fear?* I thought she'd say spiders or something. But instead, she just says two words and wrecks me:

Dying alone.

Simple. But it wasn't. Not the way she said it.

She said it like she understood it somehow. Better than anyone.

And I've been listening. To her. To the little pieces she's given me about before this town.

She told me her dad didn't know how to dad. And the only reason a dad who doesn't want to be a dad *does* do the dad thing is when there's no other choice.

Shit. It was all I could think about, sitting there: how I fumbled this game into a revelation I don't think she meant to make.

I think her mom's gone. Like *gone,* gone.

How do you even deal with that? What happened? Was she sick? Is Coley okay?

My mom is the worst sometimes—okay, most of the time—but she's my *mom.* If she wasn't here, I'd freak.

Is Coley freaking? What do I do if she does? How do I help her?

I have questions I don't know how to ask. Because she still hasn't *really* told me. So I just have to wait. Until she trusts me enough.

—Sonya

SIXTEEN

"Are you sure about this?" I ask, looking skeptically at the gloss in Sonya's hands.

"Don't you trust me?" She pouts.

"After that game of Truth or Dare?" I shoot back, arching my eyebrows.

She scoffs. "That only brought us closer together, babe." She winks at me, and my heart's about to beat out of my goddamn chest. *She calls her other friends babe,* I remind myself. I've seen her do it in the comments of her LiveJournal. It's not special, even if it feels that way.

I try to focus on the lip gloss and not how close she is. She is *so* close. I can smell a whiff of her peony shampoo beneath everything else—lotion and perfume and the blood-orange-scented lip gloss she'd painted on her own lips with ruthless precision before whipping out another tube for me.

She's a whirl of scents and moods and smiles, and sometimes I think I know her. After two weeks of almost constantly hanging out together, I'm almost *sure* of it. But then, sometimes she'll do or say something that makes me think: *Shit, no, I don't know you at all—but I want to.*

Fuck, do I want to.

"I still think that color's too dark for me."

"And I think that you should shut up and listen to me," she says. "I've spent all this time with you and you barely wear any makeup. Not that I can blame you. If I had your cute little face, I wouldn't want to hide it either!" She taps me on my nose, and it's like every nerve ending in my body floods to the tip.

"I'm gonna look goth or something," I protest, but before I can do anything, she grabs my chin between her fingers, and I can't move, suddenly, her eyes on mine. The surprise in them tells me that I'm not alone. I'm not. I'm not making this up.

If I just lean forward, I could see if her lip gloss tastes like blood orange as well as smells like it. I run my fingers through her honey-streaked hair, because I want to see if it's as silky as it looks. She looks so soft sometimes, even when she's guarded, and I rub my fingers together at night, like I'm trying to invoke the memory of hers; a spell that would summon her to me.

"Just sit still," she says, and when her voice cracks, my stomach leaps. Does it mean anything? Or is her throat just dry? Should I offer her water?

I just do as she says. She brushes the gloss over my lips and the stickiness tickles, but I hold still as her gaze drifts from my lips to my eyes, back and forth, like we're rocking on a boat, buoyed not by water but the rhythm of each other.

"Close your eyes," she says when she finishes with my lips.

"Aren't you doing this backward?" I ask as she begins to do my eyes. I fight to keep them closed as the eye-shadow pad brushes over my lids. "I thought it was eyes first, then lips."

I can hear the shrug in her voice. "I'm not sure, actually," she says. "I don't do a lot of people's makeup."

"I'm special, huh?"

My eyes are still closed so I can't see her. But the pause . . . it's enough.

"Yeah," she says softly.

She finishes up my eyes, brushing mascara on my lashes, and then dabs cream blush on my cheeks. I jerk back instinctively as she comes at me with the eyelash curler.

"I can do that one myself," I say, taking it from her.

She grins. "Don't want me yanking out your eyelashes?"

"I'm pretty sure that's a form of torture," I say, using the curler as quickly as I can.

"I think that's yanking fingernails out."

"Ew." I shudder at the thought. "I can't even imagine how much that would hurt."

"Way worse than eyelashes."

"Says the girl who hasn't torn a clump of them out."

"And you have?"

"Why do you think I don't wear a whole lot of makeup?"

She shoots me a look and I look back at her, my face stony, and then I grin.

"You're shitting me!"

"Someone's gotta keep you on your toes."

"SJ does—sometimes."

"Is she coming tonight?" I ask casually.

"Everyone is," Sonya says. "SJ and Trenton and Brooke. Alex got us an invite. Partying out in the boonies isn't really our scene, you know?"

"I don't, actually," I say. "I've hung out with your friends once, and that didn't last long."

Her gaze sweeps down, and her cheeks go pink. Is she feeling guilty? Or she's just realizing that she and I haven't spent everyday together since we met.

"How did Alex get the invite?"

"Oh, Alex knows everyone," she says. "He's kinda a social chameleon, you know."

"Again: No, I didn't," I say.

Her brow furrows. "You're kind of being a bitch."

That prickle of irritation hits my chest, spreading down my rib cage like a handprint. "Am I?"

"They're not bad people," Sonya says, before I can say anything.

"I never said they were."

"You're thinking it, though." She huffs and grabs her own gloss, leaning toward the mirror to touch up her lips.

"I didn't know you could read minds. You should market that."

The next huff is more of a laugh. "Such a bitch," she mutters around her smile, screwing her lip gloss shut. "You're lucky I like you."

I'm about to shoot back something snappy, but it dies in my throat because she's thrown her gloss onto the dresser and headed toward her closet . . . *pulling her shirt off* as she walks.

Full-body flush, white noise roaring in my ears, and my

fingertips are buzzing like magnets drawn to her skin. I curl them into my palms, nails biting in, little half-moon reminders I don't need, because I'll remember this 'til I die.

"I heard they were going to have absinthe at the party tonight," Sonya says, leaning forward and rummaging through her closet. Her hair's down, brushing the curve of her waist, and I lose myself in the swish of it, remembering how the strands felt like silk against my arm.

"Absinthe?" I echo, barely able to concentrate. Is she going to put a shirt on? Do I even want her to?

"The Green Fairy. Come on, Coley. You've gotta know—"

"I know what absinthe is," I say quickly. My cheeks can't get any hotter. "Green liquor made from anise seeds. You pour it over sugar cubes."

She plucks a striped sweater off a hanger and slips it on. "Have you tried it?"

I shake my head. "The parties I went to back home were more beer and vodka."

"I've always wanted to try it," she says, all confessional.

"Let me guess: *Moulin Rouge* fan?"

She laughs. "Why do you always get my references when no one else does?"

My face hurts with wanting to smile so hard, but holding back. I can't be transparent. I *can't.* "Just lucky, I guess."

Sonya spins to face me. "What do you think?"

The loose knit sweater slips off one of her shoulders, and my eyes follow it. I can't stop myself, and maybe, just maybe, she notices, because her eyes are wide when mine finally rise to meet hers.

We're across the room from each other, but it feels like she's inches away, the way she's looking at me.

"Coley," she says, and it's, like, on her lips my name is entirely different. Something perfect and beautiful.

"Yes?"

"What do you think?" She does a little twirl. "Sexy?"

"You look great."

She pouts; the gloss shines on her lower lip. "That's not what I asked."

I don't know what to say. Because of course she looks perfect. Beautiful and sexy and oh-so touchable. But I can't say any of that. If I do, it'll come out too true. She'll know.

With her, it's like being on a teeter-totter: I never know which way is up—it's constantly changing.

"Who are you dressing up for?" I ask.

She tucks her hair behind her ear, too casual. "Oh, you know, everyone's going to be there."

"Like Trenton?" I ask. I force myself to ask, because I've been dying to ask. Every time I've brought him up, she's found a way out of talking about him, and the curiosity burns inside me. They have some sort of history, but she's never told me exactly what.

Trenton looks at her like he has some claim on her. Like he's got the right to have her, above everybody else. I don't like it. But part of me wonders if Sonya does.

"Maybe," she says, pushing her closet door closed so she can look at herself in the mirror. There are photos and postcards taped along its edge, and I see my Post-it, the one from the first day I was here, yellow against the glass. She kept it. Tucked it between an old postcard and a black-and-white photo of the beach.

When she turns to stare at her ass in the mirror, I have to look at the ceiling and breathe. Getting your eyelashes pulled out has nothing on this.

"Are you and Trenton . . . ?" I trail off.

"What?" She stops looking in the mirror and looks at me instead.

"You know . . ." I'm pitiful. I can't even say it.

"I don't, actually," she says, and she's playing a game now, I know she is. I hate it. *I just want to know the real you. What do you want? What do you need? What the fuck do you yearn for, Sonya?* "Boyfriends are passé, Coley," is all she says in response to my silence, which isn't a real answer at all. "I'm emotionally unavailable to all." Which is just her deal, isn't it? A girl made up of lots of questions and few answers.

"Whatever." I lean forward and press my lips against her mirror, right next to where my Post-it is taped. When I pull back, the perfect dark-red stain of my lips is left behind. "Perfect," I say. "All blotted."

She's staring at me when I glance at her.

"Ready?" I ask, and it's more of a dare than any of the others I've given her.

I can dance around things, too.

SEVENTEEN

The ride out to the party takes a while. The headlights cut through the falling dark as the two-lane road winds up into the hills, where the trees thicken and the houses grow farther and farther apart.

"Are you sure you know where we're going?" Brooke asks Trenton for the third time.

"Stop asking me that!" he says. "I'm trying to concentrate on driving. If I hit a deer, it's your fault."

"It's called the boonies for a reason, Brooke," Alex reminds her from the passenger seat.

"This is taking *forever*," Brooke complains, slumping in her seat. She arches her back to look at Sonya and me in the back seat. "I don't know why you thought this was a good idea."

"Alex made it sound cool," Sonya says. "And *you* wanted to do something together."

"I wanted to *hang*," Brooke says. "I didn't want to drive out into the middle of nowhere to get eaten by a bear."

"At this point, the bear would be doing us a favor," Trenton mutters.

"Hey!" Brooke says, her eyes widening. "That's mean!"

"Oh my God, Brooke, calm down," SJ says from next to her, pulling off her headphones. "You're acting like you've never left town in your life. We're not *camping*. It's a barn party."

"Turn around before you get carsick," Sonya says, twirling her hand at Brooke, who rolls her eyes and slumps back into her seat, facing ahead.

"I don't know why we couldn't have just hung out at my place," Brooke pouts. "Like *normal*." She shoots me a sideways glance that's pure venom. Like this was *my* idea.

I shift in my seat, trying not to let it get to me. She doesn't want me here. The look both girls gave each other when they saw I was with Sonya made me think she hadn't told anyone but Alex that I was coming. Or maybe she hadn't told any of them, and Alex was just nicer and better about covering. He at least smiled when he saw me. Trenton just tried to pull on the pigtails that Sonya had styled my hair into.

"Maybe normal isn't good enough anymore," Sonya shoots back. "Honestly, you act like you just want to do the same boring stuff over and over. We're going to be done with school before you know it. Do you want to be some has-been, stuck in this stupid town, like Blake Wilson?"

"Oh my God, take that back!" Brooke says, horrified. "You know I hate her!"

Sonya laughs. "That snapped you out of it, didn't it?"

"You're an asshole," Brooke tells her. "And I'm not weird for not wanting to go out into the middle of nowhere to get drunk."

"Jamie and his friends are cool," Alex says from the front

seat. I'm starting to think he has only one mood: chill. You kind of have to be, with this group.

"Jamie and his friends grow weed," SJ mutters.

"SJ . . ." Alex's voice changes as he says it, and I suddenly am rethinking putting him in the *chill* category.

"It's not like it's a secret," SJ says.

"You can still have some fucking discretion," Alex reminds her. "Be cool at this party. I'm the one it falls on."

"I'm not gonna ruin your rep with your grower friends," SJ scoffs. "God, what do you take me for, Alex? I've known you since I was five."

"Did you know about this?" I ask Sonya in an undertone.

She shrugs. "It's not a big deal. Just be cool."

"As long as we're not, like, walking into a barn full of weed," I say.

She giggles. "It's not the right season for that, sweetie."

I flush. "I'm sorry, I don't know a ton about the fine art of growing," I say sarcastically.

SJ laughs in front of us. "Don't worry; you live here long enough, you pick up some things."

"But it'll spoil you for the shit weed they grow anywhere else," Alex calls back.

That has me laughing. "Hopefully I won't be here long enough to develop an educated palate."

"You gonna blow town as soon as possible?" Alex asks, shifting in his seat so he can look at us. His easy smile is all on me, and I can see Sonya tense next to me, her eyes flicking between the two of us.

"Aren't *you*?"

"Hell yeah. Maybe we can team up."

Is he flirting with me? His smile certainly says so. "Team Get the Fuck Out?" I suggest.

"I like it."

"I'll join," Brooke adds.

"Oh please, it's not the same. You're gonna get a legacy slot at Princeton like your sister and your dad," Alex scoffs. "Coley and I . . . we've got to fight our way out of shitholes like this." He wiggles his eyebrows at me. "Isn't that right?"

"It is harder without a silver spoon," I say.

"Ooh, damn," Alex crows as Brooke lets out a little, laughing, "Hey!"

"Sorry," I say. "Just the truth."

"No, you're right," Brooke says. "I am really lucky. My dad kind of tries to drill it into my head. He doesn't want me to be spoiled."

"You're not spoiled, babe," Sonya reassures her, reaching out and looping her arms around Brooke's neck, hugging her close.

"*You* totally are," Brooke says back, and Sonya gasps, pulling back as SJ cackles with laughter.

"My mom is stricter than yours!" Sonya protests.

"Yeah, but you've got your stepdad and your dad eating out of the palm of your hand," Brooke says.

"Seriously, it's so unfair, you get to be a double daddy's girl," SJ adds.

"Yes, it's so great that my parents fell out of love and destroyed my family as I knew it," Sonya says. "I love being abandoned." The way she says it . . . it comes out a lot more harsh than sarcastic. Brooke and SJ exchange a look, staring straight ahead as they fall silent, unable to deal with the sore spot they accidentally prodded.

"At least you've got Emma," I say.

"Yeah." Sonya nods jerkily. "I love Emma."

"She really is the cutest," I say, trying to smooth out the moment, but Sonya's eyes are still dark, like she's remembering things she doesn't want to. "Is she gonna dance like you?"

"Of course," Sonya says. "She's been in dance since she was three. Just like me."

"Oh my gosh, Emma does this little tap routine—it's *so* cute," SJ gushes, latching on to the subject change like a pro. Relief floods me as the conversation moves on, and Sonya relaxes, bit by bit. By the time we finally get on the driveway, which has a lone Solo cup turned upside down on the mailbox, she's laughing and running her mouth again.

"This is it," Alex says as Trenton turns onto the gravel road. The van rocks back and forth on the rough road that's more dirt than gravel in places. "Remember what I said about being cool," he warns us as lights grow visible through the trees.

The barn is old and red, like barns are supposed to be, I think. I'm not really up on my barn knowledge. It's lit up with twinkle lights on the outside and inside. When we get out of the van, it smells fresh and green: the hay is stacked outside in the barnyard.

There are at least thirty people inside. Music floats instead of blasting up through the rafters. It may not be harvest time for the weed or whatever, but it certainly smells like weed smoke in here. There's a thick cloud of it coming from the farthest stall. If we get any closer, I'm going to get a contact high. But maybe that wouldn't be a bad idea, all things considered.

One of those things being Trenton grabbing Sonya's hand and tugging her forward, saying, "You wanted the absinthe, didn't you, babe?"

She lets him pull her, and maybe it wouldn't hurt so much if she didn't look behind her toward me, like she *knows* it isn't right.

"Come on, Coley," Alex says. He follows the two of them, heading toward the middle of the barn, where a guy with curly hair is sitting on a hay bale, holding court, surrounded by girls and guys alike.

"Jamie, hey, man," Alex says when the guy notices us.

"Alex, great to see you." Jamie gets up from the bale and does that one-armed hug/handshake thing that guys do.

"Thanks for the invite."

"Beer's in the farthest stall. Glad you came. We'll talk later?"

Alex nods, and Jamie claps him on the back before disappearing into the crowd.

"I'm getting a beer," Brooke declares, and Alex and SJ follow her, leaving me with Sonya and Trenton.

"C'mon." Sonya moves into the throng of people, and I trail after her, hating how close Trenton is. He's not holding her hand anymore, but now his hand's on her lower back, so casual, like he doesn't even have to think it through. Because he doesn't. He gets that, with no nerves, no looks, no worries, that she . . .

I take a deep breath, the weed-scented air really hitting me. Fuck, at this rate, I won't need any absinthe.

"Hey." A girl with copper hair brushes her hand over the tops of my shoulders as I pass. I come to a stop, looking up at her. "I like your jacket. Vintage?"

"Yeah."

"Cool." Her eyes are kohl-lined, the tips wickedly sharp. "I haven't seen you around." Her eyes shift up. Sonya's watching her. "Hey, Sonya."

"Faith."

"And you are . . . ?" Faith asks, looking down at me.

"Coley."

"Nice to meet you."

"Are you the one who brought the absinthe?" Sonya asks.

Faith laughs. "Who else? C'mon, I've got my setup in the tack room."

"How's college?" Sonya asks her, pushing past Trenton to put herself right between Faith and me.

"Great. Wish I was back there right now, but alas, I'm here." Faith shrugs as we follow her into the room. It's like the size of four of the stalls outside, full of saddles and horse gear, a table to serve as a makeshift desk, with windows looking out across the field. The room smells like leather and some kind of oil, and the noise from the party is muffled here; light from the outside slants in. Trenton trails after us, trying to look unbothered. "Sonya and I used to dance together," she explains to me. "I'm a year ahead, so I got out of here."

"Yet you're right back here," Sonya singsongs in a way that tells me that she and this girl definitely took the *competitive* part of *competitive dance* seriously. Was this her former dance rival? I've seen enough dance movies to know that's *definitely* a thing. I'm achingly curious to find out more: a glimpse into Sonya's inner life, even though I get the sense that dancing is way more important to Sonya's mom than it is to Sonya.

"Not all of our stepdads can pay for summer vacations in France, babe," Faith says, patting Sonya's arm. "We've gotta work for a living. Speaking of . . . You going to Babbitt's Round this year?"

"Always," Sonya says.

Faith clambers up on the wooden table, sitting cross-legged on it.

"Did someone say there are drinks?" Trenton booms from behind me.

I wince. "That was right in my ear."

"Still your charming self, I see, Trent," Faith says, bending down and pulling out a bottle with a paper label that's been treated to look old-timey.

"You know I hate it when you call me that," he says.

"I know, Trent," she answers sunnily.

I decide then and there I like this girl.

Faith sets two glasses down on the table in front of her, pulling out a bag of sugar cubes and this fancy slotted spoon with curling scrollwork punched through the metal. It reminds me of those S holes in a violin. She places the spoon over the first glass and rests a sugar cube on top of it.

"So what are you doing hanging with this one, Coley?" Faith asks, nodding to Sonya.

"You make me sound like trouble," Sonya scoffs.

"You're a bitchy competitive nightmare, sweetie," Faith tells her.

"You are so lucky you have the good drinks." Sonya flicks her hair over her shoulder.

"I bet deep down you miss me," Faith says. "No one else can keep you on your toes. Literally."

"Just pour the drinks," Trenton interrupts.

"Like I'm sharing with you," Faith says. "Go get beer with the rest of the cave dwellers."

"I think that's an insult to cave dwellers," I mutter, and Faith grins, hot and brilliant.

"Oh, she is much too sassy to be your friend, Sonya," Faith says.

"You're surrounding yourself with bitches lately, Sonya," Trenton says disgustedly. "You know what they say about the company you keep."

"What does that say about her hanging out with *you*?" Faith asks.

Trenton's mouth flattens, his lips disappearing. He's done a bad job shaving, and I can see a patch he missed, even across the tack room. But he doesn't move. It's like he's in a one-sided war with Faith, because she completely ignores him now, focusing on me.

"Have you ever drunk absinthe?" she asks.

I shake my head.

"Come here." Faith beckons me forward, and Sonya follows me.

Faith uncaps the bottle and begins to dribble the green liquid over the sugar cube. "*La fée verte.*"

"Does it really make you see shit? Like mushrooms do?" Trenton asks skeptically.

"No, Trent, it doesn't. Rumors of it being a hallucinogen have no scientific basis."

"But it does get you a different kind of drunk," Sonya says. "I know girls who've tried it."

"That's what some people say." Faith shrugs. "It's, like, a clearheaded kind of drunk."

"But no hallucinations?" I ask, just to be sure. I am not up for a drink that's going to make me see monsters in the woods or something.

"I promise," Faith says. Her smile widens. "I'd say 'Have a little Faith,' but I'm taken."

"Oh my God," Sonya mutters behind me.

"Still a prude, honey?" Faith asks Sonya, her eyes glittering with a kind of challenge I don't even begin to understand.

"She's definitely not," Trenton smirks. "Trust me, I have hands-on experience."

My stomach curls in revulsion at his smugness.

Sonya rounds on him, smacking him hard on the chest.

"What?!" he asks in mock outrage.

"Shut up," she snarls.

I stay rooted to the spot, stuck amid the kind of animosity that has *history*—shit I wasn't here for, so I have no way of understanding. Hell, I barely understand the stuff I *have* been there for. These summer weeks with Sonya are stretching out in a whirl, little cyclones spinning me toward and away from her.

Faith rolls her eyes like she hasn't set off all this drama, and caps the absinthe, reaching for a bottle of water. "Next step," she tells me.

"I know this step." Before Faith can stop him, Trenton barges forward, pulling a lighter out of his pocket and flicking it at the alcohol-soaked sugar cube.

"Trent! Dammit!" Faith yells as the entire glass goes up in flames. She jerks backward, narrowly avoiding her bangs catching on fire, and in the process, her foot sweeps the flaming glass onto the ground, rolling toward the stack of hay bales.

"Shit!" Frantic, I spot a saddle blanket and grab it, throwing it on the flaming glass and stomping hard on it. Glass crunches beneath my feet, and the smoke putters out, the fire smothered.

"You are *such* an idiot!" Faith leaps up from the table and shoves past Trenton.

"That's how I've heard it's done," Trenton protests as she lifts the saddle blanket to make sure the fire's out.

"First of all: it's not. And second: even if it *was*, you don't light alcohol on fire in a fucking *barn*. You could've set this whole place on fire. You know better than this, asshole. You're just trying to score points with your girlfriend."

"He's not my—" Sonya starts.

"Oh my God, I do not care," Faith interrupts. She looks at Sonya, pure exasperation radiating off her. "He's going to be one of those things you look back on and cringe. I bet you."

"I thought you didn't care," Sonya says. She grabs Trenton's hand. "Come on. Let's dance."

She drags him away like I'm not even in the room—like she's got tunnel vision and the only thing she can see is proving her point to Faith. I watch them join the couples in the middle of the barn, the reek of weed smoke and beer sweat high in the air, gyrating bodies and thumping beats. Sonya plasters herself against him and he grins, his hands all over her hips like he's gotten a prize for shitty behavior.

"I can't believe she's still with that guy," Faith comments behind me. "He used to terrorize my little brother in middle school. He's such a fucking bully."

"I don't know if they're—" I stop, because I'm not sure, still. Being with Sonya is like shifting sands: you think you've got a hold on her, and then she's streaming in little pieces through your fingers. "I think they broke up," I say. "But then—" I shrug.

They're still dancing. Someone's passed Sonya a red cup, and she's sipping beer out of it as she sways with him, her other arm around his neck like she wants it to be the only thing keeping her up.

"Why is it always so hard to leave the assholes?" Faith mutters, maybe a little to herself. She touches my arm, and I turn to see she's fixed me the absinthe in the other glass. "Here," she says. "You earned it, keeping us all from burning up."

"Thanks," I say, taking the drink. It smells like herbs and black licorice and tastes the same. My eyes and lips screw up against the shock of the tiny sip I take. It's like what I think a winter forest might taste like, snow on the tip of my tongue, green in the distance. I cough a little, not downing the rest, hoping she won't notice.

"You should keep an eye on him," Faith says, leaning forward so I can hear it properly.

I raise my eyebrow, not saying anything else, waiting.

"Guys like that—bullies like that—they turn on everyone eventually," Faith says.

There's something in her voice that makes the back of my neck prickle. "What happened to your brother? The one Trenton bullied?"

"He went to live with my dad so he could go to a different school," Faith says.

"Seriously?" Trenton's still hanging all over Sonya, but now she's turned so she's facing us.

Sonya's staring right at Faith and me. I realize with a flush that we're standing *really* close.

"Like I said, bullies like that turn on everyone," Faith says, pulling my attention back to her. "Especially anyone they view as weaker than them . . . even their girlfriends. Sonya should watch out. And if you're her friend, you should watch out for her."

"I'll keep that in mind."

"Real-world shit sneaks in," Faith mutters, almost to herself. "That girl's gonna get her bubble burst."

"Huh?"

"Nothing," Faith says with a smile. "I should go find my friends. And you should go follow Sonya before he does." She nods toward the barn door right before Sonya disappears through it.

"I—" Before I can say anything else, Faith's walking away and I find myself moving, pushing through the crowd, into the cooler outside air. I breathe it in. The stars are brilliant above me: with no light pollution, I'm seeing stars I didn't even know existed shining at me every night. Sometimes I think about sitting on Curtis's porch, a blanket and some hot chocolate, trying to count them.

She's not hanging out in front of the barn, so I make a circle around it, and there she is, leaning against the wall, fumbling in her purse.

"What are you doing back here?" I ask her.

"I just needed some time," she mutters, searching her pockets. "Can you hold this for me?" She shoves her tiny purse at me and pulls out a lighter and a cigarette. She lights it, setting it against her lips and sucking in deep. She blows out in a rush, coughing a little as she hands it to me.

The filter's wet from her lips. I put my mouth where hers was and I try so hard not to think about it. Is this all we get? Our lips touching through shared nicotine? She watches me like it's all *she* can think about. Like it's inevitable, our minds making the connection our bodies won't.

We can't . . . right?

"I'm surprised you're not with Faith," Sonya says.

I raise an eyebrow. Her words are like ice. Slicing jagged and cold against me.

"She seems cool."

"Mm." Sonya shrugs, taking back the cigarette. The music from the barn thumps through the wall we're leaning against. I can feel the vibrations.

"You two competed against each other."

"She likes to think so. But it's hard to view things as competitive when I was the one always winning."

"Wow, smug much?"

"More like truthful."

"She seems like she gets on your nerves, though."

Sonya takes a long drag off the cigarette. The filter will be too wet at this rate. Someone needs to teach the girl how to properly smoke a cigarette.

"You should be careful with her," Sonya says finally.

"Careful?"

"There are rumors."

I stare at her. She stares back like I'm supposed to just know. "You're going to have to give me more than that."

"You know." Her eyebrows raise. "*Rumors.* She was *really* close to another senior cheerleader when she graduated."

It's like sinking and having no way out. The way she lowers her voice and leans in, like it's some terrible secret, and I guess it is? Does it have to be? Can't it just be simple? Because the feeling . . .

God, the feeling of wanting her is so fucking simple. Like a magnetic pull I don't want to resist.

"I don't gossip about stuff like that," I say, so quickly it has her straightening, like she's getting away from an unexpected electric shock between us.

"You—you don't?"

"Not unless the person is open about it. Um. *Out* about it."

"But what if you're just curious?" Sonya asks. "It's not bad to be curious. Or to, like, want to know."

"You gotta follow the other person's lead," I say firmly, like I actually know what the fuck I'm talking about. I don't really. I just want a way around this conversation and the look on her face, like the idea of it is unfathomable.

I know what she looks like when she's faking. But I'm not sure she's faking that.

"You and Trenton seemed to be having fun," I say, desperate to change the subject, unable to get away from what Faith said about bullies. It circles in my head—how bad did shit have to get for her brother to *change schools*? How would Sonya react if I called Trenton a bully? I think I already know, which is why I don't think I can say it.

"You know Trenton," she says.

"Unfortunately, I'm getting to."

She sucks in and then blows out blue smoke. "He's not a jerk," she says.

"Um."

"Okay. Yes. He is. Sometimes."

"Most of the time, from what I can see."

"It's just the way Trenton is."

"He needs to change," I say, and she stares at me for so long,

I think I've crossed some line. And then she lets out a laugh and it's all bitter.

"Coley, guys don't *change*," she says. "Girls just tell ourselves they will if they love us. But what actually happens is that the girl changes, so that they'll *keep* loving us."

I have to grab the cigarette from her and take a few puffs on it before I answer. "You forgot something."

"What?"

"That life philosophy doesn't have anything about you loving the guy. Why is that, you think?"

It's like all the blood drains out of her face. She takes the cigarette out of my hands and throws it down, stomping on it with her shoe.

"Love is about sacrifice," she says. "That's what my mom says. And every couple I know who's actually made it . . ." She looks at me, eyes burning from the emotional fire I accidentally triggered. "Do you think it's easy, loving someone?"

"I think love is a shitload of things. But most of all, I don't think making yourself smaller to be with someone is worth it. Ever."

"Trenton doesn't make me—"

"I didn't even say his name," I interrupt her. "You did."

Her cheeks glow red in the light coming from the barn. "You are a—"

Her words are drowned out by the screech of feedback, the music stopping abruptly. Silence fills the space, the murmur of voices halting.

"Neighbors narced about the noise," someone yells. "Cops are coming!"

"Run!" someone else hollers.

Slam! The barn door five feet away from us crashes open and kids pour out, heading toward cars.

"Shit!" Sonya says.

"Oh my God." I grab her hand. "Where do we go?"

"We need to get the others!" Sonya runs toward the barn, dragging me with her as more people scatter out the back doors.

We push through the swelling crowd as people flee. Someone slams into my shoulder and I almost go down.

"Coley!" Sonya pulls me toward her and I tumble into her chest, her arm looping around my waist. "Stay close to me!"

We make it back into the emptying barn, my heart thrumming in my chest as I spot Alex.

"There you are!" Alex stops in front of us, Brooke right next to him. "Have you seen Trenton?"

Sonya shakes her head. "Where's SJ?"

"I haven't seen her for a while," Brooke says. "She headed off with some guy."

"And you let her?!" Sonya shouts.

"Hey!" Trenton comes loping forward. "We've got to get out of here."

"We can't find SJ," I say.

He shrugs. "Too bad. Come on."

The rest of them exchange looks.

"I've got the only ride there is," Trenton reminds us, dangling the keys. "I'm not sticking around to get busted by the cops."

"If SJ gets in trouble . . ." Alex starts.

"Oh fuck this," Sonya snarls, snatching the keys out of Trenton's hand before he can stop her. "You made me ditch SJ at the club, and the bouncer nearly got her. I'm not leaving her behind again. SJ!" She cups her hands around her mouth as she hollers her name. "Alex, you and Trenton go outside and see if you can find her. Brooke, go out the front. I'll look up in the hayloft."

They scatter to look for her, and I'm just standing there in the rapidly emptying barn.

I walk the corridor lined with stalls as I hear Sonya call SJ's name up in the loft.

"SJ?" I question, peering into one of the stalls that's got extra feed stacked inside.

"Coley," a voice hisses.

My head jerks toward the sound.

"SJ?" I hurry across the way, yanking open the stall door. She's crouching there, holding her arms in front of her, stripped of her shirt, down to her jeans and bra.

"Are you okay?" I ask, alarmed. "Where's your shirt?"

"The guy I was with—we were making out. He had it tucked in his back pocket, and when everyone started yelling, he ran and I kinda froze."

"Oh shit." I immediately shrug out of my jacket and take off my own shirt, handing it to her.

"Oh my God, thank you, Coley," SJ says.

I pull my jacket back on and button it up as she slips on my shirt. "We've got to get out of here before the cops come," I say. "Hey! I found her!" I yell.

Sonya climbs down from the hayloft. "Are you okay?"

"Coley saved my ass," SJ says.

"Hey! Guys!" Sonya shouts out the back. "I found her! Let's get out of here."

The boys come loping forward, followed by Brooke. We all turn toward the big barn door just in time to see the blue and red flashing lights heading down the road.

"Time's up," I say. "We have to go out the back."

"The van's the other way!" Trenton protests.

"Shut up and run!" Sonya says, grabbing my hand and pulling me forward as sirens sound.

We bolt out the back of the barn in a group. I can't see shit as we hit the field out back, grass whipping at my ankles as I run. The air and sound blur around me, my heartbeat pounding in my chest and in my hand that's still wrapped around hers. I stumble and Sonya pulls me up and we keep going, my breath burning in my lungs as lights dance behind us.

"We need to hide," Brooke gasps out.

"We're in an open field," Trenton growls. "Great fucking thinking, Coley."

The sirens are getting louder.

I squint in the darkness, turning in a circle. "There." I point to the shadowy slope at the end of the field. "Go! Go!"

We dash toward the slope, my sneakers sliding in the soft dirt, as one by one we climb down into the gully, the tangle of plants, mud, and water knee-deep in places. We're completely hidden from view here. I peek over the top of the slope, watching flashlight beams scan across the field. I duck down as a beam swings in our direction.

"We just need to stay low until they leave," I hiss. "And then we can get to the van."

"If they find us . . ." Trenton whispers.

"Dude, just chill," Alex snaps, and *finally* Trenton shuts up.

We stay hidden and quiet, and I feel like I'm holding my breath forever, but finally the lights and the sirens fade away, and we climb out from the embankment, muddy and covered in who knows what.

"I was right about hanging out at home being a better idea," Brooke says grumpily as we cross the field and head up the road to where the van's parked.

"*Sorry* for trying to shake things up," Alex says as we come to a stop in front of the van.

"Give me my keys," Trenton says.

"How much have you had to drink?" Sonya asks.

"Are you fucking kidding me right now?!" His voice breaks as he goes from annoyed to *pissed* in seconds.

"Hey," Alex says, muscling in between them in an instant. "Stop it, man. You've had too much, and I haven't had any. I'll drive, okay?"

"As long as it's not the bitch who stole my keys," Trenton says, sneering at Sonya.

"Don't call her that."

All three of them—no, actually, all five of them—stare at me.

"What did you—" Trenton starts to say, but Sonya interrupts him.

"Oh my God, Coley, what is that?"

"What?" I look where she's staring, realizing that a leafy branch is snagged in the cuff of my jeans. I reach down.

"No!" Sonya and SJ and Alex all say it at the same time.

I freeze. "What the fuck, guys?"

"That's poison oak," Sonya says. She bends down and plucks it out of my cuff after covering her hand with the hem of her shirt. "Shit, that gully must've been full of it." She stares down at her hands. "We're all covered in it."

"Are you fucking kidding me?" Trenton asks. "This is your fault," he snarls at me. "You led us in there!"

"I don't even know what poison oak looks like!"

"Being a little itchy is a lot better than getting arrested," Sonya reminds him.

"Just do a poison-oak wash before bed tonight," SJ says. "If you don't have the medicine at home, go to the drugstore and get some."

"This is such bullshit," Trenton says.

"I don't care—we've gotta go," Alex tells us. "Keys, Sonya?"

She tosses him the keys and we pile into the van.

"You can shower at my house," Sonya tells me as Alex drives through the night, darkness and a tired, drunken hush filling the van.

She smiles like it's a good thing.

I force myself to smile back, even though all I can think is: *Holy shit, I cannot get naked when you're a wall away.*

EIGHTEEN

Maybe it's my imagination, but I'm already starting to itch when we finally get dropped off at Sonya's house. It's dark inside, and she motions for me to creep around the back after Alex lets us out down the street so we don't wake anyone up. We sneak through the back door and up the stairs.

"He was really pissed," I whisper. Trenton had spent the entire ride back muttering under his breath at such a steady pace, it put everyone on edge.

"As soon as he sobers up, he'll snap out of it," Sonya reassures me. "I'm gonna go get the first aid kit," she says. "You need to strip down."

"What?!"

Her head tilts. "The poison-oak oils, they're on your clothes and all over your skin," Sonya explains like I'm dumb. "We were knee-deep in the stuff. And we probably got it all over our arms, too, running through it. So you need to strip."

I can't stop looking at her lips as she says the word "strip." How can she act so calm?

"You can borrow some of my clothes," she says, like that's the thing I'm worried about here. "I'm going to go get the Tecnu.

You rub it all over for like two minutes and it removes the oils when you wash it off."

"I'm now on Brooke's side," I tell Sonya. "Barn parties *suck*."

Sonya grins. "Well, at least you two have *something* in common." She pauses, her expression turning thoughtful. "SJ was wearing your shirt."

"The guy she was hooking up with ran off with her shirt. She needed something to cover up."

"That was nice of you."

I shrug. "Been there."

"You've been a half-naked girl at a party?" Sonya asks innocently.

I had more meant that I'd been in embarrassing situations in which someone had saved me, but her eyes sparkle and I have to play along. "More than once."

"Really?" She steps forward and I do too. I can't not. I want her closer.

"I've also been known to dance on tables," I lie.

"With the skills that you showed me that night in my room, I have no doubt you attracted quite a crowd."

"Juilliard, here I come," I joke, and her smile—it's thunderous inside me, the way it makes my heart beat. My entire body is shaken from her presence, her entire existence. The fact that I existed for seventeen years without knowing her, and now never have to live another year without having met her.

"I'll go get the lotion," she says, and she disappears, and I'm all alone in this fancy-ass bathroom of hers. There are jets in her tub.

It's just like a bathing suit, I tell myself. I chant it silently in my head as I peel off clothes and pick off my choker. My fingers settle on the button of my shorts and my stomach leaps, like it's someone else's fingers, not mine. If I close my eyes, I can imagine it: her fingers crooked inside the waistband, nails scraping against the skin under my belly button, right above the elastic of my underwear. I prickle *everywhere* at the thought and tell myself it's the imminent poison-oak rash.

It's not. It's thinking of her. It's *how* I want to think of her. It's *why* I want to.

I need to get out of here. I just need to get the lotion and shower off the booze and weed smell and then get home. I'll tell her that Curtis will get mad if I don't show. I'll make up a curfew.

Otherwise I don't know what'll happen. I want—

So much.

My fingers tap against her sink, staccato little beats of nervousness. I breathe in and out, tilting my head back.

I could open her cupboards and see what secrets are inside. I know her peony shampoo now, and the array of body washes that's so varied, it's amazing she can fit them all along the edge of the tub. Her razors are the expensive ones that are like twenty-five dollars for the cartridge packs—I'm still cutting myself with Lady Bics—and there's an honest-to-God shower cap hanging on a hook near the tub. That makes me smile, because I've never seen anyone but old ladies wear those, and the idea of her piling her hair on top of her head and putting that thing on her head to shower is just plain cute.

I am so fucked if I think Sonya in a shower cap is cute.

"I've got it!" Sonya bursts back into the bathroom without even knocking, holding a few trash bags, a packet of gloves, and a big bottle marked TECNU.

"Hey!" My arms fly up, clutching at my bra like that's going to hide anything. They're not. I'm down to my underwear.

It's like a bikini bottom, I tell myself. *It's just like that.*

It's not. It's not at all, because there are little daisies stamped on my underwear, and the daisies have little smiley faces on them, and she's looking at them, her eyes crinkling.

"Don't you dare laugh at me," I warn her.

"At least you don't have *juicy* on your ass," she says.

"I hate you."

Fuck, Coley, what happened to *It's just like a bathing suit*?

She looks at me, and I don't think it's an oh-my-God-I'm-awestruck kind of stare. More like a Wow-Coley's-a-freak kind of look.

Fuck. Me.

"I can do it," I say, reaching for the bottle. "I don't need your help."

"We were knee-deep in a gully of poison oak for over an hour," she says in hushed tones. "Trust me, you're going to want to put this *everywhere* just in case."

"I can reach," I say pitifully, even though I can't.

"Oh my God, Coley, why do you make it so hard for people to help you?" she mutters, exasperated. "Turn around! I'm going to need your help in a few minutes to do *my* shoulders anyway. I cannot get a rash. My mom will kill me."

She's still in her clothes, and the idea of her peeling out of her shorts and sweater in front of me makes me want to unravel like a ball of yarn.

I seriously contemplate bolting. But then she'll know for sure. I just need to get through this. Get through it, take a shower, and *then* bolt.

I turn around, reaching back and unsnapping my bra. I let the ends fall away from my back, but I keep the front pressed against me. I feel rather than see her rustle up behind me, the snap of the lotion bottle, the sound of her shaking it, and then her fingers smoothing it over my back in gentle and then stronger strokes.

"You have to rub it in for two minutes," she says, and I have to close my eyes when her voice cracks, her hands dipping to my lower back. I let out a huff of breath, twisting away as I try to hide the giggle.

"Sorry, ticklish," I say, and I can hear the smile in her voice as her words follow.

"Don't you dare come near the backs of my knees when you do this for me," she warns.

"Noted."

Her hands move up my back, tracing the line of my spine, and it makes everything I've heard about being weak in the knees suddenly make sense.

"You have a birthmark," she says softly, her fingers circling over it on my shoulder. The feeling spreads out from her touch, the warmth that spreads to the tips of my fingers, pooling in my stomach into a steady throb, like a second heartbeat.

"Yeah." My voice almost cracks. "When I was little it used

to look like an acorn. But then I grew and now it's just a blob." I'm just rattling off random shit now. Why am I like this? *Least sexy talk ever, Coley.*

This is torture. Who invents a medical lotion that requires *two minutes* of rubbing it in? Sadists, that's who.

I try to hold still, but it's hard not to kind of sway into her hands. It just . . . feels so good . . . and it's maybe the most anyone's ever touched me.

"I think that's about two minutes," she says, her voice so close to my ear it makes me shiver. "Do you want me to do your legs?"

Yes.

"I can do it," I say quickly. "Let me do your shoulders first, though. The quicker the better with this stuff, right?"

"Yeah, I should get these off." She sets the lotion down on the edge of the sink and tosses her sweater next to my clothes on the ground. Her shorts follow, and I stare at our clothes tangled together on the ground instead of at her, because being in your underwear can't be like a bathing suit. Not here, in her space where she gets ready in the morning and strips everything off at night.

I finally force myself to look up because I need to grab the lotion bottle. *Breathe, just breathe. Don't stare at the peach lace against her skin and think about how it would feel under your fingers. Just put the lotion on her.*

"Ready?" She slips her straps down her arms and lifts her hair off her shoulders.

"Yeah." I snatch the Tecnu bottle from the counter and pour some into my palm. I spread it across the expanse of her shoulders, realizing she's a lot more muscular than me.

It makes sense—the dancing. The strong lines of her back entrance me, a journey of muscle and grace that only my fingers get to discover.

It's the shortest and longest two minutes of my life, and I know my face is red because I'm burning inside. But when she turns around—

She's flushed, deep crimson blooms all over her cheeks, and it's not my imagination. It's right there on her face as she leans on the sink, staring at me like she can't look away.

If I move toward her, what will happen?

Will she move back?

Will she meet me halfway?

I don't know. I never know with her.

I want to be brave enough to find out. To slide my hand up her neck and into her hair. To discover exactly what her lips taste like.

"I'll let you finish with the lotion, and then I'll take it into the guest bath," she says. "You want to take a shower with *cool* water."

I make a face.

"I know," she says. "But that's what works."

She leaves the bathroom before I can say anything else, and I slather the rest of my body with the goop, rubbing it in for the two minutes before tapping on the bathroom door. "Sonya?"

"Yeah?"

I pass her the lotion through the bathroom door. "Here you go."

"Thanks," she says. "I set out clothes for you. See you in a bit."

I turn the shower on cool water and grit my teeth before stepping under the spray. I'm gasping as soon as it hits my skin. I rinse the Tecnu off my body as fast as possible, my hair dripping down my back once I'm completely done.

Sonya's towels are so much fluffier than mine, and *enormous.* I towel-dry my hair and twist it up on top of my head in a damp knot. After I wrap myself in another towel, I peek out the bathroom door, but she's not in her bedroom. So I grab the clothes she's left on the bed and dash back into the bathroom to change. Every second I'm in her room, I'm scared she'll come back and my towel will fall off or something. That would be the cherry on top of the insane sundae of this night.

But I get back to the bathroom safely, and it's only then I realize she's left me a pair of soft cotton shorts and a tank top to wear. Sleep clothes. Not going-home-in clothes.

Her clothes. Oh my God. These are her clothes. I pull on the shorts and then the tank top and then I'm wrapped up in her and she's not even in the room and it's too much and not enough. My entire body aches, worry and heat rising from my fingertips as I tap them against my hip, trying to think, trying to ignore how soft the shorts are—worn thin like she wears them all the time, like they're her favorite.

I need to get out of here. I need to go home.

I need to *not* spend the night in Sonya's room . . . in Sonya's clothes . . . in Sonya's bed.

How am I supposed to deal with this? How can I even *breathe* right now?

I'll just go home in the pajamas. It's fine. It's not like anyone's going to see me biking down the roads this late. And

Curtis doesn't know enough about clothes to wonder. It'll be fine.

I shove my shoes back on and charge out of the bathroom without checking, and of course she's walking into her bedroom at the same time.

"Oh good, they fit," she says when she sees me.

She's changed into pink shorts and a sleep shirt that's so big that the shorts nearly disappear under them. The little glimpse of light pink is one of the most distracting things I've ever experienced, and she just had her hands all over my skin, so that's saying something.

"Thanks for the clothes and the medicine," I say. "I should get going."

"What?" She frowns. "Why? It's way too late for you to go home."

"It'll be fine. I'll bring your clothes back tomorrow."

"No way," she says firmly. "It's almost two in the morning, Coley. Half of the roads from here to your house have broken streetlights. You could get hit by a car, or some creep could get you!"

"You really think there's a serial killer rolling around town looking for victims?" I ask her.

She rolls her eyes. "Just spend the night. You told your dad you might, right?"

"Right," I mumble.

"So he won't worry. I'm sure he's already asleep. If you come crashing in at two A.M., he'll wake up and ask all these questions, and then you'll get in trouble."

"Fine," I say. "I'll stay."

Why did I say that? No! I cannot stay. I'm going to lose my mind if I stay.

"Good," she says. "Now . . ." She props her hands on her hips and nods toward the bed. "What side do you want?"

I'm doomed.

NINETEEN

So this is happening. I'm not imagining it or dreaming. Sonya reaches out and pulls back her comforter, looking at me expectantly.

"Um . . ." I say. "If you have a sleeping bag . . ."

She frowns at me like I'm *crazy.* Oh my God. Am I being even more obvious by expecting to sleep on the floor? Shit. *Shit.*

"It's just sometimes other people's mattresses are too soft for my back," I say quickly, trying to cover and of course sounding like an *old lady* while doing it. My back?! Can I just dig a hole and hide inside it forever, please?

"Well, lie back and see," she says. "Mine's not very soft."

I do as she says because I can't object without being weird now. She's right—her mattress is firm. Her sheets and pillows, however, are soft. Lying back on the pile of pillows is like sinking into something too deeply, with no tether to pull you back.

I can't do this. I absolutely cannot sleep next to her. "I'm really fine with a sleeping bag," I say, trying for a final, futile time.

"Do I smell or something?" Sonya asks, half-joking.

"Never mind," I say, because if she prods, I might just blurt it out.

"If you snore, it's fine," she assures me, climbing into bed and sliding her long legs under the covers. "Once I'm out, I'm out."

"Deep sleeper, huh?"

"Like the dead."

"I bet you're fun to get up in the morning," I say.

She flashes me a grin. "SJ once dumped me in the pool to wake me up."

"What is with you guys and throwing people in water?" I ask, thinking of the time at the lake with Trenton.

"It was funny!" she protests with a hushed laugh.

"If you say so."

She leans over and my heart stops beating because she's leaning *toward* me, so close I forget to breathe, but then I realize she's just reaching for the lamp on the nightstand. She switches it off, plunging us into darkness, and when she draws back, it's too slow to be anything but purposeful.

I've slept over at people's houses before. I've curled under scratchy Disney sheets next to other girls. But this is nothing like that.

Sonya is not like those other girls. She is every question I've ever had—about myself, about love, about touch. And she's in this double bed with me, tucked under covers together, nothing stopping us from touching.

My skin buzzes, but nothing happens. In the dark, I can hear her rustling next to me as she turns over onto her side. Her back's to me as she says, "Night!" like it's nothing.

"Night," I echo numbly, not knowing what to do. I lie there on my back, the covers tucked up to my chin, blinking in the dark. I stare into the darkness until my eyes adjust, until I'm almost used to it.

If I move, my entire body might just burst from the twisting ache of being so close but feeling so far away. So I just lie there, frozen between wanting and waiting, between question and answer.

She breathes softly next to me, so evenly that it has to be fake, right? But the minutes stretch, and when she lets out a gentle snore, I know she's not faking it. She did say she was a really sound sleeper.

I worked myself up over nothing. Maybe I'm really going crazy. Reading into everything.

No. *No.* I wasn't. This—whatever it is growing between us—it's real.

I finally tilt over on my side, facing away from her, desperate for the pull of sleep. But it's not going to work—she's too close. There's no way I'm ever sleeping, in her sheets, in her room, wrapped up in the citrus-flower smell of her, the heat of her body just inches away.

I turn once more. This time to face her. In the dark, I can barely make out the shadow of her form, let alone her face, but it doesn't matter.

I think I could summon the image of her even if I go twenty years without laying eyes on her. I think that someday, when I have gray hair and lines around my eyes, I'll be able to close them and see her perfectly, seventeen and smiling only for me.

Maybe I'll doze off if I count my breathing. They do that in meditation, I think, but I don't really know how to do that.

This is normal, I tell myself. *Girls have sleepovers. They share beds. It's normal. It doesn't mean anything.*

Her hands *lingered.* There was no other word for it. When

she was spreading the medicine up my back, they lingered on my skin. I know, because mine did the same on hers.

"Mmph."

I stiffen at the sudden noise. The mattress shifts, and I slide a little toward the middle as she moves. Her arm flops, curling against my side. Such a simple touch, but it spreads warmth everywhere. Little sparks travel to parts of my body I've never been aware of before as her fingers curve into the soft skin of my stomach.

Is she awake? She can't be. She wouldn't. . . .

Would she?

"Sonya," I whisper.

She doesn't answer.

I shift, but instead of her hand sliding off me, it causes her to cuddle up, closing the few inches between us.

Our bodies click together like puzzle pieces. She curves around me like she's a crescent moon and I'm the hidden half, something to be sheltered and cherished. I sigh into it—into her—the long line of heat sizzling up me. I want so much, so swiftly, it whips the breath out of my lungs.

"Sonya," I try again. I have to. I can't—I'm going to *combust* like this. Her hand splays across my stomach, her fingers brushing against the elastic of my shorts. I freeze, unable to move, unwilling to pull away. I can feel her hips pressed against me, where her shirt rides up and it's just skin—so much skin and so much warmth that I should be sweating, but I'm not. I'm falling into the burn of it instead, my breath finally back, and almost panting.

"Mmm," she sighs, her head dropping into the crook of my neck. The press of her lips can't be purposeful, because they flutter in a snoozy breath under my ear, but she lets out another sigh and her body relaxes, her arm tight around me.

I close my eyes, trying to calm the blood rushing to my head and . . . other parts of me. I feel like a bomb about to go off, and I suck in air, screwing my eyes shut and trying to focus. One. Two. Three. Four. Breathe out. One. Two. Three. Four. Breathe in.

I lose track of how many times I do it. I don't try to shift underneath Sonya's grip. I give myself over to it, memorizing the feel of her fingers against me, the press of her breasts against my back. She is *so* sweet, in so many ways. I didn't realize someone so sharp could be that sweet. I don't even know if she knows she's like this, melting sweet and finally free, if maybe this is only something you can see in sleep. Maybe I'm the first person to ever see it. Does she sleep next to Trenton, I wonder?

As soon as the thought hits me, I stiffen and she makes a noise, her grip tightening and her leg sliding between both of mine.

I keep breathing—amazingly, it's probably the most monumental achievement of my life—and keep my eyes closed. Time ticks by, and somehow I finally drift off, wrapped up in her in a way I've never been close to another person.

The next thing I know, light's hitting me.

"Morning!"

I squint against the bright sun, my eyes struggling to adjust, my mind trying to catch up. Everything is too bright and loud and empty. Her arms aren't around me anymore, and it's like my body hurts where she was pressed.

"I slept *so* good last night," Sonya says. "You're like Ambien, Coley."

I untangle myself from the blankets, pushing my messy hair out of my face. Oh God, I probably have the worst bedhead. I *know* I have terrible morning breath.

She looks amazing. Fuck. Of course she does. She looks like she's slept as soundly as she claimed and didn't spend the night drinking and getting tangled up in poison oak. I catch a glimpse of myself in her dresser mirror and cringe. The same *cannot* be said about me.

"I'm glad you slept good," I say.

"Didn't you?" she asks, and my head's pounding from last night, but I know when she's trying to pull something on me.

"Absinthe doesn't really agree with me," I lie. I'd only taken a sip, it had barely gone to my head. But she doesn't need to know that.

"Faith gave you absinthe?" she asks, her words spilling out quickly.

"Yeah," I say carefully, remembering how she'd acted last night when Faith and I talked. I can't help but continue, just to see how she'll act: "After you went off with Trenton, she and I had a drink together."

"I told you Faith was trouble," Sonya warns me.

"I'll take that into consideration," I tell her, even though I don't want to think about Sonya's idea of trouble, considering she'd basically *spooned* me last night.

"Whatever," Sonya says. "Don't say I didn't warn you when she, like, tries to hit on you."

"The horror," I drawl without thinking.

"What does *that* mean?" Sonya demands.

"Nothing," I say quickly, crawling out of her bed fast as I can. "I'm glad you slept good. I really need to get going. Curtis will wonder where I am."

"I'll drive you," Sonya says.

"You don't—"

"Yeah I do," she says. "You didn't bike over here, remember? I picked you up. Come on."

The drive home is almost entirely silent. I don't know what I did wrong. *Was* she awake last night? Is she mad at me for not jerking away or something? If I'd tried, I would've fallen out of bed.

Maybe she's embarrassed? I sneak a look at her out of the corner of my eye, trying to read her expression as she concentrates on the road. But when she catches me looking, she just smiles sunnily at me, and then it's back to focusing on the road.

"I'll walk you in!" she says when she pulls up to the house.

"You don't need to," I say.

"I want to see your room," she insists.

"I haven't cleaned—"

"I don't care," she says, getting out of the car before I can protest any further, so I'm the one following her up the path to the porch.

"Coley, is that you?" Curtis calls when we get inside.

"Yep. I spent the night at Sonya's," I say.

He comes out into the hall from the kitchen. "Hey, Sonya."

"Hi, Curtis."

"I made pancakes," he says. "Have you girls eaten breakfast?"

"Oh, it's okay, we're—" I start to say.

"I would *love* some pancakes," Sonya says, interrupting me. "We used up a lot of energy last night, didn't we, Coley?"

I stare at her, my cheeks turning red. "Um."

"Playing capture the flag," Sonya continues smoothly.

"That sounds fun," Curtis tells her as he beckons us into the kitchen. He dishes out the pancakes, and Sonya perches on the stool next to the kitchen island and pours maple syrup on her plate.

I take the orange juice Curtis gives me, staying entirely quiet as the two of them chatter at each other. I feel like I'm in some sort of weird dream: spending the night with Sonya, literally *in her arms*, and now I'm sitting here having breakfast with her.

Is this what it's like when you have a girlfriend? Do you just get to grow up and move in with them and wake up with them and eat breakfast with them and be . . . happy?

The idea is too strange to be real. This feeling growing in my stomach is too weird as Sonya jokes with Curtis about something called the Snowflake Festival that the town throws in the winter.

"You're going to love it," she promises when she sees my confused look. "There's a snowman-making contest."

"That sounds like something I'd hate," I say.

Curtis laughs. "We've got a Grinch right here in the kitchen."

I glare at him. "What do you know about my holiday traditions?"

He falls silent, his expression sobering. Sonya looks nervously between the two of us.

"I should go," she says tactfully. "I'll see your room next time, Coley. My mom needs me to watch my sister."

I nod.

"I'll AIM you." She hops off the stool. "Thanks for the pancakes, Curtis!"

I clear the plates as she lets herself out, fleeing the awkward situation I absolutely created. God, what is wrong with me? I can *see* Curtis is trying. It just seems to make everything worse. I don't know why.

"You okay?" Curtis asks.

"I'm fine."

He raises an eyebrow and leans forward, his elbows pressing on the kitchen counter. "I know what a hangover looks like," he tells me.

"Ten points to you," I say. "I'm going to go lie down." My eyes are gritty, like I didn't get any sleep at all.

When I get to my room, I fall back on my bed, my hand dropping down to the spot on my stomach where hers rested for so long last night. I breathe in and out, my hand rising and falling, and I swear, I can feel her hand under mine. The ghost of her breath against my neck. The heat of her hips pressed tight to mine.

My eyes drift shut and for the first time since I took the weight of her against me in her bed, I let myself revel in it. In *her.* In the two of us and the sleep-warm tangle we made under her sheets.

I hope you woke up wrapped in me, I think, willing my thoughts to float across the streets and trees and through her bedroom window. *I hope you didn't know where you started and where I began. I hope it shook you, how right it felt, waking up with your arms around me. I hope you didn't know what the fuck to do with yourself—because I didn't, last night.*

My fingers move, skirting lower, under the waistband of my shorts. No. *Sonya's* shorts. They cut a little too tight around the waist and they're shorter than what I'd wear, and on her, they'd hang on her hips, low-slung and baring so much skin.

I hope you're thinking about me too, when you do this.

TWENTY

LJ User: SonyatSunrisex00x [Public Entry]

Date: June 20, 2006

[**Mood:** itchy]

[**Music:** "Toxic"–Britney Spears]

How's everyone feeling? A little itchy? :D

xoox

Sonya

Comments:

SJbabayy:

OMG, you're hilarious. I got out of it with barely any rash. How are you feeling?

SonyatSunrisex00x:

Thanks for the tecnu tip! I'm good. No rash at all for me!

SJbabayy:

Tell Coley thanks again, will you? Also I have her shirt. She can pick it up at my place if she wants to.

SonyatSunrisex0Ox:
Cool. I'll tell her.

TOnofTrentOnnn:
I can't believe you think this is funny. It's bullshit.

SJbabayy:
Lighten up, Trenton.

TOnofTrentOnnn:
Coley never should've led us into a fucking lake of poison oak.

MadeYouBrooke23:
You know what they say about city girls. . . .

SonyatSunrisex0Ox:
Why don't you two shut up? It was dark as hell out there, and if we hadn't hidden, the cops might've picked us up. That's a lot worse than a rash!

MadeYouBrooke23:
Geez. I was just joking. Sorry.

TOnofTrentOnnn:
Gotta protect your Coley lapdog, huh, Sonya?

SonyatSunrisex0Ox:
Screw you.

LJ User: SonyatSunrisex00x [Private Entry]

Date: June 20, 2006

[**Mood:** wondering]

[**Music:** "Soul Meets Body"—Death Cab for Cutie]

bed

waking up with you
bittersweet biting wanting
do you feel it too?

TWENTY-ONE

SonyatSunrisex00x: come over

RollieColey87: right now?

SonyatSunrisex00x: we can swim. pool just got cleaned.

I look down at my arm, where the tiny patch of poison oak has mostly faded, thanks to Sonya's quick treatment. The chlorine is probably not going to help, but I'm not going to turn down an invitation from her. Especially after that party.

RollieColey87: on my way

It's been a week. We've talked and she stopped by once, but apparently her mom was pissed about her breaking curfew and made her babysit Emma all week, so we've mostly been chatting on Messenger.

Biking over there is like flying down the roads, every light turning green just for me, urging me on. I get there in record time, and when she opens the door, she's smiling like seeing me is just what she needed.

"Oh my God, *finally.*" She grabs my arm and pulls me inside. "Mom took Emma to get frozen yogurt, and I wasn't allowed to go."

"Still being punished, huh?"

"In her mind. But she never lets us get good toppings. Only healthy ones."

I make a face. "No sprinkles?"

"Sprinkles are a birthday thing."

"Sprinkles should be an everyday thing," I say, thinking about my mom and her love of Funfetti cake. She'd always add extra sprinkles.

I follow Sonya through the house, trying not to react this time when she tosses her shirt off before we even get outside to the pool. Her red bikini is all strings and strategically placed triangles, and all I can think about is how her shoulders felt under my hands. How her legs tangled with mine as we slept, her toes tickling the arches of my feet as she breathed against my neck. Her arm held me so tight, it was like even in sleep, she was afraid of what would happen if she let go. Like I'd run.

But the truth is, the second I slipped into her bed, wrapped in her clothes, I was gone.

She dives into the pool, so smooth she barely makes a splash, and I'm still catching up, watching her instead of stripping down to my own suit. I undress, but I don't jump in. I use the steps, letting my body get used to the water, cool against my heated skin. I swim toward her.

She spits water at me as soon as I get close, and I laugh,

dodging backward, splashing her in turn, and she flips over like a mermaid, shimmying off. Her dark hair's a blur that I follow beneath the water.

Floating around, just the two of us, is like catching starlight. Like she's bottled it up and spilled it out for us to play in. I drink it in, swirling around her, splashing and laughing. The longer it goes on, the closer we get, until our bodies aren't just brushing by each other, but twisting around each other, and then my back's pressed against the pool edge and her hands are on either side, so close.

"What are you looking at?" I ask her.

"You," she says.

I blink, not knowing how to answer. We're in the deep end; the only thing that's keeping me up is the sloped wall of the pool and my treading feet. But every time I move my feet, I bob forward. Close enough to touch but never quite getting there.

All I can think about is the press of her body against my back—how her knees fit into the crooks of my legs, two peas in a pod of our own making. That secret shelter of her bed, where no one could touch us.

"I wish we had some weed," she says. "I haven't gotten high since the night of the party."

"I think I read that if you look someone in the eye for a few minutes, you can get high," I say.

"Really?"

I nod. "It's got something to do with the brain chemicals."

"Ooh, sciencey," Sonya says. "Let's do it!"

"You want me to stare at you?"

"Am I that bad to look at?" she asks, batting her eyes in a way that tells me there's not a shred of insecurity behind it.

"You're ridiculous and you know it."

She pouts, which makes her even cuter, and she probably knows that, too. "I want to get high!"

"Okay. Fine." I square my shoulders and hold the pool's edge so I'm steadier. I take a breath, looking at her.

She stares back, and suddenly I'm cursing myself for suggesting this silly game, because now she's the one bobbing back and forth, in and out of my space. If I reach out, I could hook my arm around her waist. I could slide my fingers up her back, tangle with the red strings of her bikini, and . . .

Maybe there is something to the whole staring-makes-you-high thing, because my head's spinning, but maybe that's just her.

Her eyes are that golden-warm that makes you fall into them, swirling in the heat until you can't imagine anything cold ever again. They shift darker against the red of her suit and the damp slick of her hair, but in the light, they shift to honey with flecks of something deeper that you want to spend your life chasing.

I could spend my life chasing her. Devotedly. Doggedly.

But she could spend her life running. I might never catch up with her. That's what's so scary about it.

"What are you thinking?" I whisper, because I have to ask. I need to know.

She licks her lips, and I can't help it, my eyes dip down and they stay for too long. She has to notice. I'm close to not caring.

She wouldn't act like this if she didn't feel it too. She *wouldn't.*

"I . . ." she starts to say.

A beach ball comes sailing out of nowhere, hitting me hard in the head, laughter breaking through the silence.

"Trenton!" Sonya shouts as I startle away from the ball, caught so off guard that I suck in water. I surface, coughing and sputtering.

"Shit, Coley, are you okay?" Alex asks, hurrying over.

"Fine," I choke out, but I take his offered hand and let him pull me out of the water. I plop myself down on the edge of the pool and cough into my fist, my throat burning, the tang of chlorine thick in my mouth.

"Poor thing," Sonya says, patting my thigh.

"I'm fine," I say, eyes sliding back up to Trenton. "I'm gonna dry off."

I get up and stalk past him to the stack of towels, hoping he'll leave me alone. So of course he comes right up to me as I hear Sonya ask Alex if he has any weed.

"Look what you did." Trenton thrusts his arm out at me. It's puckered with a nasty rash that oozes. I rear back from it.

"Ew," I say, wrapping myself in a towel. "Get away from me with that."

"This is your fault."

"Didn't you treat it with that lotion stuff?" I ask him.

He rolls his eyes. "I didn't have time to pick any up."

"Oh my God," Sonya exclaims behind us. "What happened?"

Trenton's eyes get big and pitiful. "The poison oak got me, babe," he says, all pathetically, and my stomach turns as she falls for his bullshit and hurries over. "I did the lotion thing like you told me," he lies. "But I must've been in a worse patch of it when Coley made us hide in the gully."

"Oh, that looks awful," she says. "How have you been treating it since it broke out?"

"I dunno."

"Trenton," she scolds. "You know better than that. Let me get the first aid kit. You need some calamine on that."

"You're the best," Trenton says, but he's not looking at her when he says it; he's looking at me, his eyes gleaming.

I look away, swallowing back the sick feeling rising in my throat. *You should watch out for him,* Faith had told me. I'm starting to really see why. He isn't just a jerk. He's manipulative as fuck.

I want to get as far away from Trenton as possible, but I don't want to leave her, so I go over to where Alex is sitting, his feet dangling in the water.

"How you been?" he asks.

"Okay. You?"

"Busy," he says. "I had family visiting."

"Is that good or bad?"

"My aunts make tamales—always a good thing. But I have to entertain my cousins. And they are exhausting."

"How old are they?" I ask.

He opens his mouth to answer, but Trenton's voice rises over whatever he's about to say: "Don't put that stuff on me! It's pink!"

"Trenton." Sonya sighs. I turn to look at the lounge chairs, where she's set up the first aid kit. She's trying to smear some calamine lotion on his arm. "You've gotta let me treat that. It's gross."

"I can't have pink stuff all over my arm. Get me something that's not girly."

I can't help it, I laugh, keeping it under my breath. We're

across the pool from them, so Trenton doesn't hear, but Alex does.

"Don't you know even making contact with something pink will turn you gay?" he asks sarcastically, grinning at me and rolling his eyes. "He's right to be so worried."

"Festering, itchy wounds is *totally* better than exposing yourself to the dreaded pink," I agree solemnly.

Alex's eyes crinkle and we laugh together, loud enough that Sonya looks over.

"What are you two giggling about?" she demands.

"Nothing," Alex says, so innocently it makes me laugh harder.

"Can you please explain to him that he needs to have the lotion on his arm?" Sonya asks Alex. "This is ridiculous," she tells Trenton.

"Get me a different color calamine lotion."

"Man, the active ingredient in the stuff turns it pink," Alex says. "Just deal. If you don't let it heal, you're gonna end up with poison oak on your nethers."

Trenton's eyes widen comically. "Give me the calamine stuff," he says instantly.

"See? Easy," Alex says to me.

"You're truly a master."

"Okay, all done," Sonya says, putting the calamine lotion away. "You need to let it dry. And you need to put more of it on tomorrow. Remember what Alex said."

"You always take care of me," Trenton says, wrapping his just-treated and still totally contagious arm around Sonya, trying to pull her close.

"Trenton!" she protests, pushing him away.

"We should get going."

She's still frowning at him, her nose all scrunched up. "Where?"

"Alex's parents are on vacation, remember? We're going to hang. Say bye to Coley and get your stuff. Hurry up." He pushes her lightly to get her going, but she plants her feet, her scowl deepening to a glower that I've never seen on her face before. I'm petty enough to admit that I like that she seems so pissed at him all of a sudden.

"What the fuck, Trenton? Coley's invited, too," Alex says. "I'd love for you to come," he says to me with a smile.

"Thanks," I say.

"No thanks," Sonya says firmly, coming over and grabbing my arm. "Coley and I have other plans."

"What kind of plans?" Trenton demands.

"None of your business!" Sonya trills. "You're not in charge of my schedule, Trenton."

"Whatever," he says and stomps off like a pissed-off toddler.

"I'll see you girls later," Alex says.

"Honestly," Sonya says, pulling on her shorts and shirt. I follow her but barely have time to finish buttoning my shorts before she's walking again. "He's so obvious." She liberates a bottle of vodka from the bar cart by the pool, tucking it under her shirt. "Let's go to our spot on the tracks."

"Near the bridge?"

She nods.

"Has he always been this possessive?" I ask, trying to make it sound as casual as possible as we head down her long driveway. I can't get what Faith said about Trenton out of my head.

"Like all guys," she says.

"You keep saying stuff like that."

She looks over her shoulder, shooting me a confused look. "What are you talking about?"

"You keep talking about all this bad shit that Trenton does, usually to you, and you keep saying all guys do that."

"Yeah?"

"I don't think they do. I just think the shitty ones act like that."

Her eyebrows rise so swiftly my instinct is to backtrack. "How would *you* know?" she asks.

But instead, I meet her, barb for barb. I'm ready for her bullshit. "Oh, you know me," I say, breezing past her. "I told you about all those parties where I danced on tables. You think I haven't had my share of rendezvous with men? I've left a trail of hearts behind me!" I waggle my eyebrows, making it sound as silly and exaggerated as possible, and she bursts out laughing, all the tension in her body transforming into joy for a moment. "There you are," I say, which makes her go quiet, too fast, like a CD skipping.

"Trenton's not always bad," she insists. "I know he wanted to ditch everyone at the barn. . . ."

"That was pretty quick thinking, getting his keys," I say, grabbing my bike.

"It's not the first time I've had to do that," she says before jumping on her bike. She sails ahead of me, her hair streaming out behind her like a silk scarf as I pump my pedals to catch up.

We leave our bikes at the spot near the tracks, leaning them against the trees where they won't be found. Sonya tiptoes along the rail, her hands held out for balance, jumping back and forth in a zigzag along the tracks on her tippy-toes. There's a coltish grace in her; I see why she wins all the competitions. When she's feeling it, you can't take your eyes off her. When she's unguarded? She's incandescent.

She'd shine so brightly if she let herself. If she knew herself, trusted herself.

But who the fuck am I to talk? I can barely trust my own heart and the breath in my lungs around her. It's like she sucks it all out of me—my breath and my heart and all the pieces of my soul that are left.

"When I was little," Sonya announces, her voice grandiose enough to let me know that the vodka she'd shot was kicking in. "My mom used to put me in these little cupcake dresses, and the skirts would fly up when I twirled." She spins on one foot on the rail, a slow-motion twirl that has her laughing and almost falling. "So of course, my mom told me to stop twirling. It wasn't ladylike. And we *must* be ladylike." Sonya shakes her head back and forth, jabbering to imitate her mother. "*Be ladylike and still, Sonya. Movement is for dance class and competition and not anywhere else.*" She sighs, her shoulders slumping. "She's doing the same thing to Emma. She's gonna kill her love of it."

"Is that what she did to you?"

Sonya's silent, staring out at the bridge ahead. "I'll race you," she says.

"Sonya—" I start to say, but she's already making a run for it.

"I swear to God, this girl," I mutter to myself, and then I dash after. I can't see her; the curve in the tracks disappears into the trees here, and when I hear the whistle of the train, the fear is like an electric shock to my entire body.

"Sonya!" I pelt forward, taking the blind curve so fast the world blurs around me. All I can see is her, standing there, vodka bottle in one hand, her back to the train that's heading toward her.

TWENTY-TWO

"Sonya, move!" I yell.

She snaps back, "Don't tell me what to—"

I collide with her, yanking her off the tracks and rolling down the embankment, into the thick grass that grows around the trees. She's on top of me, her hair lifting in the breeze as the train speeds past us, whistle blowing, the sound filling my ears and my senses, her eyes wide.

The clang and rising dust around us should be chaos, but all I can see is her and all I can feel is her heartbeat against mine. It's the strangest sensation: my heartbeat slowing to twin hers, our breaths mirroring. My hand reaches out and I tuck her hair behind her ear.

She doesn't pull away. She doesn't flinch.

She leans into my touch as I cup her cheek. Her eyes close, and when her hand covers mine, it's like I know the meaning of relief, finally, after what's felt like an eternity.

This is how it's supposed to be.

The whistle begins to fade, the train disappearing around the curve, and I'm still lying there, blanketed by her body, held by her hand, my heart beating in my body even though it's hers.

She pushes herself up, just a little, freeing me of her weight when I don't want to be free, so I follow as she goes, mirroring her. We lie there in the tall grass, side by side, our legs still tangled together.

She doesn't push away again.

"Are you okay?" she asks.

I nod.

"I should've been paying attention. I'm sorry."

"It's okay. It's not like anyone would really miss me if I got flattened by a train."

She shakes her head like the idea is impossible, which cheers me. But then she says: "Your dad—"

"We talked about that," I interrupt her. "He's not really—"

"I thought your dad was nice," she says, overlapping me, almost puzzled.

"Huh?"

"When I dropped you off the morning after the party? Your dad was making pancakes. He was nice."

"I guess."

"Is he trying to do dad-ing better?" Sonya asks, her eyes getting big and thoughtful. "It's what you deserve, Coley."

I tell myself she's drunk and high on adrenaline. That's why she's pushing like this, when I made it clear last time I didn't really want to go there.

"What about your mom?"

I go very still, and her body tenses against mine but doesn't move away. Instead, she shifts closer, like she knows that soon she'll have to be the one supporting me.

"You never mention her," Sonya says.

"She's gone," I say, because I still haven't found a good way to say it. You never think of these things until you have to. You never realize how many questions could crop up that you suddenly have to change your answers to. "I mean. She died."

Sonya's fingers flex on my arm, a gentle *I'm here* squeeze as we stare at each other in the stretching shadows of the trees. We breathe together, our bodies rising and falling in the same rhythm, like we've got the same heart, even for just a breath.

"Was there an accident or . . ." Sonya pauses. "Can I even ask . . . I'm sorry. I don't . . . I'm not very good with this stuff. But you can talk to me. I can try. I want to try. I want to be good for you."

It's like she's looking right through me, holding out exactly what I need.

It's the only way I can say it out loud.

"My mom killed herself."

Silence. I wish my words could float from my lips to the water, the current carrying them away to a river or an ocean, to become part of this great big marble. Mom liked to call the earth that. They gave me her ashes, and I know she'd hate to just be in an urn; she'd want to be somewhere living and growing and beautiful. But I can't bear to even look at the urn, let alone open it. I'm such a fucking failure sometimes.

"Coley, I'm so sorry."

I nod, because I've heard that a lot. What else can you say, really? "She wasn't . . . she was really sad. She went through cycles of depression. She'd be really up and then down, but she always pulled out of it. And then—" I stop again, staring at my hands. The weight of her against me, so warm and familiar, keeps me going. Because I need to talk about it, don't I? "I don't think she was *trying* to. I think . . . she was just trying to numb the pain and she took too much, and I—" I let out a long breath. "I missed my first bus," I say finally. "I usually took the two fifteen, but I missed it and had to get the two thirty, and every day since, I've wondered . . . if I'd just taken the two fifteen like I was supposed to, maybe I would've found her in time. . . ."

Tears trickle down my cheeks, but I can't even bring myself to wipe them away, exhausted from finally saying the thing that's been churning in the choppy waters of my mind.

But then, I find I don't have to.

Because she's reaching out. She's cupping my face like I'd cupped hers, her thumb wiping away each tear like it's precious. Like I am.

"Oh, Coley, *no*." I have never known gentleness before, not until her thumb, smearing wet against my cheekbone, carrying my tears away on her skin. "You did everything you could. If you had to find her—oh my God, I'm so sorry." Her forehead presses against my temple, and I can feel tears trickle down my cheek that aren't mine.

Our tears mingle, our foreheads touch, and here, in our pain, we are one. There is no me. There is no her.

There is just us.

"I can't believe what you've survived," Sonya whispers against my cheek. "Do you know how incredible you are?"

Her hands cup the back of my neck, her thumb stroking back and forth at the base of my skull, sending shivers of emotion down my spine.

I can't stop the sound in my throat, this choked sob that just erupts from me. It's like she's drawing out everything I've been bottling up with her touch and words and assurance. I'm a shaken champagne bottle, exploding everywhere.

"I know that the reason you're here in this town is tragic, and I'm so sorry about your mom," Sonya whispers. "But I'm really happy you're here with me. That I get to know you. That you trust me enough to tell me."

I pull back, my out-of-control breath puffing across her skin as my eyes meet hers. She smiles, her hand moving from the back of my neck to tuck my hair behind my left ear, like I did for her earlier. But her hand doesn't drop. It just stays there, her fingers stroking down my jawline. I shiver. No one's ever touched me there before, and my thighs clench together as her touch softens but still doesn't part.

"Hey," Sonya says. "Olive juice."

I frown. "I—"

"Ah-love-juice," she repeats, slowed down.

I love you.

My laughter is hidden behind a wet sniff. "Oh my God," I say. "You're a total cornball."

"I am not!"

"You are. You try to hide it. But I see it." I catch her hands as she tries to pull away, mock-angry and pouting. "I see you," I say, and her wrists are caught in my hands between us, and her entire body tilts toward mine like it's where we belong. "Olive juice, too," I whisper, because this is a moment for a whisper. This is a moment to remember.

This is the softest skin on her body that I know so far—the inside of her wrists, delicate veins and the bump of bone. This is the hitch in her breath as she leans in, her eyes drifting but not shutting, fixed on my lips.

I see *her*. The girl she tries to hide.

The girl who watches my lips like she wants to devour me.

"I've never met anyone like you," she says, hushed in the silence we've created in this little bubble of us. I can't even hear the trickle of the water anymore. If a train were coming and I was tied to the tracks, I wouldn't hear the wail. I'd be a goner for sure.

But fuck, what a way to go, in her arms, her lips just inches away.

The only thing better would be what I still can't dare to think. We're on the edge, like all the other times, but she's pulled back each time. And if I push forward, I could lose.

I could crash.

Or I could stay here forever, staring into her eyes.

Is it her or me who moves? I don't know. I think it's both of us. A breaking point in sync, she and I are one heart in this moment—one breath, one pulse.

Our lips brush. Just brush. Barely there, retreat, and then back again. My lips skim over hers, a stone skipping across a still pond, and then she makes this *noise*, it hooks deep in my stomach, just seconds before her tongue's against mine, and then—

Oh.

Then.

Tangled fingers and legs, her thigh sliding between mine like that night in bed, like it was almost familiar and oh so needed. My fingers wrap in her hair before hers do the same to mine, and oh so strange and marvelous at the same time, mirroring each other. Her hand skating across my collarbone—lower, lower, the *sighs* she makes—and my fingers mimicking the movement against hers.

It pounds inside me, swirling in my head like her peony-shampoo smell and the dizzying heat of her mouth. Those three little words, stripped of wordplay. The truth of them beating in my chest like a drum as we kiss and kiss and kiss.

Olive juice.

Olive juice.

I love you.

Top left: Maya Da Costa and Myra Molloy; bottom left: Hayley Kiyoko.

SONYA (CONT'D)

(Teasing) You *promise* you'll message me?

Coley rolls her eyes with love.

And Sonya turns sweetly and walks away, ... left each other the first time they met.

SONYA (CONT'D)

You better not break your pr... this time! (Then, funny) I k... where you live! I'll hunt yo...

Coley cracks up at her then turns. She ... starts pedaling.

COLEY

I'm counting on it!!!

Her eyes well, taking in all that just happened. She's so free.

Coley beams forward, accelerating down the center of that empty road. She LAUGHS. Powerful and whole. We don't cut. We don't want to miss a second.

~~THE END~~

The fucking beginning.

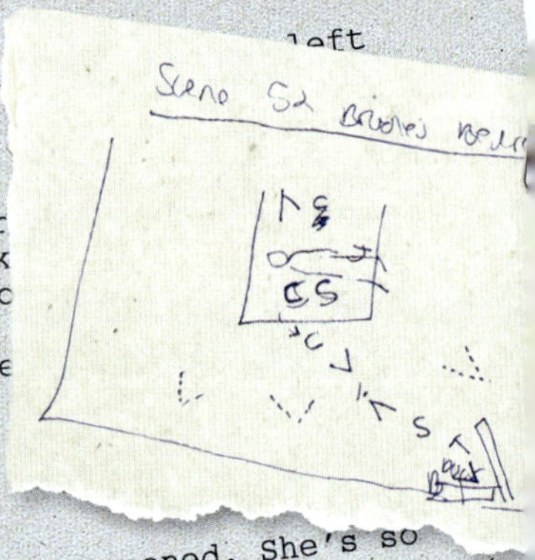

Bottom right: Maya Da Costa, Hayley Kiyoko, and Myra Molloy.

Hanging out

Coley + Sonya

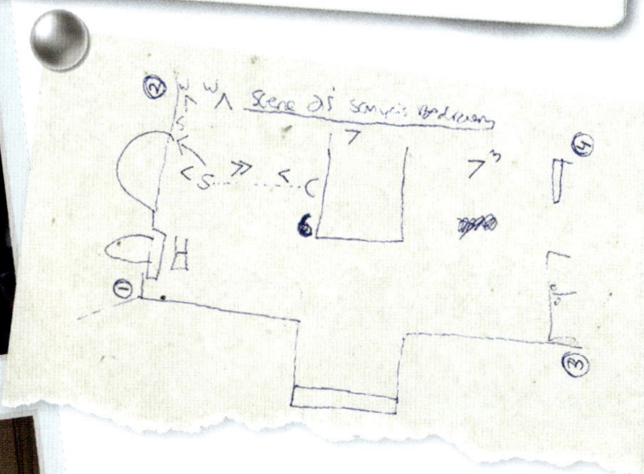

This was our original camera map for Sonya's dance scene, featuring my very glamorous drawing. We build our shot lists off of these!

Photos on left, Maya Da Costa and Myra Molloy.
Photo on right: Alozie LaRose, Levon Hawke, Maya Da Costa, and Myra Molloy.

SONYA (CONT'D)
I'm happy you're here. And I
know you.

oks at her and smiles, honestl

COLEY

Me too.

looks down, then looks back u

SONYA

...Olive juice.

One of my favorite scenes

Director Mode xx

SONYA
(Pointing to her eye) Ahhh-
(Pointing to her heart) Luuve-
(Taps Coley's nose) Juice.

Coley gets it. She's touched.

COLEY
Olive juice, too.

Top right, Maya Da Costa and Myra Molloy; middle left: Hayley Kiyoko.

Working Hard ;)

Top right: Maya Da Costa, Hayley Kiyoko, and Myra Molloy; bottom left: Shauna Carveth (key makeup), Lisa Burke (key hairstylist), and Maya Da Costa; bottom right: Myra Molloy and Maya Da Costa.

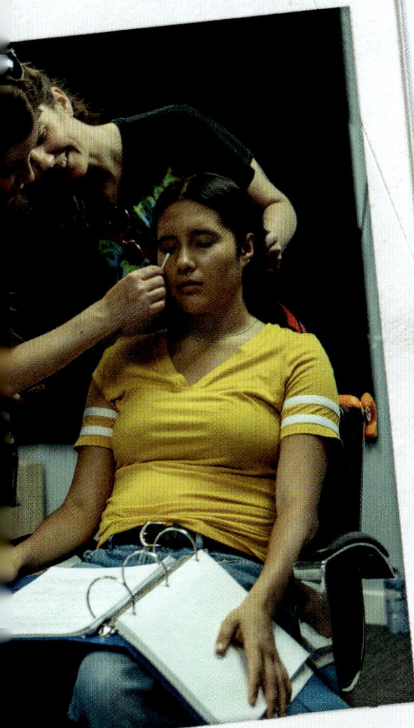

Top right and middle left: Myra Molloy and Maya Da Costa; bottom right: Hayley Kiyoko.

Quiet on set!

If you look closely, I hid the real-life jacket that inspired this scene in the shot—can you find it?

Top left: Myra Molloy and Maya Da Costa; bottom left: Sierra Sidwell, Sophia Carriere, Maya Da Costa, Levon Hawke, and Myra Molloy; bottom right: Sonya Tsypin (DP), Robert Booth (boom operator), and Myra Molloy.

Mood Lighting

My Girls Like Girls community:

By celebrating your truth, you've given me the greatest gift of all, space to be my authentic self. Thank you for making GLG what it is today; a symbol of hope and a reminder to us all that we are all worthy of love. Our community is special and I am so honored to share my life with you in it. We keep climbing forever and ever. See you at the movies!

Xx Hayley

Top left: Maya Da
top right: Myra M
and Alozie LaRose

Credits: Key Art © 2026 Focus Features LLC. Photos courtesy of Focus Features. Photographs by YK. Sketches by Hayley Kiyoko. Page design by Samantha Sadoff. All other elements by Shutterstock.

TWENTY-THREE

We don't talk. Kissing her takes my breath away, so I don't think I could, if I tried. *Making out* seems like a cheap way to describe this, learning her mouth like it's a secret I want to keep.

Even after the kisses slow, we twine together like ivy up a tree. In the long grass, as the sun sets, I drape my jacket over both of us and she cuddles close to me, her body loose and relaxed, like she knows she's safe. I'd never let anything happen to her. I'd fight the fucking *world* for her. I know I might have to, and I'm ready. She's worth it. God, she's worth it.

Her lips flutter against the skin of my neck, her thumb rubbing back and forth against my wrist. Eventually, the movement slows with her breathing, and I hold her closer as she falls into sleep, never wanting the day to stop. I want to stay here, where nothing can touch us.

I can't place the buzzing sound at first. Then I realize it's coming from her pocket. She stirs against me, waking slowly. She blinks up at me, and all I can think is that I want to watch her wake up forever.

"Hey," I whisper, reaching out and plucking grass off her shoulder.

Her phone keeps buzzing. She slicks her hair off her face and grabs it out of her pocket. "Shit," she says, leaping to her feet.

"Is everything okay?"

"Yeah," she says, staring at her phone, not even looking at me. "Yeah. I just . . ." Her gaze slides up, fixing on me for a solid, electric moment before dipping back down to her phone, paging through her texts. "I gotta go. Stuff to do."

Before I can react, before I can say *anything*, she's bolted, heading down the tracks at such a clip that if I follow her, I'll have to run to catch up.

I stand there, watching until her form disappears into the fading light.

What the fuck just happened?

I force myself to get home. Every movement is an effort, but I make it. My head's all over the place when I get to my room. When I touch my lips, after, it doesn't feel real.

I don't feel real. I'm suddenly in a world where I am a girl who gets kissed like *that.* Who gets kissed by *her.* It's a fantastical fairy tale to suddenly experience *it*—the thing that everyone's always talked about, but flipped for *me.* Princess meets princess, happily-ever-after spins in my head, and my brain doesn't even know what it should look like after the first kiss, but I'm trying.

Why did she run off? Is she okay? Did she get a text from her mom or something? I have to know. I go over to my computer and my heart actually *skips* when I see she's online.

RollieColey87: hi

I stare at her screen name, willing her to answer. But instead, she suddenly switches to an "away" message.

That's the thing about falling.

Sometimes you crash.

Come back. I try to will it through the screen, one hand on the mouse, the other still pressed to my lips, where *her* lips had been. She'd *kissed* me. Again and again, like she wanted to drink from me, desert-parched and desperate.

Come back.

But now she's just an away message, taunting me through the night every time I look at it.

My computer is the first thing I check the next morning. She's *finally* answered. Late last night, when *my* away message was on. Like she'd planned it, waiting for me to sleep, sneaking in so I wouldn't be there to respond.

SonyatSunrisex00x: hey

SonyatSunrisex00x: didn't see this. totally crashed. sooooo hungover.

SonyatSunrisex00x: vodka is not my friend

SonyatSunrisex00x: sorry for being weird last night

I stare at the messages, every bit of buzz draining from my body in a rush. I start to type. What am I supposed to say back? That she didn't need to apologize? That making out with her was the best thing that's ever happened to me? That I'm pretty sure I—

I stop typing. I need to think. Not just react.

Pulling up my browser, I click over to her LiveJournal.

LJ User: SonyatSunrisex00x [Public Entry]

Date: June 28, 2006

[**Mood:** hyped]

[**Music:** "Over My Head"–The Fray]

My girls *always* come through for me. Told @MadeYouBrooke23 that I needed to blow off some serious steam. She and @SJbabayy arranged an entire girls' night for me *and* a kickback for all of us tomorrow! AIM me for the details or comment here!

Don't know what I'd do without you two <3 <3 <3

–Sonya

I shouldn't read the comments. I know it'll make me feel worse. But I click on them all the same. By the time I'm done reading about them gushing over their girls' night, my stomach's churning. It feels like she did this on purpose; like she needed to replace the memory of me on the tracks with her *real* friends. The ones she *didn't* kiss senseless.

It's like being erased, and my skin crawls from it. There's nothing like going invisible. It makes your mind whisper that if you leave, no one will miss you. My mom thought that in the end. She was so fucking wrong.

My hand clenches over the mouse. I force myself to relax it as I click back over to Messenger. She's still online, and I wonder if she's waiting for my answer. A part of me wants to leave my away message on, to torture her like she tortured me.

Instead, I type it out, carefully and on the edge of cruel:

> **RollieColey87:** lol you *are* weird. no idea what you're talking about

And then, like I don't already know:

> **RollieColey87:** what ru doing today?

And there it is, no answer . . . and the away message again.

Something hot and horrible curls in my stomach. I thought playing her ignorance game would make me feel better. But all I feel is worse.

I'm so done with games. With lying. Especially to myself.

TWENTY-FOUR

I almost don't go. In fact, I tell myself I'm not going to. SJ was being nice when she called me up to invite me to the kickback she was throwing at Sonya's. It's payback for saving her at the barn party; she doesn't really care if I'm there. And Brooke *definitely* doesn't want me there. She and Trenton could form a club at this point. Alex . . . maybe. Sometimes he smiles at me in a way that makes me think . . . but that doesn't matter at all. Especially now.

Why would I care about some boy when *the* girl is running around in my head like a marathon?

Sonya's not avoiding me. That's what's driving me crazy. She messaged me on AIM right after SJ called, making sure I was going to come. And she *had* to be the person who gave SJ my number. So they talked about it.

Oh my God, did they talk about *it*? No. Right? She wouldn't dare.

No. Definitely not. If she can't even talk about it with *me*.

I turn over in bed, staring at the ceiling. That's why I should go. I need to talk to her in person. None of this "sorry for being weird last night" shit through AIM. We need to be face-to-face.

It's so much harder for her to hide when we're close. When I'm right there. Her friends can't see her, but *I* can. She let me in, gave me a key, and she can't just lock me out now. I can't let her. Not without telling her.

So I go. I bike over there as the sun starts to sink, and there are already a few cars I don't recognize parked in front of her house. There's splashing and shouting coming from the pool area as I ring the doorbell.

"Coley! Hi!"

To my relief, it's SJ that opens the door, not Sonya. She's positively *beaming* at me, and it makes me hesitate. I know I did the girl a favor, giving her my shirt, but she's never smiled so brightly at me before.

Be nice, I tell myself. I smile back.

"Hi, SJ." I hate how fake my smile feels. I hope it doesn't look as bad. "Thanks for making sure I got the invite."

"Of course!" She lowers her voice. "I owe you!"

"You really don't," I assure her.

"You looked out for me. I appreciate it when girls have other girls' backs," she says, and she seems so earnest, but there's something in her big eyes that sends a shiver of suspicion down my spine. I try to shake it off. I need to get better at making friends—stop being so guarded. My mom used to tell me I liked to build brick walls around me, and I hate it, but she was right. I need to knock some of the bricks free. Not all of them. But enough to create some gaps or something.

"So . . . remember that guy at the party?" SJ asks.

"The one who ditched you?"

"He texted to say he was sorry," she explains. "So I invited him to come today. He's out by the pool with Alex and some other people."

"Are you going to go for it?" I ask as we walk toward the media room. I can hear the jabber of voices and the crinkle of chip bags. There's no music, but the telltale clink of glasses tells me that Sonya's parents must be out again, if everyone's drinking.

"Brooke and Sonya say I should," SJ says. "What do you think?"

A flash of surprise hits me. "You want my opinion?"

SJ nods.

"I mean, he ditched you," I say. "Did he seem *really* sorry?"

"I think so."

"Maybe don't decide until you spend some time with him? Things can be easier to decide when you see the person face-to-face." Which is why I'm here, trying to find Sonya. I glance casually over SJ's shoulder, toward the media room. "Is everyone back there?"

"The boys keep going back and forth between the house and the pool," SJ says, rolling her eyes. "Dripping everywhere. Come on. Let's get you a drink."

We head down the hall, music starting to play and someone whooping in response. "Yay!" I hear Sonya's voice. "Come, come, come! Dance with me!"

SJ and I come into the media room just as Sonya pulls Brooke up to stand on one of the pristine white couches. She moves to the beat, her head whipping back and forth . . . and she almost instantly loses her balance, falling backward into the mound of pillows with a shriek that turns into hysterical, very drunken laughter.

"Watch out, babe!" Trenton calls lazily from where he's sprawled across the love seat, chugging a beer.

"Yeah, I think Sonya got started a little early today," SJ says in a low tone to me as Brooke scrambles down to help Sonya sit up. "She was already kind of drunk when I got here at eleven."

I bite back my response as Sonya pops back up, pushing Brooke to the side.

"Coley!" Sonya says when she spots me. She leaps forward, narrowly missing the glass coffee table and bouncing toward me and SJ. "You came! Did Brooksy text you?" She giggles. "Brooksy and Coley! That's *sooo* cute."

"You are *sooo* drunk," SJ says. "You need to drink some water before you drink any more, sweetie."

"I don't want water. I want more vodka."

"Water first," SJ insists. "I'm going to go get you some." She hurries out of the room, toward the kitchen.

Sonya rolls her eyes, slinging her arm around my neck. "Hiii!"

She reeks of something—I think it might be tequila, but I don't know my liquor well enough to be sure.

"Hi, Coley," Brooke says. "How are you?"

I frown. "I'm fine?"

"Good!" Brooke says. "That's really good. I really like your top!"

That same shiver of suspicion from when I talked to SJ snakes through me.

"You know, my parents made me get a job. At Abercrombie. If you need school clothes, you can totally use my employee discount."

"Ooh, yes, let's go shopping," Sonya says. "You'd look so cute, dressed up all preppy." She ruffles my hair.

"Drink this." SJ's back, thrusting a bottle of water under Sonya's nose.

Sonya pouts. "Okay, *Mom*."

"You're the one who started shooting tequila at ten A.M.," SJ snaps back. "I don't know what's up with you lately."

"I'm fine," Sonya insists, her arm drawing away from my neck as she plops down on the couch. I try not to laugh as she tries to unscrew the bottle and fails. Her lower lip sticks out. "It's broken."

"It's not broken." I take it from her, opening it and handing it back to her as SJ shakes her head, crossing her arms.

"We don't even have a week left with you," SJ says. "And all you want to do is get drunk."

"I'm always gone half the summer," Sonya gripes back. "It's nothing new."

Half the summer? My stomach drops at how casually she says it.

"Wait," I blurt out. "Where are you going?"

Sonya looks up at me, that telltale flush rising in her cheeks. "Dance camp," she says. "I go every year."

"You never told me," I say.

"I'm sure I did."

"No," I say firmly.

"We're going to miss her!" SJ says.

"Seriously," Brooke adds. "All I've got is my job and SJ here."

"Oh, fuck you," SJ says. "I'm great company. Be nice or I'll spend the rest of my summer with Coley."

Brooke laughs. "Watch out, Sonya, she's gonna get your girl."

Sonya's beaming expression snaps off her face so fast it makes my hand clench around the rum and coke SJ had given me. "Shut up, Brooke."

All three of us stare at her, startled into silence by the sudden vicious streak in her voice. Sonya glares at Brooke, her fingers curling into fists.

"*Any*way," SJ says, breaking the silence with an awkward eye roll. "You're still drunk. Down the rest of that water. I'm going to go hang out by the pool with Alex and everyone else. I need the chilling effects of someone who's stoned right now."

SJ disappears, and I can't help but dart a look between Brooke and Sonya with building dread. SJ is a good buffer. She always seems to know when to smooth things out. Brooke? Not so much. And me . . . I'm kind of fucked right now, because all I want to do is get Sonya alone so we can talk. But she definitely needs to sober up before that happens.

"Drink your water," I urge her, and she actually listens to me, downing the rest of it and tossing the bottle over her shoulder carelessly. It hits a vase, which wobbles back and forth, close to tipping.

"Break! Break!" Sonya chants at it, her face falling when it doesn't. "Ugh. I hate that ugly thing."

I glance over at it. It's expensive looking, that much I know. But the blue-and-gold pattern on it is pretty.

"I don't think it's so bad," I say.

"You didn't have to traipse all over Paris with your mom trying to find the shop that was selling it," Sonya moans. "Not that walking around Paris is a chore," she adds quickly, because I raise my eyebrows. "I was just wearing the wrong shoes and she knew it, and it was a whole thing. All I can think about is my blisters when I look at it."

"That's a lot of history for a vase," I tell her, and she looks down, embarrassed.

"I'm drunk."

"Do you want to get more water?" I suggest.

"If I get up, things get all spinny," she says. "Will you get it for me? It's in the kitchen."

"I'll be right back," I tell her as she slumps against the couch.

"Thank you!"

I leave the media room, heading to the kitchen, which is so clean it looks like no one ever cooks in it. But when I open the enormous fridge that's built into the cabinetry, I know that can't be true, because it's absolutely stuffed full of food you have to cook. I grab two bottles of water and a bag of chips off the counter. Maybe that will soak up whatever she's been pounding down.

When I get back to the room, Trenton's gotten up off the love seat and is sitting between the girls on the couch. A king holding court, his arms and legs spread out wide, taking up as much room as possible as Sonya sits to his right and Brooke hangs on his left, way too close to be anything casual.

"I have your water," I tell Sonya, holding it out for her.

"Oh, thanks," she says, but she doesn't take it. She's not even looking at me, her focus on Trenton as he continues telling his story.

". . . and then we grabbed the food and drove off before he could take the cash," Trenton finishes with a sneer. "You should've seen the guy's face! He jumped out the window and started chasing us. Can you believe it? What a lame-ass. Fifty dollars' worth of food and he never saw it coming."

"He probably got blamed for it," Brooke says.

"Already feeling the plight of the working people now that you have a job?" Trenton asks.

"No! Not at all," Brooke says quickly. "I'm only working because my parents made me get one. My dad is on a whole responsibility kick."

"I can always help you get fired," he offers.

"Trenton!" Brooke giggles like it's the funniest thing.

"Here," I say to Sonya, holding out the bottle of water again.

"Thanks," she says, but she's staring at Trenton and Brooke like she's trying to solve something.

"I'm gonna . . ." I don't even bother to finish the sentence. No one's paying attention to me.

I head to the bathroom, turning on the tap and sticking my hands under the cold water. I press my damp, cold hands to the back of my neck, trying to calm down.

You shouldn't have come. That's all I can think as I grip the edge of the marble sink and stare in the fancy mirror.

A knock on the door jerks me out of my pity-fest. "Occupied," I call, hating how strangled my voice comes out.

A pause. Then a softer, more insistent tapping. "Coley? It's me."

It's shameful how fast I scramble to unlock the door.

She breezes right past me, heading toward the mirror. "My eyeliner is all smeared," she says, popping the mirror open and grabbing a makeup bag tucked inside. She clucks her tongue at her reflection when she closes the mirror again. "Why didn't you tell me how bad I looked?" She begins to clean the smeared eyeliner with a makeup wipe.

"You don't look bad."

"Liar," she scoffs.

"What is going on with you?" It trips out of me, unwilling and too honest, hanging there between us.

She looks at me in the mirror, the eyeliner pen poised in her hand. "What are you talking about?"

I lick my lips, that rush of *pitiful* almost sucking me into an ocean of doubt. But I resist. I remember. Her lips against mine. Her hands on my stomach. Her body clutching mine. "You didn't tell me you were going to dance camp."

"Hmm," she says, leaning forward and starting to line her eyes. "I thought I did."

"You didn't."

"Sorry," she says, sounding like she doesn't even understand what she's apologizing for. "I guess I'm just used to all my friends knowing. I've been going to camp since I was seven. It's part of my summer routine."

"Are we . . . are we going to talk while you're gone?"

"Oh, I don't know," Sonya says, her attention sliding back to her makeup. She finishes her right eye and moves on to her left while I just stand there, feeling about two inches tall.

"What does that mean?" I snap, trying to gain some kind of strength. But she's got me in her palm, ready to crush.

"Camp is about training," she says. "I really need to focus. And you . . ." She finally looks at me and her eyes sweep up and down me, assessing in a horrible, stomach-clenching way. "You're kind of a lot of drama, Coley."

My eyes burn, but I blink away the tears. I need to get out

of here. I can't move. I'm rooted to the spot. "Did I . . . did I do something? Are you—"

"What?" she interrupts, entirely exasperated. It's like a knife to my throat.

"Is this about—"

"I'm just *busy*," she says, overriding me again. "I have a life, you know? I have training. Friends at dance camp I only see every summer. It's overwhelming, prepping to dance with some of the best people in the country. I'm overwhelmed, okay?"

"Okay," I say from numb lips.

"I have a lot going on right now," Sonya says again, a broken record. "I can't handle this." She gestures at the space between us.

"You can't handle what? You can't handle me? Or you can't handle *us*?"

Her mouth twists into a mean line. "Coley, you're at a party," she says. "Go mingle. Stop sitting around looking so sorry for yourself."

"I'm just gonna go," I say.

"What?" The eyeliner falls into the sink with a clatter. "No!"

"You're fucked up," I tell her.

"So?" She smiles. "Go get some drinks so you can be like me!"

"No," I say. "You're *fucked up*, and you know it, Sonya."

It drains off her face, all the drunken joy, as my words sink in.

Knock! Knock! Knock!

It's frantic, the sound.

"Hey! Let me in!" calls a voice. "I gotta pee!"

"I'm out of here," I say, brushing past her standing there, stunned into silence. I bolt past the guy who's trying to get in the bathroom, heading down the hall before I hear her belatedly call my name.

"Hey!"

I just need to get to the front door. She won't follow me out into the driveway.

"Coley!"

I jerk backward as she grabs my arm in front of that giant staircase. I whirl, stumbling into her.

"Get off me," I tell her.

She doesn't let go. And I'm so weak, I don't pull away.

"Are you mad at me?" Sonya demands.

I can't help it, I laugh. "Are you fucking kidding me?"

"No! I—" She blinks, bewildered and rapidly sobering in front of me. "I'm sorry, I guess?"

It makes me so mad she's pretending she doesn't know what she's sorry *for.* Maybe she can't even admit it to herself. Fuck, I don't know if I can, either, but I've been trying. I'm *trying* here. I'm trying to understand—myself, her, what's going on between us, and she keeps putting her fingers in her ears and going, "Lalala."

"Get the fuck away from me," I tell her, finally shaking her off.

"I don't want you to be mad at me," she says, her eyes so big—bigger than I've ever seen them, *begging* me to understand. "I told you, I'm really overwhelmed."

The beat of the music from the other room surrounds us like a heartbeat as I stare at her. "What are you so *overwhelmed* about?"

"I—I told you! Dance camp—"

"If it's a camp you go to *every summer*, what's so overwhelming about it?"

"I don't know! It's just that *everything* lately has been so much harder."

"You *make* things harder," I tell her. "We were fine. We were great. We were . . . we were *getting* somewhere. And now you're acting like an entirely different person. Like I don't matter."

"I know. I know." She nods so rapidly I'm afraid it'll make her dizzy. "I'm sorry. I suck, okay? I *know* I suck."

She sways toward me, her hand closing around my wrist. When I don't pull away, her hand travels up my arm, her eyes reveling in my shivering as she draws her fingers up my shoulder, my neck, to tuck a strand of my hair behind my ear.

"I really suck," she says.

I sigh, giving in to her, hating her a little bit for it, even as I lean into her. "You don't suck, Sonya."

"I promise I'm sorry," she says, stepping closer. "I know I get . . . Today just sucked, okay? I . . . fucking olive juice."

I melt. I don't want to, but I do. Then and there, half in her arms and wanting to be fully in them so badly.

"Olive juice, too," I mutter to the ground, not wanting to give her the face of my full attention.

Somewhere in the house a door slams and someone laughs loudly—Trenton, I think.

"Come on," Sonya says, grabbing my arm.

"Where?" I ask, resisting.

"Do you trust me?"

I stare right back at her, all challenge and spark and *Why should I?* "I don't think I should."

Her fingers flex on my wrist. Not a warning or a reassurance, but an omen. *I could take your hand. I could change you with three little words. Don't you know I have that power?*

"If you don't try, you'll never know for sure," she says, and when she tugs on my hand, I follow, not answering, refusing to give her what she wants, but unable to stop myself from trying to get what I want.

She leads me back into her bedroom. She doesn't turn the lights on, and the curtains are drawn, making it feel dark and secret and too small in a good way. This time, there is no hesitation or lingering near her bed. We fall onto it together, giggling and thumping against the mattress as Sonya twists and finally drops my hand to scramble for the bottle.

"It's supposed to taste like strawberries and cream," she says, holding out the bottle to me to examine.

I make a face. "Last time we drank fruit-flavored stuff, it didn't work out too great."

"This will be different," she insists, taking the bottle back from me. She picks up a remote from her end table, pointing it toward the boom box. It lights up, the blue light dancing over her face in the dark, and the music starts to pulse through the room, covering up the sounds from the party below. I watch as she uncaps the bottle.

"Come here," she says, sitting cross-legged on her bed, rumpled blankets and the skirt of her sundress splayed across her knees. Shadows stretch across her face as she balances the open bottle on her palm, her eyes widening when it almost falls.

I move on the bed until we're sitting across from each other. Our knees brush and then touch, and I don't pull away; I just let it happen.

"Close your eyes," she whispers.

I hesitate.

"Trust me," she says, even softer. Begging for a shaky treaty between us.

I give it to her. I close my eyes.

I let her wash over me as she leans into me.

"Drink," she urges, laying the bottle against my lips, soft like a strawberry kiss. I tilt my head as she tips the bottle and it rushes into my mouth, too sweet and on the edge of cloying. I swallow as she speaks, her words wrapping around me, the only thing connecting me to the world.

"This is the sacred healing drink of the ancient times. Each swallow will fill you. Breathe it in as you feel each cell of your body turn to gold."

I almost giggle, but she's tipping the bottle into my mouth again. "Your old self, the one you're stuck in, it will melt away with each sip. And you'll get closer and closer to the person you're meant to be."

My heart clenches at her words. *Is that what you want?* I think, my head beginning to spin from the too-fast gulps of the too-sweet liquor. *Do you want to leave the fake self behind? Or do you want to leave* me *behind?*

"Think about her," Sonya continues. "Confident and free. No worries. No pain." Her voice hitches a little, and I can't help myself: I reach out, my hands cupping her knees, holding them. Holding *her.* "Wouldn't it be nice to be someone new?" she asks.

I start to nod, but there it is again, the bottle against my lips, like she's determined I'll be as swirling tipsy as her.

I open my eyes to find her searching my face in the dim light, looking for a deeper answer.

"Hi," I say, holding out my hand. "I'm Coley. Not sure we've ever met."

She reaches out and grabs my hand, but she doesn't shake it. Her fingers and mine interlace, the most intimate of holds, unmistakable as our palms slide together. "Funny," she says, with that wicked smirk. "It feels like I've known you forever."

As the track changes, the music slows. I tug her up, strawberry-sweet going to my head, making me brave. Our hands still clasp—I never want to let go. "Dance with me."

Her arms go around my neck, the bottle still dangling from her fingers. Her face turns into the crook of my neck even though she's taller, her breath hot against my skin.

My arms around her waist, our bodies swaying not exactly to the music, but a rhythm of our own. Our breath and pulses meld as our bodies brush and then press . . . and then there's no space, there's just us, and the clothes that are in the way. I want to pluck them off my body, to feel more of her skin beneath my palms and fingertips.

I want to learn every inch of her so I can map her in my mind each night we're apart.

"Why do you always feel so good?" she mumbles into my neck, almost like she's not expecting an answer. "It drives me crazy. I lie in bed at night, and it's all I think about."

My eyes widen at the confession.

She lifts her head, pulling back so she can look at me. "*Why*, Coley?" she asks earnestly, and that stab of heat turns to ice as I realize there's pain in her eyes. "Why is it like this?" she asks me. "I didn't—I didn't ask for *any* of this."

"Sonya—" I start to say.

She shakes her head, the bottle falling from her fingers onto the ground, ignored by both of us in the wake of her denial. "I'm not like this," she says, and I don't want to think about what she means, because she clutches me closer as she says it. Gathers me to her chest like someone's going to tear me away. "I'm not like this," she repeats, and tears spill down her face, dripping onto my shirt even as she clutches it tighter. I hold her back fiercely, wanting to comfort, not knowing how. Not knowing what—

"I'm *not*," she insists, and she wrenches herself away from me, she *tears* away from me like it's the only way, like it's physically too much.

Like she's going to break if she doesn't run.

I stumble back, stunned.

"Sonya—"

"I need some air. I need to get out of here."

"Wait—" I reach for her, unthinking, just reacting, but she's darting for her bedroom door, turning the handle, jerking it open.

"Oh my God." Brooke giggles, her fist raised, poised to knock on the door Sonya's just jerked open. Trenton's right next to her.

"There you are," he says. His expression shifts when he catches sight of Sonya's wet, puffy eyes. When his gaze snaps to me, a chill fills my entire body as something in my brain whispers, *Run.*

"Why are you crying?" Trenton asks Sonya urgently.

"Nothing," Sonya says. "A sad song was playing. I just need a minute."

But he keeps looking at the space between her and me, like he can trace our steps back, like he *knows* just a minute before we were wrapped up in each other like nothing else existed.

"What's going on?" he asks, stooping down so he can stare at Sonya directly in the eyes, too much accusation to be concern.

Sonya just shakes her head, tears trickling down her cheeks.

"What did she do?" Trenton demands. "Hey." He surges toward me, and I scramble back, my hip ramming into Sonya's dresser. "What the fuck did you do? Did you lock her in here?"

"What?" I almost laugh at the thought. "Fuck off."

"Trenton, stop!" Brooke warns.

"Whatever," he says. "Sonya, come on." He grabs her arm, steering her out of the room. "Sonya!" he snaps when she looks over her shoulder at me, the door swinging shut, leaving me alone with Brooke.

The silence that follows is the kind that makes you want to dig a hole, shrivel up, and bury yourself inside. Brooke is staring at me like she's got a million questions and all the answers would disgust her.

"I think you should leave," Brooke tells me, finally breaking the excruciating silence.

"It's not your house," I say, because all I can think about is how Sonya looked over her shoulder at me. Like she couldn't help herself. Like she needed one last look.

I need to make sure she's okay. She looked like she was about to have some sort of panic attack.

"You should really listen to me," Brooke says. "They'll be back together by the time school starts. She barely has any time for her real friends when she's in girlfriend mode. You're going to get left behind. Might as well do a classy fade-out instead of whatever *this* is." She waves her hand and curls her lip, and I have to bite the inside of my lip to keep myself from reacting.

"Thanks for the advice," I say sarcastically.

"I'm trying to help."

"If you say so." I walk past her, leaving her in Sonya's bedroom.

Anyone with any observational skills can tell Brooke has a big thing for Trenton. I wouldn't be surprised if they were hooking up behind everyone's back. But her insistence that Trenton and Sonya will be back together by the time school starts is still a dagger in my heart, because the way she said it was so sure and bitter. A resigned sort of truth that wasn't just about getting to me—it was also about warning herself.

Is this what it's like to be a summer fling? Is this the thing Brooke and I suddenly have in common with each other? I don't want to think of it—being someone's secret. But that's what I am, aren't I?

I push the question out of my mind, hurrying down the stairs two at a time. More people have arrived since Sonya and I went up into her room. The downstairs hall is thick with them, and I have to push to make my way through. I don't recognize anyone, but it doesn't matter. All I'm looking for is her.

"SJ, have you seen Sonya?" I ask when I spot her next to the drinks, talking to a guy that was probably the one who'd ditched her before.

"Yeah, few minutes ago. She was headed back there." SJ jerks her thumb toward the kitchen.

"Thanks."

But she's not in the kitchen when I get there. I'm almost about to leave—I'll message her, I guess—when a giggle floats through the cracked door that I thought was the pantry.

I move toward it, slow motion, my hand closing over the knob, pulling it open to reveal the laundry room.

Pulling it open to reveal *them*.

TWENTY-FIVE

Sonya's perched on the washer, her legs wrapped around Trenton's waist, making out like they're trying to prove how sturdy the washer really is.

I don't know if there's really a word for what I'm feeling; it's like I'm a deck of cards being shuffled, speeding through heartbreak/betrayal/jealousy/hurt/why/sonya/*why?*

She kisses him, her legs tight around him like she needs to keep him there, but I know she doesn't. I know what it's like to kiss her: you'll stay there forever to make it last just another second.

Her tears are dried like they weren't even there, and I can't stand it. I can't torture myself like this. This is sick. *She's* sick. He's a fucking bully and maybe something worse, I don't know, but I'm not going to stick around to find out.

I turn and run before either of them can see me. I push open the sliding glass doors that lead to the backyard. The pool's been abandoned for the drinks inside, floaties skimming lonely across the water.

I'd grab my bike and go, but my temples are pounding, spots dancing along my vision, and I need to sit down and breathe, blink them away before I can get on my bike.

I slump down on the cement bench at the edge of the patio, burying my head in my hands, trying to count my breaths and losing count on seven. Then three. Then fifteen.

Shit, I can't stop thinking about them. Has he undressed her yet? Are they going to fuck right there on the washer?

Hot tears gather at the corners of my eyes, but I sniff angrily, staring at the sky, blinking them back.

She doesn't deserve them. She doesn't. Not until she actually talks to me.

"You okay?"

My head jerks up. Alex stands there, hands in the pockets of his coat. I didn't even hear him walk up.

I shrug. If I talk, I might start crying for real. Who the fuck knows, after this day? These weeks. Sonya's existence in my world.

He pulls out a perfectly rolled joint, lighting up, not offering me any. Rude. A part of me wants it. To float away. To soften the horrible edge of my heart that Sonya has honed to a razor. I'm bleeding with each breath, my own weakness for her carving me up.

"Can I?" I ask him.

"Only if you talk to me," he says.

I glare at him.

"You look like you really need to talk," he adds.

"You're so altruistic."

I take the joint when he offers it, breathing in the smoke. It's almost sweet—something I've never experienced before with weed. I hold it in my lungs as long as I can, breathing it slow.

"Sometimes my friends are a lot," Alex says, out of nowhere, as I hand him the joint.

"Why are you friends with them?" I ask, curious despite myself. "I mean, I kind of get the impression you're the odd man out."

He takes a hit and then breathes smoke out. "Do the rich kids not hang with the poor kids where you're from?"

I shrug. "It was a lot more separated in my school. Is this a small-town thing or something?"

"It's a Sonya thing," Alex says.

My eyes widen.

"Not like that." He laughs. "I mean she's the reason we're all friends. In first grade, there was like this fall festival thing and there was a petting zoo with a pony."

"Why do I have the sense that this is not a cute story?" I say, taking the joint he offers back.

"So it's me, Sonya, Trenton, and SJ," Alex says. "Brooke didn't move here until fifth grade. And we're petting the ducks and the chickens, and there's a very cute pig."

"Was there a goose?" I ask, pulling on the joint, letting it cloud my head further. I'm barely focusing on what Sonya's doing in the laundry room, losing myself in the idea of little Sonya at a petting zoo. "Geese are very mean."

"I've heard that. No geese, though. But there's a pony."

"Is the pony mean?"

"The pony's nice. Until Trenton decides he should ride it."

"Oh no."

"Yup. He clambers on that pony's back and kicks it like he's got spurs on. With a whole '*Yeehaw*' whoop and everything."

"Shit."

"Pony rears back. Tosses him off. But that's not enough. I think Trenton, like, triggered some sort of trauma inside the poor thing, because next thing we know, it's rampaging around the petting zoo."

"Where were the adults?" I ask, incredulous.

"Getting funnel cake. The petting zoo was supposed to be the safe place to park us."

"Whoops."

"Sonya freezes. Right in the path of the pony! And you've gotta understand—she didn't get tall until middle school. So she's really tiny. And the pony's barreling right toward her. It's gonna trample her. Trenton's on the ground after being tossed. SJ's screaming her head off. And I . . ." He laughs.

"You got her out of the way," I finish.

"How did you know?" Any other time—or maybe if I were a different girl—his smile would spark hot in my stomach. It's so wide and free, and it makes his dark eyes seem endless. I see why a girl would want to get him alone and bask in his attention.

"Did she tell you about how the pony rampage made us all friends?"

I shake my head. "No," I say. "Rescuing someone just seems like something you would do."

He rubs the back of his head, bashful. "That's nice of you."

"Just truthful," I say. I mean it to be kind of a dismissal, something to put space between us as I realize, suddenly, that there's very little between us. It doesn't feel bad. Like I said: if I were a different girl . . .

Is that what Sonya wants? Was that what she was talking about, as she tipped the strawberries and cream in my mouth like a blessing? Does she want me to be some cookie-cutter girlfriend because she can't even wrap her head around the idea of *girlfriends*?

Could I do it? For her? Alex is close and smiling down at me, his eyes settling on my lips from time to time, like he's thought about it. Like if I wanted to, I could lean forward and—

So I do. It's almost like an experiment in my mind. Hypothesis: this will make me feel better. Test: lean forward, lips against lips.

His reaction is immediate. No hesitation. Why would there be? This is how it's supposed to be. No fear. No worry. This is *right* . . . right?

His hand slides over my shoulder to cup it carefully, like I'm glass. His mouth moves against mine, and I close my eyes, grasping for *it*—that bubbling hot feeling in my stomach I got when I just *thought* about her, let alone touched her or kissed her.

It's not there. His lips are soft and his hand is warm but it's just . . . nothing.

No. It's worse than nothing. It's like a closing of a door in my mind. There's a dead-end sign on a path that I was supposed to go down.

I *know* now. I can't run away from it the way she does, now that I know what it's like to spark and burn under another girl's hands. What it is to blossom at the mere thought of her. Kissing Alex is a wet match, fizzling dark compared to her. It's not his fault. It's not my fault.

It's just . . . who I am.

There it is: the truth. No running from it anymore. It's living in me, and I can try to kill it or try to grow it.

I break away from him, the sob coming out of my mouth before I can stop it.

"Coley?" His face shifts to concern. "Did I do something? Are you okay?"

"I'm sorry."

"No, no, please don't apologize. If I pushed—"

"No," I assure him. "You're great, Alex. I'm just . . . I'm a fucking mess." Tears trickle down my face, and he makes a worried sound, digging in his pockets and coming up with a crumpled napkin, holding it out to me.

"Oh, Coley," he says. "We're all fucking messes."

I laugh through the napkin, using it to mop up my face, but the tears are still glimmering in my eyes, on the edge of spilling.

He reaches out to kind of nudge me awkwardly in the arm. Like a bro would do. "It'll be okay. Whatever it is. I promise."

I look down, hating to ask for a favor after I've just kissed and rejected him, but I've got to get out of here. "Can you drive me home? You were right about the weed being stronger. I'm feeling it."

"Of course," he says. "Let's go."

As we get up, I hook my foot on the uneven edge of the patio, stumbling into him.

"Careful," he says, catching me.

"Whoo, sorry, that joint was . . ." The world spins a little. I laugh and lean into him, my head swirling for a second. "You sure you're okay to drive?"

"I have a lot higher tolerance than you," he tells me. "But I can walk you home if that makes you feel better. Up to you."

"Too far," I say. "I don't want to even bike."

"I'll drive slow," he promises.

The sound of the glass door sliding open jerks my attention to the left. People spill out, SJ and Sonya, closely followed by Brooke and Trenton. They stare at us, and I pull away from Alex, but it's too late.

Trenton lets out a braying laugh. "You fucking dykes now, Alex?"

"Oh my God, Trenton!" Brooke hisses, covering her face, but not her smile.

I don't even think about me. How fucked up is that? My eyes flick to Sonya—how can she *stand* this?—but she won't even look at me directly. She's staring at Alex instead, her eyes alight with a kind of fury that makes me want to scream *What gives you the right?* But I can't. I can't do anything.

All I can do is leave. God, I want to get out of here so bad.

"Can we go?" I ask Alex.

He nods. "My car's this way." He calls over his shoulder as we walk away. "You're an asshole, man. You need to think about that shit."

"You need to learn to take a joke," I hear Trenton yell distantly behind us, but luckily, we're far enough away that Alex doesn't turn back to respond.

Alex's truck is a lot nicer than I expected. It's at least fifteen years old, but the interior is pristine, like he really cares about keeping it up—a stark contrast to the general filth and stickiness of Trenton's van.

The drive is quiet, like he understands I just can't handle it.

But after a few directions, he pulls up to my house, and that good-guy energy that had him tackling Sonya out of the way when they were five rises to the surface. He pulls the parking brake and shifts on the bench seat of the truck, solemn.

"I could say a lot of things here," he says. "But fuck if I know which is the right one."

It *almost* makes me laugh. But I don't have it in me. I'm too raw. She's cut me open, over and over, and I don't know how to heal.

"I feel like I'm never gonna be normal," I confess.

"Why would you want to be?"

"God, that's such a guy thing to say," I tell him.

"Maybe," he says. "But maybe I'm right. It's better to just be yourself."

"So you're gonna go back to rescuing people from rampaging ponies?"

"If there's an angry pony, I'll be there, hand to God," he says solemnly, and my throat swells with how much I appreciate him. I don't know what I would've done, biking the long way home, Sonya pounding in my head like a pulse.

"You've been through a lot," he says.

I frown at him, but I don't have to wonder for long, because he continues. "I, uh, heard about your mom? I'm so sorry, Coley."

"You heard about my mom," I echo, my ears roaring, his words static-cling in my brain. How—

Oh. I know how.

"Yeah, Sonya, she—" He stops, his eyes catching on my face, words fading as the realization hits him. "Oh shit. Coley—"

"I've gotta go." I scramble for my seat belt.

"I'm sorry. It was being talked about like it was something everyone knew—"

I tear out of the car, trying not to listen to him, trying not to throw up as I run up the path to the house. For once, Curtis isn't there, so there's no interrogation. There's just the dark house and the hallway and then, thankfully, my bed.

It's only when I throw myself down on the bed and shiver

at the breeze of the swamp cooler that it hits me: I don't have Mom's jacket.

I left it at Sonya's.

It's like I'm a grenade and someone's pulled the pin. *Pow.* Tears slick down my face, and I curl into a ball, drawing the blanket over me. It's not nearly as comforting as Mom's jacket, and I know the ache inside me is so much more than that.

I don't want to see any of them ever again. I don't even know if I want to see *her* again. But as soon as I think it, I want to take it back, even though I didn't even speak it out loud.

God, what's *wrong* with me?

TWENTY-SIX

How could she tell them about my mom?

The question's still circling in my head the next day, over and over. Sonya's filled me with questions. About her. About myself. About the world and my heart's capacity for *everything*: hate and love and jealousy and spite and *anger*.

Oh God, I'm so angry at Sonya, but even more, I'm angry at myself.

I shouldn't have trusted her. That's what this means, doesn't it? But I did; I told her everything. I spilled my fears and my truth and the gnawing wound and wondering inside me, that terrible "what-if" that I'll never be able to shake. And she turned around and told her friends like it was gossip. Somehow, this feels like I've betrayed my mom just as much as Sonya betrayed me. I was stupid and careless, lost in the whirl of Sonya, and now I'm here. Where everyone knows I'm the girl whose mom killed herself.

How fucking *dare* she?! I want to tear her hair out. I want to scream at her. I want to fall on my knees and cry and ask *why* while she holds me.

That's the worst of it: I still want her. How can I still want her when she's so cruel?

My mouth flattens as I jerk up in bed, my mind made up. She may not want to see me, and at this point, I don't know if I want to see her. But I need to get my mom's jacket back. So I grab my stuff and head toward the front door. The soft strumming from the living room should've clued me in—but I almost don't notice Curtis sitting on the couch, playing one of his guitars.

"Hey, Coley."

I stop halfway toward the front door. "Hey, I'm just heading out."

"Where are you going?" he asks. "You've been busy lately. In and out of the house. Not that that's a bad thing," he adds. "I'm glad you're making friends. But I was hoping we could have dinner together at least once a week."

"Sure," I say distractedly. "But I left my jacket at Sonya's," I say. "You know, Mom's jacket? Or, I guess, your jacket."

He smiles. "It's your mom's jacket," he says. "She had it way longer than I did. And it looked way better on her. And on you. Why don't I drive you?"

It's not ideal. "I can bike—" I start to say.

"No, this way we can go to dinner. There's this great hibachi restaurant that I've been meaning to take you to. I like to eat there on Fridays."

"So I've been messing up your routine?" I ask.

His face falls, but then he smiles determinedly, which makes me feel like a total ass. "More like giving me reasons to create a new one," he says, putting away his guitar.

"How many of those do you have?" I ask, gesturing to it while he grabs his keys.

"A few," he says. "A lot fewer than I had when I was younger. I sold some. And my motorcycle."

"You had a bike?" I ask, suddenly a lot more interested.

"I did," he says. "An old Harley. Do you like bikes?"

"Mom always said they were too dangerous," I say, following him into the car. "Sonya lives on Kingsley Street," I tell him.

"That's a fancy neighborhood," he remarks, pulling out of the driveway. "Your mom was right: motorcycles are really dangerous. I don't want you riding them."

"That's totally hypocritical."

"I'm finding that being responsible for a kid is kind of all about that," he says.

It startles a laugh out of me. "I don't think you're supposed to admit it," I tell him.

He shrugs. "I want to be honest with you, Coley. That seems like the best method here, doesn't it?"

I'm quiet. I didn't realize we were going to have a heavy talk. I've just walked into it like a trap, because it's not like I can get out of the car. Well, maybe at a stop sign. But he'd probably get angry if I just ran from the car to avoid a conversation like a big coward.

"I'll be honest with you if you're honest with me," Curtis continues.

"Okay," I say slowly.

He smiles, relief obvious in his face. "Good."

We're quiet as he pulls up to Sonya's house. "I'll just be a second," I tell him. "She's really busy getting ready to leave for dance camp."

I get out of the car and ring the doorbell. As the chimes

fade, I hear it: the sound of laughter. It grows louder as someone comes toward the door.

"Someone get the cupcakes," I hear Sonya's voice call before she opens the door, half-turned away from me. She's wearing a ridiculous headband that says BON VOYAGE. Her smile snaps off her face when she sees me, and she snatches the headband out of her hair.

"Hi," I say through numb lips. Shit. *Shit.*

"Is that the guys?" I hear SJ's voice call. "Tell Trenton I want my burger!"

She appears in the hall from the back room, Brooke hurrying behind her, and they're wearing the same headband that Sonya had been wearing.

The world fades in and out, my ears ringing as it hits me: Sonya's not busy packing like I thought she'd be. She's busy having a goodbye party with her friends.

She just didn't want me anywhere near it. Near *her.*

She can't even look at me. She's staring at the ground.

"I'm here for my jacket," I say.

She finally looks up. Her face is like *ice.* "Oh?"

"Yeah. I left it. In your room." I don't add *when we were half a second away from making out again,* but it's implied. The swift rise of red to her cheeks makes a vicious sort of pleasure twist inside me. She feels it. I *know* she does.

"You can go get it, I guess," she says with a shrug, like she doesn't care.

"Could you come?" It's me at my bravest, forcing those three words out.

"I guess." She looks to SJ and Brooke. "Sorry, girls, just a second. If the boys come, let them in. I'll be right back."

I walk up the stairs, acutely aware of her just two steps behind me. The whole way, we don't talk, and when she closes the door behind us, it's nothing like before. It's not a secret bubble, just the two of us; now it feels like a trap. One we both lured each other into.

"It's around here somewhere," Sonya says awkwardly, going over to her bed and looking around. She finds it in her laundry basket, which makes no sense unless she tossed it in there. "Here." She thrusts it out to me, but when I grab it, she holds on to it. She uncurls her fingers slowly, like it hurts to let go, but when she looks at me, her face is so smooth. Like glass. "Is that all you need?"

No, I think. *I need a lot more from you. Starting with a fucking explanation about* everything.

"Yes," I say, like a coward, as my anger simmers and scorches me instead.

Sonya just keeps standing there, statuelike. I remember, suddenly, what she'd drunkenly told me that day on the tracks. How her mom didn't want her to twirl around in her dresses when she was little. How she used to always tell Sonya to *be still* when she wasn't dancing. Is that what's in her head right now? Is she pulling her real self inside her skin so tight she'll never let her out again, now that she knows what happens when she does?

I want to hug her. I want to scream at her. I want to tell her that it's okay. I don't know if it is; I don't know if that's a lie.

But if I touch her, if I open my mouth, it'll come out: the anger, the confusion, the *everything* that swirls in me when it comes to her. My entire body vibrates like I'm a plucked guitar string and she's the one who just keeps picking at me. I have to get away. I have to leave. If I don't . . .

I don't know what I'll do. I don't know who I'll become.

I want to find out. But I'm scared. Of me. Of her. Of this.

This push and pull. This buzz that fills me every time I'm near her. Who knew you could literally vibrate with need? Not just want. *Need.* There's a difference.

She taught it to me.

I force myself to walk past her toward the door, and as I do, our arms brush and the hitch in her chest is loud and it's like my entire body feels it and it echoes through the room and through my body and through my *soul,* because it's not just a sign. It's another in a series of confirmations, stacking up in my head.

And I just *break.*

"Coley." She whispers my name like it's a sweet sound she wants to taste. I lean in to let her taste me, unable to resist her pull. Helpless. I am always helpless when it comes to her.

Her eyes flicker down to my lips as she licks her own. I lean closer, my hand slides up her arm, soft skin, warm girl. We're a heartbeat away from each other. . . .

She snaps her head back, that icy expression back on her face. "What are you doing?" she asks, calm as you please as she spins me in yet another direction, whirling too fast to know which way is up.

I latch on to the first thing I think I know: "I know you like me," I say, almost like a reassurance. She has to know I feel the same after everything. She's just scared.

But she's not saying anything. She's just standing there, getting colder by the second.

I keep talking, to fill the silence gaping between us. "You kissed me," I say, and *there*: she flinches. She's not made of ice.

The girl I know. The girl who kissed me and danced zigzag

across those train tracks. The girl who loves to twirl. *That* girl is in there, dying to get out and shine.

"You spent all your time with me," I continue, because she's standing there so still, like she's trying to turn into a statue. "You basically said you *loved* me."

She laughs. Small and uncomfortable and crawling up my spine like something slimy. "I don't know what to say."

"Really?"

Her eyes flare, irritation crackling in the space between us. "You're being silly, Coley. I'm like this with all my friends. Some girls are touchy-feely. It doesn't mean anything. Especially not what you're thinking." She shakes her head, and it's almost scolding, the way she does it.

The embarrassment hits me with a bewildered rush. I want to protest. I want to fight for—I don't know—us? But she's saying there isn't any *us*. That there never *was* an us. That I'm *imagining* it.

I'm not. *I'm fucking not!*

"I know you told your friends about my mom."

Sonya's fingers curl into fists, and even from here, I can see her nails digging into her palms. Does she want to hurt me? Or herself?

"Are you even going to apologize?"

Her chin tilts up and when she says nothing, I'm the one who wants to wound her.

"You're making really shitty choices," I tell her. "And I'm not even talking about whatever it is between you and me. What you did—you had no right. Only a really terrible person doesn't apologize when they've done something that bad. That was fucking *unforgivable*." The last words come out like a snarl as I try to hold back the tears. I leave without even waiting for a response, trying to breathe around the burning hurt in my chest. I hurry down the stairs, walking right past Sonya's mom, who says, "Coley, aren't you staying?"

"No, sorry, I was just picking up my jacket. My dad's waiting for me. Bye!" I call, waving behind me as I bolt to the front door and tear out toward where Curtis's waiting.

"What's wrong?" he says instantly when I get in the car, trying to rub the tears off my cheeks before he sees them. Fuck. Another thing I've failed at.

"Please just take me home," I beg him.

"Of course," he says. "We can do dinner another night." And to my relief, he doesn't ask any more questions. He drives me home without saying a word and lets me fiddle with the radio and play my choice of songs, and he doesn't even complain, though I can see his mouth twitching at my music like he *wants* to say something.

When we get home, I can't even make it to my room. I just collapse on the couch and turn on the TV, desperate for some kind of distraction. I can't think about her denial. I can't think about being crazy—I know I'm not. I know it was real.

It *is* real. When we brushed together, I wasn't the only one to feel it.

Maybe it's just physical for her. Maybe it's not emotional. Maybe that's why she doesn't think it's real. But it *is*. If I could just get her to open up—

Oh God, I need to stop. I need to breathe. I switch the channel, landing on some animal show. I watch the lions prowl the savanna, trying to lose myself in the narrator's description of their lives and how the pride survives.

I hear Curtis order delivery in the kitchen, and when it arrives, he settles down next to me.

"What are you watching?"

"Some lion thing," I say, taking the container of lemon chicken from him when he offers it.

We eat and watch in silence, and maybe for the first time, I don't feel angry at him.

I just feel glad I have someone.

TWENTY-SEVEN

LJ User: SonyatSunrisex00x [Public Entry]

Date: July 5, 2006

[**Mood:** elated]

[**Music:** "Milkshake"—Kelis]

I have *arrived*! I know everyone's *dying* to know all the details of dance camp, so I'll spare you that torture, lol. But I am safely tucked away in my little cabin and dancing my heart out and missing all of you!

Tell me what's been going on while I've been away! It's been seventy-two hours and I'm already perishing from lack of news.

xoox
Sonya

Comments:

SJbabayy:

We miss you, sweetie! Things are boring here without you.

MadeYouBrooke23:
Speak for yourself. I'm working my ass off.

SonyatSunrisex00x:
Retail getting to you?

MadeYouBrooke23:
You know it.

SonyatSunrisex00x:
You're going to make so much money, though! That's awesome!

T0nofTrent0nnn:
Yes, it's so awesome she gets to be a cog in the retail machine.

SJbabayy:
Oh, shut up, Trenton. No one asked you.

LJ User: SonyatSunrisex00x [Private Entry]

Date: July 5, 2006

[**Mood:** !!!]
[**Music:** "Smile Like You Mean It"–The Killers]

Fuck my life.

First of all, my leaving party *sucked*. It was the opposite of fun. Coley just had to talk and try to get me to talk and there's nothing to talk about! There can't be.

And then she got so hurt. Like it was all my fault. And I told myself it wasn't. I got so drunk after she left.

It isn't my fault. But then I had the entire drive to camp with just Mom in the SUV with me, and all she wanted to do was listen to self-help stuff on audiobook, so I tried to think instead.

And then I started wondering if maybe it was a little my fault.

I did tell SJ about Coley's mom.

My mom tried to talk to me once the self-help audio ran out, but all she wanted to talk about was dance, and that made me think about how we don't talk about anything *but* that and fuck. . . .

I think my problem is all the thinking. Ha.

I haven't even gotten to the cherry on the fucked-up sundae that is my life right now. Camp was supposed to be my sanctuary. My break from all this summer drama and weirdness and these . . . I dunno . . . these feelings. A respite from it all. That's what Madame Rosard calls camp.

That's how I've always thought of it. But Faith is here. She's not just a counselor this year, she's Madame Rosard's assistant. She's in *all* my morning dance classes and is running our starting stretch.

The girl has gone mad with power! She's been on my ass ever since I arrived and saw her. Like she's my personal watchdog or something.

First it was "Oh, Sonya, put your luggage on this rack for cabin 4." And then it was "Oh, Sonya, push the luggage rack all the way to cabin 4 for me." And then she *follows* me to "make sure I get set up okay." And my mom just smiles and nods and waves me off like it was fine and I don't even deserve a hug or a real goodbye.

And my roommates were all happy to see her! Even Gaia, who is *my* camp friend, not Faith's, and oh my God, why couldn't Faith have stayed home or stayed at her stupid college or something? Anywhere but *here*. This is my place! She graduated! She shouldn't be here.

She keeps smiling at me, all smug, like she *knows* something.

I hate her. Why can't she just leave me alone?

—Sonya

TWENTY-EIGHT

She's not just physically gone. That's the thing. Sonya's gone from my life the way I'm gone from her heart.

Was I ever in it? I couldn't have been, if she was able to discard me so quickly. A blink, a tilt of her head, and I was gone. Dismissed like a lip gloss she no longer wanted to use.

"I wanted to show you something," Curtis says.

It takes me a moment to drag my eyes away from the TV. I've been planted on the couch for what seems like weeks, but it's just been a few days. Time's lost all meaning, just like everything else.

Does she even think about me as much as I think about her? She's probably dancing her heart out, laughing, while I'm crying in the shower, and every time I smell citrus or flowers I think of her.

Curtis's holding something in his hands, and when he sits down next to me and hands them over, their smooth edges beckon me.

"I just found them," he says.

I stare down at the photos and suddenly all thoughts of

Sonya are driven from my mind. It would be a blessed respite, but the photographs bring a different kind of pain. They're of Mom and Curtis and me; I must be two or three, dressed in a puffer jacket in the snow. God, she looks so young. Almost unrecognizable.

Not because of how young she looks. But because of how *happy* she looks.

My fingers trace down the photo, circling around the tiger's-eye pendant she's wearing. She really did keep it, all these years. What did that mean? Did she still love him, even at the end? How could she, after he decided staying behind was better than being with us?

"Your mom was so funny," he says. "I never laughed more than when I was with her. We had a friend, this snobby Harvard guy who was kind of slumming it, hanging with our crowd. You probably know the type. But he used to call your mom 'a true wit.' It was the one thing he got right. She really was."

He's quiet for a moment as I shift to another photo. Mom alone this time, in profile, a floaty red dress that tied around her neck, one hand resting on her pregnant stomach, the other pointing to the camera—probably at Curtis. Her head's tilted toward the blue sky, the smile on her face so free. She doesn't know what's to come. She doesn't know who I'm going to be. How Curtis's going to leave us. How she's going to leave me.

Would she do things differently, if she had some sort of crystal ball that told her what was to come? Was there some sort of path we all could have taken that would have left us whole and intact—a family?

I have to keep my hands from crumpling the photos. I place them on my lap, unable to continue flipping through them.

"She was a woman of big highs and big lows," Curtis continues, like he knew her. Like the sixteen years I spent with her isn't comparable to what, the *handful* he spent with her in their twenties? The anger sparks inside me like a forest fire: it starts slow and then spreads, fast and greedy for any fuel that'll grow it further. And the more Curtis talks, the more fuel he gives me: "I know how hard it was for her, when she was low," he continues. "If you're feeling like that, Coley—"

I jerk up from the couch, the photos spilling on the ground. He immediately crouches to gather them like they're precious, and that flares the anger hotter. Of course he thinks pictures are meant to be handled with care. Not actual people.

"Why would you show me these?" I demand.

His eyes widen, his hangdog expression making me want to slap it right off his face. "I was happy I found them. And I'm . . . I'm happy you're here, so I can share them with you."

"The only reason I'm here is because Mom's *dead*."

He has the audacity to tear up then. His eyes fucking *glimmer* with tears, and I hate him. I want to scream at him: *You don't get to cry over her.* But she cried over him, long after he was gone, so really, who the fuck am I to tell him that?

"Did you know she was wearing your precious necklace when she died?" I demand, and his eyes widen, the words hitting him just like I wanted. "You weren't taking care of her," I say, and now that I've started, it's like I can't stop; the words rattle out almost as fast as the feelings. "You weren't there for her. Not for the highs. Not for the lows. *I* was. I was there. Every day. You have no idea what it was like."

"I want to know," Curtis says. "I want you to talk to me about what you've been through—what you're feeling. I really want you to feel like you can share with me, Coley."

I'm shaking my head the entire time he's talking, it feels so fake. "Don't you think it's too fucking late?" I ask, and it doesn't even come out angry, it comes out honest and bewildered, because how can it *not* be too late?

He rubs a hand over his stubbly mouth, looking exhausted but determined. "I know my loss is not the same as yours," he says slowly. "But losing your mom taught me that I'm not going to stop trying to grab on to the things I want, even if I think it's too late."

I'm quiet, because that kind of trying . . . it just seems like too much. I think I lost that kind of hope in pieces: first when I lost my mom and then when I lost Sonya.

"You and I . . . we're what's left of our family," Curtis says. "I know it's not ideal. I know it should be her here and not me. I'm sorry, kid. I really am. And I know you don't know me. But I'm trying to change that."

I stare hard at him.

"I really want to know you," he tells me.

"Only because you *have* to."

I leave the living room before he can say anything else.

The Polaroids stay scattered on the ground.

I crawl out my bedroom window. It's maybe a little dramatic, but the idea of walking past him to get to my bike makes my stomach churn with nerves. I *hate* this. I want to be able to relax in my own space, but I can't because it's not my space, it's *his*. No matter how much he insists it's my house, too. I don't feel that way.

So I climb out the window and grab my bike, pumping my legs with purpose. I fly over the pavement, the rush of the wind in my ears and hair my only goal. I let it drown everything out—the tightness I feel every time I'm around Curtis, the mess that Sonya left my heart in, the secrets that twist deeper and deeper inside me, like they'll never see the light again.

Everything blurs to green and brown and gray around me as I speed down the road. I almost don't register the spot of red until it's too late. I squeeze the brakes, the wheels skid across the pavement, and I almost tip over the handlebars in front of the stop sign.

Cars whiz in front of me on the cross street, and I pant, my entire body thudding with relief and dread. Fuck, I almost biked right into traffic. I need to get myself together.

I take a right, heading to the 7-Eleven down the street. Leaving my bike outside, I go in, making a beeline for the back. The same redheaded cashier from the first time I was in here glances up when the doorbell chimes, but then returns to his crossword.

Sonya conned him so easily. It seems like a lifetime ago now. I was dazzled by her nerve, clumsy in my own attempts at stealing the champagne. I was so afraid she'd think I wasn't cool. That was the beginning, wasn't it? The start of *us*.

I just wasn't smart enough to remember that for something to have a beginning, it also has to have an end.

But can we even have a beginning or middle or end when she won't even acknowledge it *existed* in the first place? *I'm like that with all my friends*, she said.

I should've asked her if she made out with SJ, too. Or Brooke. That would've been better than the humiliating spectacle I made of myself. Why is it that you always think of the best comebacks days later? She's probably forgotten all about it by now. She's off at her camp, dancing away, having fun with her friends. I could torture myself and look at her LiveJournal. I've been tempted, but so far I've resisted. She's made it very clear what she thinks, and I have to figure out how to deal with that.

Maybe I should just run away. Then I wouldn't have to deal with any of this. It's not like Curtis would work hard to find me.

The second I think it, I know it's stupid. I need to finish school at least. I can't let a girl stop me from doing that. Even a girl like Sonya.

"Can I help you?" asks a pointed voice behind me.

I jerk out of my thoughts, realizing that I'm holding the beer fridge door open and staring into the cooler for who knows how long. The cashier is leaning over the counter, frowning at me.

"Sorry," I say quickly, closing the fridge and going to the next one, grabbing an iced tea. "Brain fart."

"You should try one of these," he says, tapping his crossword book when I come up to the counter to pay.

"I'll keep that in mind," I say, handing him the money. "Thanks."

I walk outside, uncapping the tea and sipping it, letting out a disgusted sound. Shit. I'd grabbed the unsweetened kind.

"That bad, huh?"

I look up. The girl who works here—the one who almost caught me with the champagne last time—is leaning against the pole where I've parked my bike. A cigarette dangles from her bright red lips.

"Wrong kind," I say, walking toward her. "You're . . . Blake, right?" I have to look at her name tag to get it right.

Blake stubs out her cigarette and pulls out a sandwich from her pocket. It's so random, she has me blinking at her.

"Do you want some?" Blake asks, holding out the sandwich.

I shake my head. "Thanks, though."

She nods, still staring at me. "You kind of spaced out in there," she says.

I flush. I hadn't even realized she was inside. "I'm having one of those days." I let out a laugh. "Fuck, I'm having one of those *years*, you know?"

Blake nods solemnly. "Life, dude."

I let out a laugh, because it's succinct and not very deep, but it's also pretty true.

"Is it a love thing?" Blake asks.

"It's a lot of things," I answer.

She takes another bite of her sandwich, chewing thoughtfully. Then she reaches out and pats my shoulder. A piece of tomato falls from the sandwich and to the ground, narrowly missing my shoe. "Whoever broke your heart's an idiot," she tells me solemnly.

I don't know why it means so much for this strange girl to say that to me, but it's like someone's taking a tiny Band-Aid and placing it on my messy heart. It's not a lot and it's not a very big Band-Aid, but it's *something*. To my utter humiliation, tears prick at my eyes.

"They're stupid," Blake insists.

"She is," I agree, and then my eyes widen, because I just said it out loud, like it was nothing.

But Blake just takes another bite of her sandwich. "It's cool," she says, like she understands I'm about to freak out. "You smoke?"

I nod.

"I just got off work," she says. "Come on. Come to my place. I'll smoke you out. You look like you need it."

TWENTY-NINE

Blake keeps all her windows rolled down. "I don't have any AC," she explains as we drive down the street. I've left my bike chained up at the 7-Eleven and the hundred-degree heat swirls in my hair. I scrape it into a ponytail, rolling the elastic off my wrist and securing it, even as strands fight their way free.

Her car's the definition of a beater. Not that I can really judge, since I get everywhere via bike. But her rearview mirror is duct-taped to the window, and the back seat is more duct tape than upholstery.

Blake pushes a CD into the player, and the sound of Nine Inch Nails blasts through the car. I try not to wince at the volume.

"I live out near the creek," Blake tells me, like I'm supposed to know where "the creek" is. I swear, sometimes it's like it never occurs to any of these people that someone doesn't know this place.

"That's nice," I say, because what else am I supposed to say. *What creek?* Then she'd ask where I'm from originally and then I'd start thinking about Mom and then I'd just . . .

I want to fucking *forget*. Everything. Just for a little bit. The idea of getting really high sounds like heaven right now. I want to laugh at stupid cartoons or something and eat my weight in Cheetos.

Blake seems content not to talk much as we drive. It's strange, but I'm grateful for it.

The farther we get away from town, the more I realize "the creek" is far away.

"Wow, you really live out in the sticks," I say as she finally slows down to pull onto a dirt road.

Blake laughs. "I don't think I've ever heard someone call it that."

"It's not bad, is it?"

She shakes her head, pulling to a stop in front of a weathered house with a rusty roof. I squint in the sunlight to check, but yep, it's a *tin* roof. I guess I thought they retired tin roofs in favor of shingles long ago.

A dog barks at the chain-link fence surrounding the house.

She leads me inside the cramped house. It's cool inside from the shelter of the trees around it, and the narrow hallway with beige carpeting she leads me down is dark. So is her room: she's got black curtains and a bed with a Buzz Lightyear comforter. A lava lamp is the only other light source.

She throws herself on the bed, and I creep slowly around the books and stuff stacked around her room in crooked piles.

"You like to read?" I ask.

"Sometimes," Blake says. "Mostly fantasy stuff. You?"

"Not really a fantasy fan," I admit. "But maybe I haven't found the right book."

She uproots a bong from underneath her bed. "Smoke?"

I nod, coming to sit next to her. The first hit is smooth, cooled by the bong water. But four hits in, it gets increasingly clear she needs to clean her piece. But by then I'm so stoned it doesn't even matter. I just lie back and stare at the popcorn ceiling of the old house. The world starts to spin a little, and I sit up, trying to clear my head.

"Bathroom?" I ask.

"Right in there." She points to the door off her bedroom.

I walk purposefully into the bathroom, my head fuzzy and slow as I splash water on my face. It helps a lot. But then I catch a glimpse of myself in the mirror as water drips off my chin. In the cramped bathroom, all I can see is myself. I'm caught in my reflection, and all I can feel is hate. I hate Curtis . . . Sonya . . . myself . . . Mom.

Sometimes I hate her so much for leaving me. And I hate myself so much, all the time, for not being there to save her. For not being enough to keep her here.

How could I not be enough to keep her here?

"You okay?" Blake asks quietly.

I shake my head again, unable to do anything but tell the truth in that moment, my brick walls crumbled by Sonya's destruction, punched through by her betrayal.

I turn my head, looking at Blake. In her own way, she's cute. Like a wicked fairy that does nothing but cause trouble and laughs when her plans unfold on the unsuspecting humans.

"You sure you don't want another hit?"

"No," I say. "I want something more than that."

Her thin eyebrows rise so much they nearly hit her hairline, and I flush, remembering how I'd slipped and told her that my love problem was about another girl. This girl accidentally knows more about me than anyone else in the world, and that thought hits me all at once in this tiny bathroom, my hands still gripping the sink that's speckled with toothpaste.

"Do you have scissors?" I ask, my voice cracking a little as it rises in a question.

A slow smile creeps across Blake's face. "Why? You gonna stab a bitch?"

I laugh. "Just get them."

She disappears. I can hear her rooting around in her room before she returns with them in her hand. "They're sharp," she warns before she hands them to me.

"Better for stabbing," I say, and she giggles, too high and too long, as I grip the scissors.

I pull my hair out of its ponytail, tossing the elastic into the sink.

"Do you want my help?" Blake asks.

"Do you know how?"

She shrugs. "I do my hair."

I look at her bleach-blond do. It's a little more than fried. "I think I can do most of it. I might need your help with the back."

"Cool," Blake says, sitting down on the edge of her bed, watching me from that spot. "I'll be your studio audience then. *Go Coley!*" She laughs at herself. She doesn't seem to notice she's the only one who's laughing.

My hair hangs loose around my face. I take a hunk of it, running the scissors along the length, trying to measure in the mirror. How far am I willing to go?

Sonya'd twisted the strands around her fingers like they were precious jewels. As if she could wear me like a ring. And I wanted her to. I wanted to be a part of her, inside her body and heart and mind. But instead, she's the one who's imprinted on me—not the other way around. I'm being haunted by someone who isn't dead but who seems to want to be dead to me, and what the fuck do you do with that? How do you deal with it?

My fingers tighten around the scissors.

Snip.

Brown strands fall into the sink. I stare at them, the surge of power crunching like glass inside me. *Snip. Snip.* Swaths of hair fall, and with each one, I feel even more powerful.

"Looking good!" Blake says, between another bong rip.

Just a few more cuts.

When I'm done, the sink's full of hair and I'm shaking my head back and forth, the choppy swing of it brushing my jaw.

"Cuuuttteee," Blake says, getting up and grabbing my hand. I put the scissors down, letting her draw me down onto the bed. She balances the bong between her crossed legs and runs her fingers through my new do. I close my eyes, trying not to enjoy the feeling—trying not to compare it—and failing at both.

"Wanna see something cool?" she asks.

I nod.

She lights up the bong, sucking in the smoke. When she blows it out, it's in tiny little rings, until she starts laughing again.

"How long did it take you to learn that?" I ask dryly.

"Oh, forever," she says.

I lean back on the bed, closing my eyes. "Good use of your time?"

"What the fuck else is there to do in this shitty town?" she asks me.

"Why don't you leave, then?"

"I love how you say that like it's easy," Blake says, looking me up and down. "You one of those rich girls like Sonya?"

The mention of Sonya, so casually and dismissively, is like taking a bullet. A reminder that she knows Sonya and her friends, and probably a lot better than I do. I shake my head, like it'll shake the ghost of her away from me. "Sorry," I say. "You're right."

"I *am* gonna get out of here someday," she says. "I've got plans."

"Yeah?"

"Plans to hit this bong." Her words dissolve into more laughter, and this time I laugh along with her, because she's weird and a little funny and maybe a bit scary, but aren't all girls in some ways? Maybe it's better to feel this way now, instead of like with Sonya, that long, slow, drawn-out roller coaster. I hadn't known how much hurt she'd be able to wrench loose in me. If I'd known, would I have jumped? I fell so hard. Can you even stop a fall like that? Is it inevitable?

Is the hurt?

Blake's head tilts toward mine on the bed, looking at me. "You're kind of hot and cold, aren't you?"

I blink, because the answer is *definitely*, but I don't think that's what she wants.

"I can't tell if you're about to laugh or cry," she continues, and the flash inside me, it's twisting guilt. I should go. I'm a fucking mess, chasing distraction in any form, even if the form is another girl.

But I'm weak. I just stay there, on Blake's lumpy bed, and I lie.

"Maybe I'm being weird," Blake continues.

"Aren't we all?" I ask. "Just a little?"

She looks at me, thoughtful.

"Or a lot," I add, and her smile cracks her whole face crooked in this sweet, lilting way. Like she can't be bothered to give you anything but a tilted smile.

"What did you think when you met me?" Blake asks.

"I thought *Shit, this girl's gonna bust me for shoplifting.*"

Her laughter is a screech—too loud, but lacking such self-consciousness I marvel at her for a second, wondering what it would be like to be that split-second free.

"You're funny," she tells me. "Funny, funny Coley."

I can see it happening before it does. It's so strange, almost fake—like I'm watching it on a movie screen, which makes it feel even *more* fake, because girls don't get to make out with each other in movies.

Blake leans forward and kisses me. An awkward, pot-scented slide of lips on the edge of messy. I kiss her back, clutching at her like a doomed lifeline. I hate myself for the thought that snakes around my brain: that I've erased our last kiss. Mine and Sonya's. The one I didn't even know was our last kiss.

She knew.

Sonya knew *everything*. She'd held all the cards and played them like she was the only one who knew the rules—because she was the one who made them. Why was it so easy for her to walk away? Is that all this ever is? Girls just using you to see if they like you. Trying you out like a pair of jeans. Then deciding *No, not for me.*

Isn't that what you're doing? The thought slides along my body like Blake's fingers, the combination stomach turning. Not because of Blake.

Because of *me*.

I pull back, breaking our kiss. I need to go. I need to run. Just like Sonya.

"I'm pretty high," I say, but my eyes close as Blake's fingers trail through my now-shorn hair. It feels *so* good. Almost like . . .

Don't finish that thought. Don't think about her.

"Me too," Blake says, almost like it's permission. Like whatever happens is no big deal, just because of that. Is it an out? Or an excuse?

Her fingers trail down my temples, tracing the sweep of my cheekbones. Soft touches, evoking memories of a girl who I learned was anything but soft. God, I just want someone to love me. To touch me like they love me. Like they cherish me.

No. I want *Sonya* to love me. To touch me with love. To look at me with devotion.

"You're really pretty," Blake murmurs. "Has anyone ever told you that?"

Sonya did. But I don't know now if she meant it. If it was a game.

I shake my head, like that'll make the lie real.

When Blake kisses me this time, my eyes close and I drift into her touch. Her lips brush across my body, followed by her words, and if I keep my eyes closed, I can imagine she's someone else.

It's wrong. It's unfair. It's, quite plainly, *fucked.*

Instead of Blake's voice, I hear Sonya's. Instead of Blake's lips, I feel Sonya's fuller ones. Blake's fingernails aren't painted black in my mind, but periwinkle.

"I like your smile," Sonya tells me, her fingers trailing over my collarbone teasingly, her head pillowed on my stomach like it belongs there. "And your brain," she continues, lifting up to skim her body against mine. I have to fight myself to keep from arching into her. "The way you think . . . you're pretty smart." She laughs. "Pretty and smart. Get it?"

"I—"

"I like you," she interrupts, and I reel at hearing it, stated so plainly.

It yanks me out of my fantasy just as she kisses me, because Sonya . . . she *wouldn't.* She wouldn't say it so plainly.

She'd never *admit it.* Not even to herself.

Blake's lips are moving against mine. I'm in her bed in her little house.

And I'm a piece of shit who just—

I pull away, breathing hard.

"Are you . . . ?" Blake blinks at me, confused.

I blink furiously, desperate to keep the tears from creeping in.

"Sorry," I say. "I just remembered—my dad expected me home for dinner. If I don't show . . ."

"I get it," Blake says. "My dad was an asshole, too."

"He's not," I say, almost automatically, and then I frown at the impulse to defend Curtis, of all people. What the fuck is wrong with me?

I'm just falling apart all over.

"I'll sober up and drive you home," Blake says. "Come on."

But when she holds out her hand, I can't bear to take it.

THIRTY

It's late when Blake drops me off. The house is dark. I'm halfway to my room, thinking I've gotten away with sneaking in, when the lights flick on. I freeze, feeling Curtis's presence behind me. *Fuck.*

"Coley," he says.

"Yeah?" I turn around and try to look as innocent and unstoned as possible.

I know I reek of weed. I should've taken up Blake's offer to shower, but the idea of doing that was too much like that night with the poison oak and Sonya. I hate that. That *everything* reminds me of something that happened with her.

"What did you do to your hair?"

"Cut it," I say, surprised he actually noticed.

"Okay. Fine. Where were you?"

"I was at a friend's."

He frowns. "I thought Sonya went to dance camp."

"I am capable of making more than one friend," I say, even though I'm not so sure. I *am* sure that what Sonya and I had wasn't *friends,* no matter what she said. I have no idea what

Blake was. I need to find out so I can feel that I'm not just as bad as Sonya.

"I think you and I need to make an agreement," Curtis says, stopping me from heading down the hall. "You need to be home by midnight."

"That sounds more like a curfew than an *agreement,*" I say, crossing my arms.

"Fine. It's a curfew," he says. "I need to know where you are and when you're coming back. That's why you have a cell phone."

"The service sucks at my friend's house," I explain. "She lives out in the woods. I didn't get your texts until we drove back to town."

"Then tell me that before you go," he says.

"Why don't you just let me live my life, and I'll let you live yours?"

"Because I'm responsible for you, Coley!"

"Bullshit! I'm responsible for me! I've been responsible for me *forever.* I've been responsible for more than me! Stop acting like I'm a kid. If you really knew what Mom was like when she was low—" I stop myself, breathing hard as he stares at me.

"Just because you can take care of yourself doesn't mean you should have to," Curtis says.

"Oh, fuck you," I snap, unable to stop myself this time. "Your first instinct has always been to put *you* first. You ditched me. You ditched Mom. All because you didn't want to *move?*"

"It was more than that, Coley," he says.

"Explain it to me, then," I say, my mouth flattening my words into a weapon. "Because when good guys break up, they don't stop being dads. Only bad guys think you can stop being a dad."

He's silent.

"You didn't fight for me. You didn't even *try*. No summer visits. No phone calls on Christmas. Not even a card on my birthday." With everything I list, it's like I'm opening old wounds, feelings spilling out of me instead of blood. "You were the first person who ever taught me that I'm someone nobody missed," I continue. "That I'm disposable. You're not supposed to be disposable to your own dad. Do you know what it was like, growing up and realizing that? Understanding that there was this big hole where you were supposed to be?"

He just stands there and takes it, and I'm lost in the rush of actually *saying* it. The things that have been in my head, long buried because I used to tell myself when I was little that there was no use wondering about him when I'm never going to see him again.

Except now here we are. Stuck together. The most fucked-up of life's tricks. But I can scream and cry and accuse him all I want now.

I can push him until he shows his true self instead of this kicked-puppy version. I want to meet the man who left us. I want to see that Curtis instead of whoever this is.

I just need to push the right button. Sonya taught me that. Sonya taught me a lot of things about hurt and love and how thin the line is between them.

"Why don't we make a deal," I say. "You'll put up with my shit and I'll put up with yours. Like roommates. And the morning I graduate, I'll get the fuck out, just like you want me to."

I don't know if I've ever seen someone go so white, so fast.

"Is that what you want?" he asks, so swiftly and ragged that it startles me.

"That's what *you* want," I insist.

"No," he says. "That's the *last* thing I want. You're a year away from being an adult. And I missed most of your life so far, and I can keep telling you how sorry I am for it. Because I am. But I also can make sure I don't miss any *more* of it. All I want is for you to be happy and safe, and the way you've been acting reminds me of—" His mouth snaps shut, his eyes going wide at the stumble. It's like he knows it's the wrong thing to say.

Because it is. Any rage that had slowed to a simmering mess bubbles up into a boil in a second.

"The way I've been acting reminds you of Mom," I finish for him. "And you don't want to even consider that, right?"

"Coley—"

I spin, knocking past him so hard on my way down the hall I'm afraid he'll fall. Then he'll really kick me out, and he'd be justified. I slam the door to my room closed and lock it tight, but even crossing the room to my bed is too much. I just sink to the ground, my back sliding against the door. Hugging my knees to my chest, I press my forehead against the tops of them.

But unfortunately, Curtis is learning how to dad, because I hear his footsteps down the hall, and they don't keep going past my room to his. Instead, they stop in front of my door and then he knocks.

My hands tighten around my legs.

"Coley?" he says through the door. "Will you please let me in?"

I shake my head, which is so stupid because he can't see.

"I know I fucked up," he says. "Now and back then. But the only way we get through it is by talking to each other."

I am so sick of talking. Feeling. Existing.

As soon as that last thought hits me, I reject it, my entire body shuddering at the thought. *No.* I can't think that way. That's the kind of stuff he's scared about.

That's the kind of stuff *I'm* scared about. That vicious edge my mother drew too close to, her mind telling her no one would miss her . . . when *I* would. I *do.* I don't know how to do anything *but* miss her. I miss her so, it's hard to think about anything to do with her, because when I do, it hurts too much. I've blotted out two entire lives—hers and mine before she died—and now I'm a hollow shell: all the love and memories and the sense of belonging scooped out of me.

"I never thought it'd be this way," Curtis tells me through the door, sounding as broken as I feel. "I always thought . . . Fuck, Coley, I always thought she'd come back someday. That one day, there'd be a knock on the door and when I opened it, you'd both be there. And I realize now . . . it was wrong to just wait for something to happen. That every time I pictured it—and I did picture it a lot, Coley—you were both frozen at the ages you were when she left."

"*You* left," I snarl through the door.

There's a soft thump against the wood. I press my hand against the wood, wondering if his is on the other side. I want him to feel the heat of my anger through the door.

"I left you behind," he says. "I kept you but only in my mind, where you were three years old all this time. That's on me. That's my loss and yours, and I'm sorry. I was a coward. But I didn't leave your mom. She left me."

I can't help but ask, because I can't ask her. It's been circling in my head since I discovered he made her tiger's-eye pendant. "Do you still love her?"

When he answers, it takes forever. That's the thing about the truth: it's hard to get out.

"I'll always love her, Coley. Just like I always loved you, and I always will."

THIRTY-ONE

There's a shaky sort of truce between me and Curtis since the other night. We tiptoe around each other, like we were doing in the beginning. But it's so fucking lonely—days spilling into each other, endless aches that can't be filled, wondering what Sonya's doing, if she ever thinks about me.

When Blake calls me to hang out, I'm spiraling down into what-ifs again, and I promised myself I wouldn't, so I tell her to pick me up. This time, I actually tell Curtis where I'm going. That truce and all. I'm trying to be responsible.

I don't want him to be scared I'm going to swirl down into the dark like Mom. Figuring this out was . . . not great. I shouldn't care how he feels or if he worries. But he keeps trying and I don't have anyone else. So I kind of have to try a little, too, I think.

"I'm going out, okay?"

He looks up from the couch, where he's sorting through records. "Where?"

"My friend Blake's; she lives out by the creek. She's picking me up."

"Okay. Be home by midnight."

"Have fun with your records."

"Do I detect sarcasm?"

"I mean, it's kind of old-fashioned, isn't it?" His record player has its own little case in the living room next to his guitars.

"Classic, Coley," he says. "It's *classic*."

"I'll take your word for it."

"I could play you some—"

"Oh God, you're not going to make me listen to your old-guy music, are you?"

He laughs. "I have never felt so uncool. 'Old-guy' music?"

"I dunno what you like!"

He shakes his head, looking mortally offended and deeply amused.

Outside, a horn honks.

"That's Blake," I say.

"Go have fun. We'll talk music some other time. You can have me listen to what you like, okay?"

"You won't get *any* of it," I tell him very sincerely.

"I might surprise you," he says.

As if, I think, but before heading out, I give him a little wave to keep up the peace.

Blake opens the passenger door from the inside for me before I can reach for it. "Hey."

I have a plan this time. I've spent a few days agonizing over it: how shitty I felt for thinking about Sonya when I was with Blake. I can't pull that again. I need to get to know Blake beyond her being a little weird and a lot loud. That's what you do, right? Just, spend time with a girl and get to know her? It's like I'm triple-guessing myself now, tinged by everything with Sonya. There's still no road map.

"Have you always lived out here?" I ask, as we head back toward her house, windows open, the fresh scent of hay in the air from the semitruck in front of us carrying a whole load of the stuff.

"Yeah, my mom inherited the house. It's been in my family forever. The only thing my grandpa didn't gamble off."

I don't know what to say to that. *That sucks?* Because it seems like it probably does. But at least they still have the house? Life's little twists, even when some of it's good, some of it's bad.

"So it's just you and your mom?" I ask when we get to her house and it's just her and me again.

"No, my dad's around, but he kind of just checks out when he's home," Blake says casually, rooting around in the fridge and pulling out a pie tin. She sticks two forks into the center of the remains of the cherry pie and breezes past me, heading toward her room. I follow, and she's already spread out on her bed, the pie balanced on one of her lumpy pillows as she digs around for her bong.

"You want a hit?"

I shake my head. Maybe part of the problem was getting too high last time. Better to have a clear head. I sit down at her desk instead of next to her on the bed, trying to keep some space.

"I'm running low," Blake comments. I flush, wondering if I should've offered to . . . I dunno . . . get some weed? I don't know the etiquette here: there's a lot more pot here than down south.

I lean against her desk, my elbow scraping against something sharp and papery. I look down and frown at the white packages spread across the desk. MEDICAL GRADE NEEDLE 16 G.

"Blake," I say slowly. "Why do you have all these needles?"

"Drugs," she says cheerfully, taking another hit.

I stare at her, my skin prickling . . . and *fuck*—

Smoke billows out of her nostrils as she does that screechy laughter thing again. "Ha! Your face!"

I feel a little sick; heat rushes to my face.

"I'm starting my body-piercing training next year," Blake tells me. "I just need to save up a little more money."

"That's . . ." I fade off, because I can absolutely see Blake enjoying poking holes in people for a living. "Fitting," I finish. "And cool. I could never."

"Squeamish, huh? Want me to do yours?"

"My *what?*" I ask, my mind going to all sorts of places.

She laughs. "Wow, you're turning red. Your cartilage, maybe?"

I touch the top of my ear. A little hoop or stud there would be nice. Especially with my shorter hair.

"I'd like that."

"Fuck, yeah," she says.

We set up in her bathroom and I'm impressed with how prepared Blake is. She's got needles and sterilizer and prepackaged sterilized hoops she lets me pick from. I choose silver over the gold, because the gold reminds me of Sonya and I want something that's mine. Silver, like a crescent moon, whispering wisdom in my ear. I need as much wisdom as I can get these days.

"So how did you get interested in this?" I ask as she preps my ear and marks the piercing spot carefully.

"Did my own ears with a sewing needle and ice when I was little," she says. "Then I went and bought a bunch of earrings at Claire's and charged the other little girls twenty bucks to do theirs."

"Hard core."

"What can I say, sometimes mutilation pays," Blake says. "Deep breath."

I obey and feel the sting of the needle in my ear. She has steady hands—maybe *because* she's so stoned?—and before I know it, there's a little hoop winking in my ear. She cleans the area diligently and hands me a bottle of saline solution and a little card with aftercare instructions.

"Wow," I say. "You're prepared."

"You've gotta train seven hundred and fifty hours to get your license," Blake says. "But I have to make money for the training."

She wanders back into her bedroom as I stare at myself in the mirror. Short hair, new piercing. It's not a whole new Coley staring back at me, but it's *something.* At least I'm trying to drag myself out of this endless circle of loathing and wondering if there's ever any good.

"So you're gonna do your hundreds of hours and get out of here?" I ask, coming to sit next to her on the bed. She grabs the pie and spears it with her fork, the munchies kicking in.

There is something free about her that fills me with this weird mix of envy and embarrassment. I don't think I could ever just not care like she seems to.

"I want to get to a bigger city so I can learn how to tattoo," Blake explains. "I've been planning my first piece since I was twelve. Wanna see?"

I nod and she plops the pie tin in my lap as she gets up and rummages around in her sagging bookcase, pulling out a sketchbook that's so worn and stuffed that the spine is cracked and the cover is held together with rubber bands.

She snaps them off the book, and pages spill out. As she

sifts through them, I get a flip-book experience of her art in flashes. A graveyard, the stones shadowy charcoal smears across the ground. A bunch of hands, reaching out of the ground. They get progressively less human and more zombielike the farther down the page. A self-portrait, a lot harsher than it should be. Is this how she sees herself? A cat, black—of course—hissing. She finally finds the sketch she's looking for, picks it out, and places it between us.

It's another angel, but her wings aren't shades of charcoal. They're not feathery, but leathery, and they spring out of the angel's back, bloody and painful, thorns springing up around the edges. This angel's head is stooped, like the wings are too much of a burden for her.

"She seems sad," I say in the sudden silence between us. I reach out for it before I can even stop myself. To touch it, I guess? But Blake snatches it away and carefully tucks it between the pages of her sketchbook.

"Yeah, well, she's part of the drawings I did after I dumped my gay ex and had an abortion," she says with a shrug. "Pregnancy hormones are shitty as hell. They totally messed with my head. I don't recommend it."

"You don't recommend getting pregnant by a . . . wait—" I shake my head, trying to gather all the information she's just dumped on me. "Your ex is gay? Do you mean gay as in . . ."

"Gay as in gay," Blake says. "Though I dunno, maybe he's bi? I'd have to ask him, and we don't talk. I mean, he was good about the abortion: he paid for half, like he should've. But he's, like, in his head about the whole liking-guys thing." She rolls her eyes. "He thinks too much. It's not a big deal."

"Do you really think that about being gay?"

She looks at me, and for a second her gaze turns fierce. "Anyone who tells you otherwise is a fuckwad," she says, and I've never thought of anyone's voice as deadly before, but now I know what it sounds like.

I let out a laugh. "That's . . . you've been through a lot. I'm sorry if it's been tough."

"Aw." Blake leans forward and bops me on the nose. "This is why I like you. You're so cute! The world hasn't hurt you yet."

I smile shakily to hide it, the way her words strike me. That casual assumption. *If you only knew.*

But I can't tell. God, I *can't* tell.

I trusted her. After train-track kisses and Sonya's hands, spreading lotion down my back in the soft silence of her bathroom, her bed just a wall away. I let myself trust her and then she just shattered it. Not just with the push and pull where she'd yank me in only to flinch away like it wasn't her idea in the first place. But the fact that she told all her friends about my mom . . .

How could you do that to me?

"You're sweet, Coley," Blake tells me, bringing me out of my thoughts, leaning forward to kiss me. I want to believe her. I want to be the girl that she sees in me, because I'm not. I'm the opposite.

Now *I'm* the one wearing the mask, *my* lips sliding over a girl's, hiding myself while she spills her secrets. Sonya would laugh at me now.

She'd say, *I taught you well.*

I guess the students always become the masters.

THIRTY-TWO

"I think we should go out," I say.

It's my fourth time hanging at Blake's house. I got here late, so it'll be dark soon. The days between the hangouts have dragged on. I'd like to say I've completely lost track of the time since Sonya left, but I'd be lying.

"There's nowhere to go," Blake scoffs.

"We could go to the lake."

"No way."

"Get something to eat?"

"I'm not hungry," she says. "I haven't smoked today. I ran out of weed last night."

"Shit," I say.

"This sucks," she complains. "I hate messing around sober."

I sit up. "Do you want me to go?"

"No, you fucking weirdo," she says. "I know someone. Who sells. We can just go grab some."

"Do you have the money?"

"He owes me a favor. Or a few million, really," she says. "After all, I made sure he wasn't a teen dad."

My eyes widen as she gets up. "Your ex deals weed?"

She grabs her keys off her desk and then her studded wallet. "You sound so scandalized, Coley-Bear," she mocks. "You're the one who's been smoking up his weed when we hang."

I flush. "It's different."

"So sweet and innocent," Blake laughs. "Come on. Let's corrupt you a little." She holds out a hand and I take it. Because I know she's been hurt, and I know deep down, you don't tell someone the stuff she told me unless you care. Unless you've got wounds you're looking to heal.

Blake blasts her music as we drive twenty over the speed limit, up winding roads we should really be taking slow. My head's spinning by the time she comes to a stop in front of a cluster of dilapidated mobile homes spread across a barren piece of land. The area's been stripped of all trees; a few stumps are the only hint of what came before.

Blake parks in front of a yellow mobile home that has cement blocks for steps.

"That's his," she says. "I'll go see if he's home. Stay here."

She gets out and heads to the front. I watch her through the windshield, something funny building in my stomach when I notice she doesn't knock on the door. She tries the knob first. Then she turns in a slow circle on the cement-block steps, like she's counting the cars.

Dread rises in my chest. Something's not right here, and I roll down the window. "Hey," I hiss.

Blake's head jerks toward mine and she hurries over to the car. "Keep it down," she says.

"Is he here?" I ask, even though I know the answer.

"Don't think so."

"Should we just go, then?" *Please, let's just go.* It's like nails are tapping against the back of my neck in warning. My heart's beating like I've been running for miles.

"Nah," Blake says. "I need to smoke. And he owes me."

"Blake!" But she's already heading back toward the mobile home.

I watch as she tries one of the windows and, to my horror, gets it open. Shit. Shit. She's really doing this. She's *stealing* from her drug-dealer ex. This is insane. This is dangerous. Curtis's going to kill me if someone else here doesn't.

My hand closes around the door handle, my thighs tensing, my heart screaming *Run, run, run.* But there's nowhere to go! We're miles away from *anything.* I'm stuck. I'm stupid and fucking *stuck* while this crazy-ass girl pulls risks I'd never—

The crunch of gravel behind me sends my clamoring heart into a full-on stampede. Panicked, I glance in the rearview mirror as a truck pulls up behind Blake's car. Blake's disappeared into the mobile home. I crouch down, hoping whoever's in the truck didn't see me. But what if they did? The windows are open. I can't roll them up now. Fuck. Fuck. We're doomed. We're going to get beaten to death.

The truck's headlights light up the driveway, and I cringe as I hear the door slam. Someone's gotten out. I slowly peek up, high enough to see the side mirror. The shadowy figure heads toward me, and when I see the bat in his hand, my entire body screams at me to run.

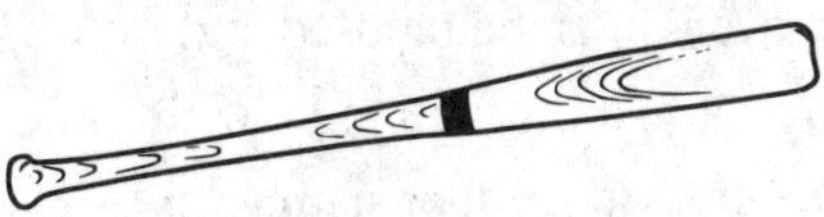

Nowhere to go, no one to call, all alone again.

Panic soars through me as the footsteps grow louder.

"Hey, what are you—" says a male voice. I blink at the words, recognition skating along my rapidly firing brain, but not connecting. "Coley?!"

I blink up at Alex, who's staring down at me with an expression of total confusion. He looks at the fuzzy handcuffs hanging from Blake's rearview mirror and then toward the mobile home.

"Oh, you've gotta be fucking kidding me," he says. "Is she inside my place?"

Before I can answer, Blake answers the damn question by choosing that moment to climb back out the window, a baggie of weed clenched between her teeth.

Alex charges forward, bat swinging, leaving me behind, trying to piece together everything in my reeling brain. *Alex* is Blake's maybe-gay ex?

"Blake! What the fuck are you doing?" he yells.

"Payment, baby!" The bag of weed falls out of her mouth as she laughs. Alex lunges for it, dropping the bat as he does, but she's too close. She drops to the ground and grabs it, dancing away from him. She kicks the bat out of the way, cackling.

"Blake, give that back," he says. "That's a fucking *ounce* of Indica."

"Oh, it's an ounce of Indica?" she mimics him, her face screwing into a horrible imitation of him.

My stomach twists horribly as I watch them. Is this what life is? Is this what love is? Just being used and fucking people over? Is this what I have to go through to be with someone?

Behind me, I hear a car door slam.

And there he is: the person who will absolutely make this terrible situation even worse. Trenton comes strolling up to Blake's car, like Alex isn't chasing a giggling Blake all over the yard and doesn't need his help. Just hands in his pockets, totally chill, *totally* focused on me.

I want to dig a hole and hide. But I don't have time to roll up the damn windows as he leans into the car.

"Well, look at you," he says, over Blake's giggles and Alex's yelling. He still hasn't caught her. "Finally taking yourself out with the trash?"

I stare straight ahead. If I look at him, I'm afraid I'll do something like burst into tears out of sheer humiliation.

"Trenton, can . . . you . . . fucking . . . help?" Alex bellows, finally getting ahold of Blake around the waist. She swings wildly against his grip, and Trenton darts forward just as Blake kicks back, hitting Alex hard in the knee. He goes down with a shocked, gutted noise.

"Shit! Blake, you bitch!" Alex gasps.

With a bat in his hand, Trenton leaps toward Blake, and she *bolts*, dodging around him and galloping toward the car, still clutching the baggie of weed at her side. She yanks the door open and backs out, narrowly avoiding the minivan, the biggest smile in the world on her face as the boys chase after us, Trenton swinging his bat at the car. But it's no use—she's gotten away. *We've* gotten away.

But it's like my heart doesn't know that.

She's still laughing as we speed down the tree-lined street, and when she glances over to beam at me, her laughter thickens. "Oh, sweet Coley-Bear," she coos. "Did I scare you?"

"Pull over," I say.

"Wha—"

"Pull over!"

The car bumps down the uneven road until she pulls over to the shoulder. I get out of the car. I can't be inside there with her right now. Those moments before I realized the dealer was Alex . . . I thought, fuck, I thought so many things and none of them were good, and all of them were *terrifying*.

"Are you gonna puke or something?" Blake asks.

I look over my shoulder at her.

"Get in the car," she says. "It was *funny*."

"No, it wasn't," I say.

She rolls her eyes. "Come on, Coley."

"No."

Her face hardens, her mouth flattening. "Fine! Have fun getting home, bitch!" And she drives off.

I pull my phone out. There's a part of me that hopes I *don't* have a signal. Yeah, it's like fifteen miles to town. But walking fifteen miles home is almost better than the alternative.

But I have a signal. Which means . . . *fuck*.

I take a deep breath. Then I punch in the number.

When he answers, I start crying. I'm crying so hard I'm not even sure he hears half of the story I spill, right there on the side of the road. But I do know he hears the last question, because it echoes in my brain, hours later, when I'm calmer.

"Dad, can you come and get me?"

Is this what I have to go through to be loved by a girl?

THIRTY-THREE

I'm sitting there on the side of the road, knees to my chest, butt in the dirt, arms wrapped around my legs. My chin dips into the divot my pressed-together knees make, my teeth gritted together to keep from chattering as I rock back and forth.

It's not cold. But it doesn't matter.

My eyes ache from crying. They've dried up, my tears, tacky and grubby down my face and chin, collecting in the span of my collarbones. But I can't get my heart to stop beating like I'm a rabbit on the run from a fox.

If I loosen my arms from my legs, I'll run. Just bolt like a wild thing, trying to seek some sort of freedom.

So I hold myself tight. A straitjacket of my own making, trying to hold it in.

But there's too much. It's too much.

All being myself has led to is pain. I tried to open up to Sonya, and she tossed me aside like I meant nothing. I tried to get to know Blake, but everything we did reminded me of someone else, and now I'm here, left behind on the side of the road.

Tossed aside.

Everyone's always leaving. Curtis did it first, when I was little. Mom lost her grip and couldn't stay. Sonya kissed me like I was the first and last and only, then shattered me and twirled away like it was nothing.

Like I was nothing.

By the time Curtis pulls up, I'm crying again. He jerks the car to a stop and *jumps* out like I called him and told him I was carjacked or something.

"I'm okay," I say, but I can't stop *crying*. The more I try, the more I cry. It bubbles out of me: tears and snot and the humiliation and fear and *relief*.

He came to get me.

"Sweetheart." He grabs my shoulders, and I tense, thinking he's going to *shake* me or something. But no, he's, like, *checking* to make sure I'm okay. He kind of pats the tops of my shoulders like *all clear*! And it's so awkward that any other time, it'd be funny.

But then he pulls me close, hugging me tight, and it's not awkward anymore.

Suddenly, it's exactly what I needed, and his shirt is getting completely wet with my tears.

"Can we go?" All I want is a shower and my bed and to never see Blake or Alex or Trenton ever again. Which I know is so not going to happen because of this stupid small town and, oh yeah, school in less than two months. I love how I've cemented my reputation as an absolute freak to everyone before even stepping inside school.

"Yeah," he says. "Let's go home."

I buckle myself in, fiddling with the AC vents for something to do as he pulls back onto the road.

He's silent as we drive. For *miles*. I sit there, my stomach thrumming with anxiety, cheeks wet from tears. But eventually he cracks. There's a small thread of pride stitched on my heart that it's not me who breaks first.

"Do you want to tell me what happened?"

I stare out the window because looking at him is *not* an option.

"I fuck everything up." The words—the truth—are out there before I can stop them.

"Why would you say that?"

"I hate myself. I hate *everything*."

"Coley," he says, voice deepening with concern.

I concentrate on the trees, picking them out in my head as we pass them. Pine. Pine. Redwood. Oak.

"She hates me."

"Your friend? Blake? What did she do?"

"No, not her. Sonya."

He falls quiet.

"I'm the one who should hate her," I continue. "I hate myself that I don't. Is that what love is? Never hating the person even when they deserve it? Because it's a crock of shit, Curtis."

"I—" He glances over at me, trying to process. I just charge ahead.

"I don't know why I'm not enough for her. Why am I not enough for *anyone*? Mom gave up on me. She must've hated me, too. She couldn't stand to be around me in the end. Sometimes I think that's why I missed my bus that day. So I could just have a few more minutes without her hating me."

"Oh, Coley." Without another word, Curtis pulls over again on the side of the road. A truck that's been tailgating us breezes past. He turns in his seat, his hand coming to rest on my seat, inches from my shoulder.

"Your mom loved you," Curtis tells me.

"Not enough."

He's quiet for a long time, the truth of it settling between us like a new scar we share.

"Maybe not in that moment," he says finally. "I don't think she was thinking about anything but her own pain in that moment. But as a whole? Every day? Your mom *loved* you. She fought for you. And I know she was so proud of you."

"You don't—"

"I do," he interrupts me. "Coley, I'm the one that packed up all her stuff. Her journals. Her sketchbooks."

"Did you read them?"

He lets out a long breath. "I read the most recent one. The one that covered the last year before she—"

I want to summon some sort of outrage, but I can't. A part of me gets it. A part of me wants to read them now that he's mentioned them. A part of me never wants to touch them. *Ever.*

"I wanted to understand some part of how this happened. How you'd been living," he explains.

"Did her journal give you answers?"

"It gave me a lot of questions," he says. "Questions I think only you can answer for me. In time."

"And you think we have time?"

"We have as much time as we're willing to give each other, Coley," Curtis says sincerely. "We can start over. You and me. That doesn't mean the past is forgotten or even forgiven. I know forgiveness and trust are things that are earned. But you deserve to heal. To love yourself."

"I don't think I can do that."

"I do."

I want to believe him. Having that kind of hope . . . I don't know if it's possible. But I'm never going to find out if I don't try.

"How can anything get better?" I ask him.

"By us being honest with each other instead of circling each other like we're in a boxing ring," he says. "I am on your side. I want to be on your team, not fighting you. I want to watch you graduate high school and then college and, hell, maybe you'll get a master's degree."

"Uh, have you seen my grades?" I ask skeptically.

He laughs. "Okay, then I want to see you start your career. Find your partner in life. All that stuff. I want to be part of your life, Coley. I know I missed too much. But I don't have to miss any more. We can be here for each other. For the bad parts and the good parts."

"Sonya gave me the good parts," I whisper. "And then she fucked me over. She didn't just leave," I confess. "She told her friends about Mom."

"Oh, honey." He reaches for me, and then I'm in my father's arms, leaning across the parking brake, an awkward but oh-so-needed hug.

"You were the good part of whatever you had with her," Curtis says fiercely. "You are the good part of *everything,* sweetie. We can't control what people do—how they betray us or even why. How they leave our lives. So many people are running scared. And sometimes they run back to us and earn back our trust. But the ones who don't come back—or who don't work to earn back what they lost from us—we have to learn how to let them go."

"It's so hard," I confess.

"But when you let go, you can take all that love you had, all the energy, and funnel it into yourself instead. Because there is so much for you to love about yourself, Coley."

"I wish I could see it," I say.

"You will," he says. "I'm going to make sure of it. I promise."

Sitting there in the car with him, it feels like he means it. And he's right. He and I, we have each other. That's it.

Trust is earned. And I think, bit by bit, he's earning mine.

THIRTY-FOUR

LJ User: SonyatSunrisex00x [Public Entry]
Date: July 8, 2006

[**Mood:** elated]
[**Music:** "Maneater"—Nelly Furtado]

Next time you boys tell me dancing isn't hardcore exercise, I want you to go through the stretching session I just went through. Oh, wait, you'd be crying five minutes in!

I've got muscles I didn't even know existed throbbing in protest.

—Sonya

Comments:

T0nofTrent0nnn:
I've got something else that's throbbing.

> **MadeYouBrooke23:**
> *TRENTON!*

LJ User: SonyatSunrisex0Ox [Private Entry]

Date: July 11, 2006

[**Mood:** Annoyed]
[**Music:** "Numb"–Linkin Park]

I've been booking solo studio time each night just to get away from it all. Madame Rosard told me I needed to make sure to socialize. I couldn't just throw myself into the work. But, like, isn't that the point of all this money my parents are paying?

She didn't like it when I said that. I almost got put on dishwashing duty. If I get two more warnings, they're going to call my mom. So I just need to make sure no one sees me do anything that warrants a warning.

The first time I booked studio time so late it was mainly because my roommate invited Faith to hang out in our cabin and I couldn't stand that know-it-all smile of hers. Why does everyone like her? She's so smug. Like she's won at life.

I wouldn't be so proud if I were her. I heard her mom doesn't even speak to her anymore. Her parents split up because of her. Her dad took her side and her mom . . .

Love isn't very unconditional, no matter what they say. I learned that when my mom and dad split up. A family breaks and it doesn't leave a scar; it's a wound. Sometimes it doesn't heal.

Some things are hard to heal.

I don't want my family to break. To be the thing that splits it apart completely, just because I can't control—

How can Faith stand it? Her parents *split* because she couldn't control herself.

Or does it hurt, and she just hides the wound?

If she is hiding it, I want to know how.

I want to learn.

I need to.

Because I hurt her.

Not Faith. I couldn't care less about her.

Coley.

I fucked it all up. I mean, Coley kind of fucked it up first, acting all . . .

Why did Coley have to act like that? Why did she have to talk about it? It was fine until she wanted all *that.* She should've known better. I'm not Faith. Coley's not Faith. We don't get to *be* Faith.

You only get to be Faith if you're willing to lose things like your entire mom or all your friends. Why would Coley be willing to do that when she already lost her mom? It makes no sense.

Nothing is worth being the thing that breaks everything apart.

I could never be worth that.

Could I?

–Sonya

LJ User: SonyatSunrisex00x [Public Entry]

Date: July 15, 2006

[**Mood:** feeling the love!]

[**Music:** "A Thousand Miles"–Vanessa Carlton]

I got the cutest care package today! @SJbabayy, thank you so much!!! I have the little ballerina hanging from my bunk. My roommates were jealous at first, but I shared the cookies with them! You are so sweet! <3

And @T0nofTrent0nnn, do you *know* how much trouble I could've gotten into with that card you sent me? Cartoon penises spelling out "I miss you"? Seriously? Are you five years old?

–Sonya

Comments:

SJbabayy:

So glad it got there safe! The ballerina made me think of you!

> **MadeYouBrooke23:**
>
> *I can't believe you sent her a care package without me!*
>
> **SJbabayy:**
>
> *I couldn't find you! You're always disappearing these days.*

T0nofTrent0nnn:

Just making sure you're missing me, babe.

LJ User: SonyatSunrisex00x [Private Entry]

Date: July 18, 2006

[**Mood:** I don't even know]

[**Music:** "Chasing Cars"–Snow Patrol]

Sometimes when I lie in my bunk at night, my body just aches.

And it's not my muscles or the hours of dancing. Stretching doesn't relieve it.

It's deeper than that.

It's like it's in me so deep I can't heal it.

Someone else has to.

She has to.

Coley sneaks in, at night. Into my head, into my heart, into my body. Slips under my skin, sparks stirring to life, and I can't stop her. I don't want to.

It's all I'll ever get of her now.

It's the only time I feel alive. Laying there in the dark, thinking of her, of us, train-track kisses and hushed voices in bathrooms, her fingers trailing up my stomach. But in the dark, alone in my bunk, my mind wanders and her fingers trail down instead, along with mine in real life.

It *hurts,* wanting someone so much. Knowing you can never have them again. Lip biting, blood bursting in your mouth as you get there kind of hurt.

This is all I get: memories in the dark and my hand and she . . .

Coley will be like Faith someday. She'll shake off our town and move back to L.A. or San Francisco and she'll meet some hot liberal-arts major in college, I bet. Some beautiful girl whose parents don't care. A girl who brings her home and doesn't think twice about holding her hand when she walks through the front door.

Coley will get everything she deserves. Some girl who'll give her the world. And someday, she'll say to that girl, *Did I ever tell you about the summer after my mom passed away? About the girl I met?* And she'll laugh at the memory of those kisses that I'll still be holding on to as precious, because she's shared so much more with someone else. They won't be important anymore.

I'll be just a wisp of memory. Another girl will be her life.

Maybe if I stay still enough, I'll turn to stone.

Maybe then my mother will be happy.

Maybe then this aching will stop.

Why can't I let her go?

—Sonya

LJ User: SonyatSunrisex00x [Public Entry]

Date: July 25, 2006

[Mood: blissful]

[Music: "Dirty Little Secret"—The All-American Rejects]

Sorry to not update from my sacred spot in the woods! I've just been having the time of my life! I'm gonna be unstoppable this competition season! Watch out, girls!

—Sonya

LJ User: SonyatSunrisex00x [Private Entry]

Date: July 25, 2006

[**Mood:** pissed]

[**Music:** "Bring Me to Life"—Evanescence]

Everyone is on my ass lately. My mom is, every time I have a family call, even though all I really want to do is talk to Emma. I know Mom and Madame Rosard talk. They're friends. Gossiping friends, I bet. Which means Mom knows how I'm screwing up in class.

At least I can avoid Mom, except for the phone calls. Faith, I can't avoid, and oh my God, she will not stop. I can't nail this routine in class. And I get it: Madame Rosard was getting frustrated with me. *You're off your game, Sonya.* She actually said that to me!

Oh God, is she saying that to my mom? I'm going to come home to a whole new white-board schedule where she's allotted me five minutes of break time every three weeks at this rate.

Madame Rosard was tapping the floor with her cane like she does, but it was off-beat. When she goes off-beat, you're fucking up.

She brought me up to the front of the class and it was like, *Sonya, you're better than this* over and over and over again until, I swear, I was dizzy no matter how much spotting I was doing. And the entire time, Faith was standing there by the mirrors with the rest of my class *watching*.

And then! Oh my God, it was so excruciatingly humiliating. Then Madame Rosard brings Faith up to show me how to do it! And I still can't nail it!

And that's why I'm not waiting for Faith after class so she can walk me through it again. Like I'm a five-year-old who's just learning.

Camp was supposed to be fun. It was supposed to be a break. My sacred place! This is *my* camp! My place! And Faith just keeps ruining it with her smug I-know-all-your-secrets smile. Ugh. I hate her. She's just another terrible reminder of this summer.

I should TP her cabin. Teach her a lesson.

–Sonya

THIRTY-FIVE

LJ User: SonyatSunrisex00x [Private Entry]

Date: July 28, 2006

[**Mood:** drunk]
[**Music:** "Too Little Too Late"—JoJo]

It was an accident.

That's what I wish I could tell Coley.

I didn't mean to tell everyone about her mom. I just told SJ. And I had a good reason, I thought, but I guess maybe I didn't.

I didn't know if I'd done the right thing when Coley told me. I didn't know if I should've said something different or better, and I was so worried about messing up that I messed up. And SJ is so smart about deep emotional stuff because she's been through some shit.

But then Brooke overheard us talking about it, and it spread and spread, and I'd hoped Coley wouldn't find out.

But she did.

And she hates me. And that should be good, right? I should be glad.

I can't want a girl like that.

I just can't.

—Sonya

LJ User: SonyatSunrisex00x [Public Entry]

Date: July 30, 2006

[**Mood:** jubilant]
[**Music:** "Hey Ya!"—Outkast]

One more week everyone, and then the bitch is *back!*

I hope you're planning something fabulous for my return.

I expect champagne. Streamers. Glitter. A stripper jumping out of a giant cake!

You know, the works. I've been away working my ass off and I deserve to *party* when I get home!

—Sonya

LJ User: SonyatSunrisex00x [Private Entry]

Date: July 30, 2006

[**Mood:**]

[**Music:** "My Happy Ending"—Avril Lavigne]

My mom called me today. Not the other way around. That's how I knew I was in trouble.

I was right about Madame Rosard reporting back to her. Mom started out all sweet, which of course put me right on edge, because Mom is not sweet. But when it was clear I wasn't buying it, she launched into her whole spiel.

She said she's worried about me. This whole summer I've been acting strangely. "Disconnected" she called it. She kept asking me if I was having boy troubles or something. She said that teenaged boys are flighty, but she knew that Trenton cared about me, deep down, even if he was a flirt, and I wanted to tune her out, because God, of course it has to be a boy, right?

It can't be that Mom's got a stranglehold on my life and a step-by-step plan for my future and didn't even consult me about any of it. Or that I get to see my dad in bits and pieces and he tries so hard but it's not the same as living with him and eating breakfast together and going to bed at night knowing they're there in the house with you.

I see how Emma looks at herself in the mirror sometimes. Like she's already looking for flaws. And she's a baby; she doesn't have any flaws. And then I ask myself when did I start doing that? Her age? Younger? And I ask myself: Where did I learn that? And the answer isn't a good one.

How am I supposed to love myself when everything I was taught steered me away from it?

Be silent, Sonya. Be still. Mom used to tell me that when I was little. I think maybe it's why she put me into dance in the first place: she thought I could burn up all the energy so I could be her pretty little doll the rest of the time.

I'm not a pretty little doll, though. I'm a broken doll. A fucking mess.

No one wants me.

No one should want me.

Why did Coley want me?

Why can't I stop wanting her?

—Sonya

LJ User: SonyatSunrisex00x [Private Entry]

Date: July 30, 2006

[Mood:]

[Music:]

It's after midnight and I'm hiding in the computer room like some sort of loser. I had the studio booked late, and then no one came to kick me out at ten like usual, so I kept going, because Faith's going to gloat if I still can't get Madame Rosard's choreography down right.

When I finally packed up to go, I heard something down the hall in studio C. Giggling. I thought someone was having a secret party or something.

I guess the "or something" was right.

I've never seen two girls kiss before.

Isn't that strange? To have experienced something as common as a kiss before you've ever seen it. It's a fuzzy idea in the visual, until it's not.

They were kissing in studio C. Faith and Orion, Madame Rosard's other assistant. Up against the mirror, finger-interweaving, my-smile-against-yours, I'm-about-to-lift-you-onto-this-barre kind of kissing.

I couldn't move. They couldn't see me, and I just stood there for like a full thirty seconds before my legs starting working again and I ran all the way here to the computer lab and I just . . . I want . . .

Is that what Coley and I looked like that day by the railroad tracks? Soft and so happy it's like you're full of light?

Does it really look like it feels when it's right?

Because Faith and Orion . . .

They were beautiful.

—Sonya

To: RollieColey87@aol.com
From: SonyatSunrisex00x@aol.com
Subject: [UNSENT EMAIL] I'm sorry

Dear Coley,

I'm sorry. That's the thing I need to say first. I'm sorry about telling SJ about your mom. I didn't mean to, but that's not an excuse. I fucked up and I need to own it. I'm sorry. I'm so fucking sorry. I don't think I'm very good at forgiveness . . . which means it's kind of messed up that I want yours so bad.

I miss you. I think about you all the time. I can't stop. All I want is to touch you. To kiss you. To lay down in bed with you. I replay moments in my mind—the freckles on your back, the lotion between my fingers. . . . I wanted to turn around that night, after the party, when we were alone. I wanted to turn and stand there and let you look at me. I wanted you to see all of me as much as I wanted to see you.

I wanted more than that. I wanted everything. I dream about it—waking up tangled with you, and when I wake up and you're not there it's like someone's punched me each time.

I don't know how to do this. I don't know how to want someone so much and not have them and I know you'd laugh. Spoiled little Sonya, not getting what she wants.

But I can't breathe. I can't think.

You make me want to throw my life away, and I can't.

I won't.

But God, do I want to.

—Sonya

LJ User: SonyatSunrisex00x [Private Entry]

Date: August 2, 2006

[**Mood:** furious]

[**Music:** "Hide and Seek"—Imogen Heap]

I can't believe Faith. Who does she think she is? I should report her. Go to Madame Rosard and tell her what an invasive, nosy *bitch* Faith is.

And she knows I can't! That's what makes me so mad about this. She knows I won't. Because I'd have to tell them what she said.

Who calls someone that? Who says those things? Assumes them? Like she knows me better than I do. She only knows things because of what she did!

She cornered me today. I should've known something was up. I thought she was going to get on me about the choreography again and how I'm not creative enough in my movement for modern dance. But instead, she said something that made me want to die.

She told me I needed to be careful about logging out of the computer in the lab. She said I'd forgotten the other night, all soft and slow, like she was breaking it to me. Like I wasn't seconds away from killing her because I could see it on her face.

She'd read some of it. Maybe my email to Coley. Maybe even my journal. My private entries are supposed to be *private* and now . . .

I literally wanted to throw up all over her feet. I thought about it. It would serve her right.

But she kept talking. I could barely hear her until she said it:

Lots of us go through self-loathing closet-case phases, Sonya. It's okay.

Like she was lesbian Jesus giving me permission! Like I was one of *hers*. Like I had been part of an *us* somehow this whole time and didn't know!

I really thought I was going to throw up. But she kept talking. All gentle like she was worried about me. About how she wants to help, and how hating myself isn't going to get me anywhere.

So fake. So rude. So condescending. I don't need her help or her nasty assumptions! I don't need anyone.

I told her to get out and she finally listened, and then I rushed over to the computer lab to change all my passwords, just in case.

Faith acts so casual about it. Like it's *easy*. Like you can kiss girls in dance studios whenever you want and hold hands with them down the street and bring them home to your mom like you would a boy. Like that love is something you can reach out and grab. Like . . . like . . . it's something you can just *have*.

I don't get to be Faith. All I get is the memory of railroad-track kisses and Coley's eyes, shining at me like I was her only, and I'll never get that again. Someone looking at me like they know me because they actually *do*.

And now I know: to go through life unknown when you've had a taste of the other side is a lot more bitter than sweet.

But it's what I've got. It's all I've got.

—Sonya

THIRTY-SIX

We make a list. Me and Curtis. After he picks me up from the side of the road and the whole shit show with Blake, we make a list. It sounds so corny—hell, it *is* corny. It's corny how excited he is to sit there and make one. And it's maybe a little pitiful that I kind of like that he's excited. But we make a list of stuff to do.

The first thing he puts down is taking me to the hibachi grill, which we were supposed to go to when Sonya was still in town. But there's other stuff on the list, too. He puts down *Introduce Coley to The Cardigans,* and I put down *Introduce Curtis to some music written this century.* When he puts down *Take Coley to the gem show this fall,* I have to ask what that is. Apparently people sell crystals and gems and stuff at the fairgrounds every year.

"That sounds like the perfect setting for a heist movie," I tell him, and he laughs so hard I think he's faking it, but then it goes on too long to be anything but real. When he's finally done, he dabs at his eyes and shakes his head. "Your mom had a running joke about that because I used to drag her to them."

"No way."

"One time she got really bored because I was taking forever, and she sketched a whole diamond smuggling plan on a napkin. I wish I still had it."

"I don't think the life of diamond thieves is for either of us," I say. "But I'll go to the show with you, if you want."

"I have a feeling you might like the crystal-skull booth."

"There are crystal skulls?" I perk up, and he laughs again, in that way I'm realizing he does when I do something that reminds him of Mom.

Maybe it's not about being mad that he knew a whole different version of her than me. Maybe it's about getting to learn about her through him, and vice versa. Teaching him back. It's all either of us has anymore.

We decide to tackle the first thing on our list—going to the hibachi grill that very night. Makoto's is the kind of place that bustles, warm and full of the kind of noise that you associate with family. Laughter and claps and the sharp *snick* of knives and spatulas against the grills as the chefs cook the food for the customers.

Curtis and I take a table around one of the grills with a few other people—a smiling older couple who greet him by name, and a family with a little girl who's in awe over the onion tower the chef builds for her on the grill.

"Curtis! Long time no see," says the older man.

"We've missed you," adds the woman, smiling at me. "This must be your daughter. I'm Myra. This is Dan."

"This is Coley," Curtis says.

"It's so nice to meet you," Dan says.

"You too," I say.

"Myra owns the auto shop in town," Curtis says. "My old car would not be running still without her."

A lady mechanic? "That's so cool," I tell her.

"You ever want to learn how to change your own oil, you come to me," Myra says. "Something every car owner should know."

"Right now, I'm just a bike owner."

"Good for you," Dan says. "Builds strong lungs, biking all over."

"We'll have to get you your license before winter," Curtis says casually, like it doesn't make my heart leap, the idea of that kind of freedom. "I'll teach you to drive, if you want."

"Speed demon like you?" Dan snorts. "She'd be better off taking real lessons."

"Shush," Myra scolds as I grin.

"Your dad and I used to ride motorcycles together," Dan tells me. "Definitely get real lessons."

"I'd love to learn how to ride," I say.

"No way," Curtis says firmly.

"No fair," I shoot back, but I keep it light.

"Maybe when you're eighteen," he says. "But only if you wear the right gear."

We put in our orders, and they fall into a familiar chatter with each other, yet it doesn't feel lonely or like I'm on the outside—probably because they keep asking me questions.

Hibachi grills like Makoto's are so Americanized and the food will never come close to what Mom used to cook for me when she was having a good day, but it's really yummy and a welcome reminder of her. By the time we get up to go, I'm pleasantly full and I've got enough for lunch tomorrow in my takeout bag. I'm starting to see why Curtis has a weekly tradition with this place. It makes us feel closer to my mom. As we walk out, we pass a sign I hadn't noticed going into the restaurant: HELP WANTED.

"We'll see you two next week?" Myra asks as we walk out to the parking lot.

"We'll be here," Curtis says.

"Sounds fun," I add. "It was really nice meeting you."

"Wonderful meeting you, Coley," Myra says. "Bye!"

They wave before heading to their old Chevy.

"They're really nice," I say to Curtis as we walk toward his car.

"I'm glad you liked them. We've been friends for a long time."

"So you're not the kind of guy who fixes his own car," I say.

He laughs. "My talents have always been more geared toward things like music and jewelry. Your mom used to joke that she was handier than me. But it was more of a truth than a joke."

"We once blew out a tire on the Grapevine, and she changed it herself, right there on the nonexistent shoulder," I say, smiling at the memory, even though at the time, I'd been kind of scared. "There were cars and semis whizzing by a foot away. Mom's in this white sundress and floppy hat, and by the time she was done, she didn't have one speck of dirt or oil on her."

"Of course she didn't." He smiles, so fond and sharp with memories, and it doesn't hurt this time that I recognize my smile in his face. It doesn't hurt that he's smiling thinking of her. It aches to talk and think about her. But things that are healing ache just as hard as open wounds.

"So we did one of my things on the list," he says as we come to a stop in front of his car. "You get to choose the next one."

He's right. We agreed to alternate. I think about the things

I put on the list and then look over my shoulder, where the HELP WANTED sign is taped to the window. One of the things I'd added to the list was *Get a job*.

"I'll be right back," I say.

I dash across the parking lot and duck back inside the restaurant. The hostess looks up from her stand. "Hi," she says. "Did you forget something?"

"I saw the help-wanted sign as we left. I was wondering if I could get an application?"

"Oh, cool, of course," she says, pulling one out of the drawer and handing it to me. "Our manager is here tomorrow, if you want to drop it off while he's here."

"Great. Thank you."

"You're welcome. Good luck."

Curtis's waiting for me in the car when I get back.

"What was that about?" he asks.

I show him the application. "Maybe if I get hired, there's an employee discount."

"Now that would be useful."

"Okay, what do you think about this?" I hold out my arms, knowing it's absolutely ridiculous that I'm asking Curtis of all people to give me fashion advice. But I've never gone to a job interview before, and I'm not sure if the blue button-up shirt and jeans are okay. I made sure to button it up so you can't see the lace of my camisole out the top, just along the bottom.

"I think you look great," Curtis says.

"Do I look like I'd be a good hostess?"

"Very reliable," he says. "I do have something for you, though."

"Yeah?" I walk into the living room and sit down next to him. He hands me a long velvet box. I flip it open, and for a moment I just stare down at it.

"I noticed you like those tattoo chokers," he says in the wake of my silence. "So I thought you might like this."

"You made this." My fingers touch the finely braided silver wire of the choker, perfect ovals of tiger's-eye studding the intricate wirework.

"Everyone needs a good-luck charm," he says. "You know, people associate stones with a bunch of different things. In some spiritual traditions, tiger's-eye is a protective stone. In others, it's said to bring clarity to the wearer."

"Do you believe in that stuff?"

"I don't know," he says. "My philosophy has always been to just be open and listen about stuff like that. I figure everything in the world is made up of some kind of energy. Different energy gives people different vibes."

"Vibes?" I can't stop the smile on my face. "You sound like a hippie."

"I think some beliefs are what you make of them," Curtis says. "So if you think the tiger's-eye will give you clarity, maybe it will."

I lift the choker out of the box, my thumb pressing into the center of one of the stones. I need all the clarity I can get. But my heart is what needs protection. Sonya will be home in a few days. School will start at the end of August. I won't be able to avoid her or her friends once that happens.

I need to be ready. Distracted. That's why I want this job so much. It's the perfect distraction. If I can work and go to school, I'll be so busy that I'll never have to think about her unless I run into her. And I'll find a way to avoid that, too.

I'll find a way to uproot her from my heart, bit by bit.

I have to.

"Do you like it?" Curtis asks me.

I smile and I tell him the truth: "I love it."

THIRTY-SEVEN

To: RollieColey87@aol.com
From: SonyatSunrisex00x@aol.com
Subject: [UNSENT EMAIL] no subject

I want to hate you, you know. Gaia snuck in vodka and I had some, and now I'm here, in this shitty computer lab, instead of in my nice bunk with my friends, and it's your fault, Coley. All your fault. I just want to hate you. It'd be so much easier. Maybe you don't care. You said you wouldn't forgive me. And why would you? I'm a fucking mess. Just like Faith said. Messy fucking Sonya. Never knows what way's up. But I did know. I *did.* I knew everything before you. Or I thought I did. I was sure I did. How can you be so wrong about yourself? How can you not know something so— No. You did it. I'm not. I need to hate you. It's not even wanting. I need to. I have to. If I don't . . . Fuck, what do I do if I can't?

—Sonya

THIRTY-EIGHT

"The couple at grill two is waiting for water," Kendrick tells me as I finish up the drinks for grill 4.

"On it," I say, adding two water glasses to my tray and balancing it on my palm. My first few days working at Makoto's, I was afraid of dropping the drinks all the time. But one week in I feel like a pro.

"You're the best," Kendrick calls behind him as he prints out a check.

I move through the restaurant, dropping the drinks off at the grill farthest from the kitchen first, and then delivering the waters. I pick up empty plates as I go, enjoying the sounds of the chefs cooking and that perfect burn of chili-scent that tells me someone ordered a dish extra spicy.

I like the rhythm of it, the restaurant, I mean. Ever since my first day. There's always something to do—and, yeah, most of the time that *something* is cleaning. But sometimes it's watching the food prep in the back or listening to Chef—I don't think he has another name, it's just Chef—talk about his time traveling. That guy's been *everywhere*.

"That six-top should be coming in soon," Jackie tells me as

I come up to the hostess stand to check on her. "How are you holding up?"

"Much better ever since you recommended me these clogs," I say, wiggling my foot at her.

"You need the best you can afford in food service," she says sincerely.

"I never thought about my feet hurting until doing this job," I admit.

"What are you two talking about up here?" Kendrick asks.

"Shoes," Jackie says.

"Always a good subject." Kendrick grins. "Are you staying for family meal tonight, Coley? Chef wanted a head count."

"Family meal?" I ask, confused.

"I forgot, you've been doing the lunch shift," Kendrick says. "At dinner shift Chef serves a staff meal after we close."

"It's really fun," Jackie adds. "You should stay."

"Yeah," I say. "That sounds great."

"Yay!" Jackie claps her hands together.

"Incoming," Kendrick says, and the six-top Jackie mentioned come walking in, and just like that, we're back to work.

At the end of the night, Kendrick and Jackie dim the lanterns that light the restaurant and flick off the neon sign that says OPEN. Ten of us gather around one of the tables where Chef's set out bowls of miso soup and rice and a vegetable curry full of potatoes and carrots.

As ten hungry restaurant workers fall on the food, I suddenly understand why it's called a family meal. It's like having eight brothers and sisters and you're all ravenous and Chef's looking on like some sort of benign grandpa.

"Make sure Coley gets some curry!" Kendrick protests, pushing a bowl toward me.

"Thanks," I say, spooning some over my bowl of rice.

"Gotta look out for my trainee," he says solemnly and then winks like he's in an old movie to make me laugh. Out of all my coworkers, Kendrick is the funniest.

"Is Tye coming tonight?" Jackie asks Kendrick from across the table.

"Yep! He should be here soon."

"Coley, do you like it?" Sam, one of the prep cooks, asks me.

"It's delicious."

"Best thing about night shift," Sam says.

The bells on the front door jangle, and a tall man around Kendrick's age comes strolling in, a box in his arms.

"Tye!" Several people call his name when they see him.

"Hey guys," he says. "Chef, here are your mushrooms." He hands the box over to Chef.

"Perfect," Chef says. "I have your payment in the back when you're ready. Now go eat!"

"Yes, Chef," Tye says, walking over to Kendrick, sitting down in the empty seat next to him, slinging his arm over Kendrick's shoulders. "You miss me?" he asks Kendrick.

"Always," Kendrick answers, his hand coming up to grab Tye's, their fingers interlacing.

I look away, and then back, to make sure I'm seeing what I'm seeing. No one else seems to be even looking at them holding hands. Everyone else is just eating and talking, and Chef's examining the box of mushrooms like Tye's handed him a box of gold.

"I see we have a new face." Tye smiles at me. "You must be Coley."

"This is my boyfriend, Tye," Kendrick says. "He grows the mushrooms for the restaurant."

"It's nice to meet you," I say. "How do you even grow mushrooms?" I ask, wincing as it comes out, because it sounds so silly, but it's better than me staring at their hands, so casual and easy wrapped up in each other. It's just so normal.

Kendrick makes a face. "Don't get him started!" he warns, and Tye nudges his shoulder against his boyfriend, laughing.

"Oh you, shush," Tye says. "So the first thing you need to know about mushroom growing is—"

His words are drowned out by a chorus of "rule number four!" from the rest of the table.

"What's rule number four?" I ask Tye, leaning forward as they keep chanting it.

"Thou Shalt Not Talk Mushroom Growing Anywhere but the Kitchen," Tye says.

"The mushroom talk got that intense, huh?" I ask. "Were people taking sides? I hope no one was rooting for the icky button ones. But I guess some people will always go for the underdog."

Tye's eyes glint with humor. "Kendrick said you were funny."

"I try. Sometimes I succeed."

"Coley is Curtis's daughter," Kendrick adds.

"Really?" Tye smiles. "Your dad's cool. He made us these." He holds out his arm, showing me a simple bracelet with strips of redwood inlaid in the silver band. Kendrick wears a similar one on his left wrist.

"Those are gorgeous," I tell them. "He's really good, isn't he? I never knew he made jewelry until I moved here."

“Someday I’m going to ask him to make us matching rings,” Tye says, with a kind of beautiful promise in his eyes.

Kendrick’s face softens at Tye’s words. “You’re so sentimental.”

“Someone in this relationship has to be,” Tye teases back, and then he steals Kendrick’s bowl of curry and launches into a talk about the fine art of mushroom growing, despite rule number four.

THIRTY-NINE

"Coley, you home?" Curtis calls when he gets home.

"Hey," I call, when I hear the front door open from my bedroom. "I'm getting ready for work."

Curtis peeks his head in my room. "Hey. I missed you this morning. How are you doing?"

I shrug, going for honesty: "It'll be better once I get to work."

Every day that passes means we're closer and closer to Sonya's homecoming. She'll be back from camp any day and I've been so good: I've avoided her LiveJournal and all the spots her friends hang out at. I've focused on my shifts and my friends there and I've gone to family meal every time when I've worked the dinner shift.

It feels good. To work hard and then afterward, to gather and eat and laugh with everyone. To share silly jokes about repeat customers or gossip about the horror-show first date we were front-row to at table 2.

But it also feels tenuous. Like it's a bubble I'm holding in my hands and the slightest pressure will pop it.

I can't let anything pop it. I need it, this feeling. Of being welcome. Of being strong.

"I'm really glad working at Makoto's is going so well," Curtis says, jerking me out of my thoughts. I've been brushing the same piece of my hair for too long. I hastily tuck it behind my ear.

"I love working there," I say. More honesty. At this rate, I'm going to be fully truthful with him. It's weird to imagine, but I guess that's where we're at now. Huh.

"My shift's only four hours. Do you want me to bring home food?" I ask.

"As long as I get to choose the music as we eat."

"Fine," I say, like it's some great imposition. More truth? I've kind of liked the last two albums he's played for me. I know, I was surprised, too.

"I got this for you," he says, pulling out a booklet from his back pocket and handing it to me. It's a driver's manual. "So you can take your test to get your learner's permit."

"Thanks," I say. "I'm not sure I'll be able to save up enough from Makoto's to buy a car, though."

"Let's focus on getting your permit first," he says. "Myra can help us find something safe for you when the time comes."

"Handy to be friends with a mechanic," I say, checking the time on my phone. "Crap. I really gotta go. You want your regular order?"

"With extra edamame. Here's the money for dinner."

I take it from him. "See you later."

It's about twenty minutes by bike to the restaurant, and I go hard for the last mile, so I still make it there ten minutes before my shift starts. I splash water on my face in the break room while Kendrick ties his apron around his waist and tosses me one. I wrap the ties around my waist, adding half a dozen pens to the pocket. Hostessing requires writing just as much stuff down as the servers, and the servers are *always* trying to borrow my pens. By the end of the night, I'll be lucky if I have two pens left.

I apply lip gloss in the mirror, staring at myself.

There's something about restaurant clothes that make me feel grown up. Maybe it's because most of the black clothes I own are winter clothes, so I've been wearing a skirt and V-neck sweater most days. I need to buy some more black clothes. Maybe I should take Brooke up on her employee-discount offer. The thought hits me and I wince, the lip-gloss wand halfway to my lips.

"What's *that* look?" Kendrick asks.

"Just thinking about stuff earlier this summer."

"Oh?"

Fell for the wrong girl. Just say it, Coley. You can say it.

"Yeah, I kind of fell for a girl I shouldn't have."

Kendrick doesn't even blink at my admission, and that thrills me even more than saying it. His casual interest thumping through me is an entirely new experience. "Was it unrequited love?"

"Not really," I say. "More like confusing and messy and . . . wonderful, sometimes."

"And now?"

"She's just . . ." I look up at the break room ceiling, trying to figure it out. "I don't think she's where I'm at," I say finally. "I wish she was. But she won't even admit—" I stop myself.

"You and Tye," I say. "I've watched you. Not in, like, a creepy way," I add hastily, and he chuckles. "But when we clean up from family meal, the way you move around each other. With each other . . . it's like a dance only you two know."

Kendrick smiles gently. "I guess it is like that, when you don't have to hide."

"It's kind of scary," I admit.

"Lots of good things are," he says, and then Jackie comes in, still in her gym clothes, and the workday really begins.

"Do you want a smoothie or something?" Curtis asks as we walk out of the grocery store with our cart.

"I'm good," I say. "I was gonna run in there, though." I point to the tattoo-and-piercing shop in the corner of the shopping center. "I want to get a stud for my cartilage piercing."

"I will get a smoothie and you get your jewelry. Meet back at the car in ten?"

"I'll be there," I say.

I walk to the tattoo shop and head inside. There's sample artwork all over the walls and a big jewelry counter in the back.

"Be with you in a sec," a voice calls. So I go over to the jewelry case to look. Lots of hoops and barbells that look like they're designed for tongue piercings. It flits across my mind for a second—what it would be like to kiss a girl with one—and then I shake it out of my head. My eyes snag on a little turquoise stone in the corner of the case.

"What can I do for you?"

I straighten at the words and then my stomach twists, because Blake's standing there, her bleach-blond hair in space-buns on either side of her head.

"Coley," she says, eyes widening in surprise.

"Um. Hi." Shit. I should just turn around and leave, right? But I take a deep breath instead. Small fucking towns are the *worst.* This is what it's going to be like—running into Blake, into Trenton and Alex and Brooke and SJ.

Running into Sonya.

I just have to learn how to deal.

"Hi," Blake says.

We stare at each other, and at first, I think it's my imagination, but it's not: there's a dull flush rising in her cheeks.

"I was gonna ask to look at that turquoise stud in the corner," I say, pointing.

"Cool." She grabs it out of the case and places it in front of me.

"So," she says.

I don't say anything, I just pick up the earring's case and check the price on the bottom.

"I'll take it," I say.

"Great." She grabs it and goes over to the cash register.

"Did you ditch the 7-Eleven job?" I ask, handing her the cash.

She nods. "This is better." She gives me my change.

"This is too much," I say, counting it.

"I gave you my employee discount," she says casually.

I'm so taken aback I just blink at her. "Thank you?"

She nods again. Sagely this time, like she's gained some sort of wisdom. How stoned is she?

"I've got someone waiting, so I gotta go," I say. "Bye."

I'm almost to the door when she calls out.

"I was kinda shitty, wasn't I?"

I don't even know what the hell to say to that, because *duh.*

"I can be like that," she continues, and the way she says it, it's almost like an apology.

"I'm sorry, too," I say. "I was . . . I was going through some shit."

"Looks like you still are," she says, still a little too observant to make me comfortable. She smiles as I shift from foot to foot. "You're still too fucking sweet about the world, Coley-Bear."

I don't bother to tell her to not call me that. She'd probably laugh.

"My dad's waiting for me," I say. "I should go. Bye."

"See you around."

FORTY

"We've got a birthday at grill three," Jackie tells me as she comes back to get drinks for her table. "I'm going to get everyone together. Can you help Kendrick in the kitchen plating the pineapple tower? He'll show you how."

"Yep."

The back kitchen is mainly prep, but it's still hotter than the rest of the restaurant, and a different kind of loud, as the kitchen staff move and work around each other.

"Behind you," I call, moving through the narrow aisle between the fridges and the prep counter. Kendrick's at the end, slicing a pineapple for a special birthday tower of fruit.

"You ready to sing?" he asks.

"Oh no, not that," I groan.

"You haven't had a birthday yet?" He grins as he begins to arrange the pineapple spears on the plate.

"Not yet. But they taught me the song on my first day before I got handed over to you to train."

"I won't ask you to beat the drum this time. That takes time and skill."

"I have no rhythm," I warn him. I start to help arrange the pineapple slices on the platter once he shows me how.

"That's okay. You'll be drowned out by the rest of us."

"Do *any* of us have rhythm?"

"It'll be okay," he assures me with a grin. We finish creating the pineapple tower just as Jackie peeks her head into the kitchen. "Is that pineapple tower ready? I've got everyone ready up here. It's a little girl, so the chefs are going to give her a show."

"All ready," I say. Kendrick picks up the platter carefully, and I follow behind him. The entire front-house staff is assembled outside the kitchen. Luckily no one hands me a drum, but I see Cameron, one of the servers, holding one. He begins to beat it as the group of us walk toward the customers sitting at grill 3. There's a bunch of gift bags clustered at sneakered feet, and the bottom drops out of my stomach as my eyes fly up to see Sonya sitting there next to Emma and the rest of her family.

Kendrick places the platter down in front of Emma, whose eyes are as wide as saucers at the tower of fruit and the sparkler candle that's piercing the top piece.

Sonya glances at the group of us and then her eyes *jerk* back toward mine, a double take for the ages that should make me triumphant but just makes me feel like someone's grabbed my guts and twisted.

She cut her hair; it brushes her shoulders now, instead of hanging below them. When? Why? Did she take scissors to it in a bathroom, angry and trying to purge what we had from her, like I did? Has she felt even a *fraction* of what I've been feeling, all these weeks away from her?

Everyone around me begins clapping their hands to the

rhythm of the drum. I can barely hear them. All I can see is her. But I follow along with Kendrick when he nudges me as the chefs sing to Emma.

Emma cheers and blows out her candle at the urging of her parents. Sonya hugs her sister, but she's still staring at me.

I have to get out of here. I can't exactly flee the restaurant, but I can stay busy.

"I'm going to check the reservations," I tell Jackie as we disperse.

"Great," she says. "Can you wipe down the menus while you're up there?"

"Absolutely," I say, grateful to have an excuse to stay away from the grills as much as possible.

The hostess stand is the most beautiful thing I've ever seen—a reprieve. A breather. I need a second. Just one second to get it together.

My fingers curl around the wood stand, my heart thumping in my throat. *This was inevitable,* I remind myself. *It's happened. It's over.*

"Coley? Hey."

But it's not. Fuck. Of *course* it's not. Of course she followed me.

I stare at the phone, praying for it to ring, but it doesn't save me. So I grab a pen and focus on the reservation book in front of me.

"Hey," I say, glancing up for a second to shoot her a quick smile before going back to writing a name in the book. I'll cross it out later. "Did you need something? More water for the table?"

"What are you doing here?" Sonya asks.

"I'm working?"

"Since when?"

"Like a month or so."

"Your hair," she says, gesturing to her shoulders. "You cut it."

"Oh yeah, ages ago."

Kendrick comes over, a stack of menus in his hands. "Can you take these for me?"

"Of course." I grab them.

"You sticking around for family meal?" he asks.

"Yeah," I say, acutely aware that Sonya's watching us.

"Sorry," I tell Sonya, as I set the menus on the stand and begin to sort them so they're all facing the right way. "Fridays are always busy. Tell Emma happy birthday for me." I smile at her, small but not trembling, even though I feel like it. My legs shake behind the hostess stand. If she reaches out and touches me, it'll be over. She'll know it's not as solid as it looks, the strength I'm showing. But it's not fake, either, and that makes me feel stronger.

A frown twitches across her face at my dismissal. "We should catch up," she insists.

"I've got work," I say.

"What about after?"

That familiar pout plays across her lips, and for a second, I go down the rabbit hole, remembering how they fit against mine.

"Do you really think we have anything to talk about?"

"C'mon, Coley. Don't be like that."

Prickles spread down the back of my neck. No. She doesn't want me to be *like that.* Because what I'm being is honest. And she can't deal.

"Fine," I say. "I'm off at eleven."

"I'll see you then. It'll be great!"

She goes back to her parents and Emma, and I watch her for a second, wondering if she'll ever really get *great*. Then the phone rings and I get back to work, trying to ignore the clock ticking toward eleven.

She's waiting for me as the staff trickles out into the parking lot after family dinner. She leans against the car her mom lets her borrow sometimes, watching me. It's about ten minutes before Curtis picks me up. He doesn't like me biking home at night.

"You can go home," I tell Kendrick, who usually stays with me until Curtis comes. "My . . ." I pause, because what is she? We're not friends. Were we ever that? No. It was always something more. Something she didn't want to name and ran from. Something that changed me and pushed me forward in the end, instead of backward like I'd thought. I guess for that I can be grateful. Someday, at least. When the hurt fades.

If the hurt fades.

"She and I need to talk," I say to Kendrick, and he nods like he understands, because I guess he does.

"You're amazing," Kendrick says quietly. "Don't forget that, okay?"

"Yeah, yeah," I say, waving as he heads out. Only then do I go over to her.

"Hey," she says brightly.

"Hi."

She tucks her hair behind her ears nervously. "I like your hair."

"You said that before."

Her brown eyes sweep down, staring at my feet and then back up again. "Yeah, I guess I did."

Silence. I can't stand it.

"So what's up?" *Just get this over with, Coley.*

"It's really good to see you," she says earnestly.

"Okay." I breathe it in, trying not to let it affect me, the way her eyes rove over me like she's been hungry this whole time.

"Can I—can we hug?" Her voice breaks on the last word, and that fucking *breaks* me. I hate that I cave so easy. I'm stepping forward just like she is, and then there we are.

Her arms wrapped around me, the curve of her waist, long lines of muscle under my hands—I dreamed about this each night. I hate to admit that. But she felt like home before and she still does.

When we pull apart, she doesn't pull back. Instead, her cheek slides against mine, achingly slow, and her hands cup the back of my neck as our foreheads rest together. She smells like peonies, that scent so familiar and so missed and so dreaded all at once. In the parking-lot light, her skin glows. My fingers want to chase the light up her arms, along her collarbones, across the tight stretch of her jeans. My hands clench in the fabric of her shirt when she whispers in the tiny space between us: "I missed you. So much."

It breaks the spell. I don't know why, maybe because it's exactly how I felt this whole time. It's a reminder of the hole she left in me.

I gently step away from her. Her fingers trail down my shoulders and then away, her eyes wide at the rejection.

"Why are you telling me this?" I ask her.

"We haven't talked—"

"Whose fault is that?"

Her mouth snaps shut.

"You're the one who asked to talk now," I tell her, trying to be gentle because . . . fuck, because I have to. Because you have to be gentle with the people you . . .

I thought this would be easier. But I guess it's going to take practice to not fall right back into her.

"So talk," I say, hating the little spark of hope inside me that this time, maybe, she won't dance around it.

"I like you," she tells me and it's like kick-starting my wounded heart. "It scares me how much I like you," she continues. "And I don't know what it means," she says, kind of swaying back and forth. "I don't know if it means I'm like—" She stops, running her hand through her hair, that casual heart-stopping flick, jerky and nervous for once. "Maybe it's just you? That's what I've been thinking. That you're, like, an exception. I'm just attracted to you. I mean, I know you're wrong, but this feels right—"

"Wait, what?" I interrupt, her words crashing like a bulldozer into my building hope-high. "You think I'm *wrong*?"

She stiffens, her shoulders squaring defensively. "Well, you know what I mean."

"No, actually, I don't," I say. "Why don't you explain it to me, Sonya?"

Sonya flinches, the anger under my words hissing through my teeth.

"You're fucked up, if you think like that," I tell her, brushing past her. I don't care if Curtis's not here yet. I'll head toward the road I know he's coming down.

"There's nothing about me that's wrong," I say as she follows me.

"I didn't— Wait—"

She grabs my arm. I freeze, and then we're both standing there, staring where her fingers encircle my wrist like it's the strongest tether in the world.

But I guess love is the strongest tether, isn't it?

"I'm sorry," Sonya says. "I didn't mean—" She licks her lips, desperation crawling into her voice and eyes. It makes my stomach swoop in the worst way. She's hurting. She's *denying*. She's going to fucking hate herself if she keeps doing this, but I can't make her love herself. All I can do is love myself and hope she can get there someday.

"I don't know what to do," she says, tears gathering in her eyes. "You changed my entire world. I never thought . . . I wasn't . . . I wasn't *like* this before you! You've confused me more than anyone I've ever met."

"Do you think I wasn't confused?" I ask her. "Do you think I wasn't *changed*?" I shake free of her grip, and she lets out a shaky sob.

"I have feelings, too," I say, hating how my voice rises. "You changed me. And you hurt me. You *betrayed* me. I shared something about my life and my mom and my grief with you, and you treated it like gossip for your friends!"

"I'm sorry," she sobs. "I'm so sorry about that. You have no idea. Coley, I care about you so much—"

"You don't care about me," I say. "If you did, you'd let me move on instead of trying to waltz back into my life like nothing's happened so you can get the attention you want!"

"It's not about me getting attention," she insists. "But the idea of you with someone else— Fuck, Coley, it *kills* me."

"Are you fucking kidding me? *You* left me!"

"I want you to be happy," she insists. She licks her lips nervously. "Even if I can't be the reason, I want you to be happy."

"Then leave me alone," I say firmly, wishing that I felt as sure as I sound.

"But I want to be the reason you're happy!"

I'm silent, waiting.

"I can't sleep at night," Sonya says. "I was so distracted at camp that my dance teachers were calling me out all the time. All I could do, sitting in my cabin or at class or *anywhere* was think about you. I couldn't get away from it and I tried. I tried so hard. But I can't do it, Coley. All I want is you."

"Stop," I say shakily, because it's all the right words but so, so late. "Why are you saying this?"

"Because I want to be with you," she says.

"Then *be* with me!" I shout, unable to stop myself.

"I can't!"

Two words. Crushing me. But it's enough to wrench the truth out.

"Then leave me alone!"

"I can't!" she says again, and it breaks my fucking heart as she starts crying so hard that she has to lean against her car's hood. I want to reach for her, I want to be a comfort.

But God, what will that make me if reaching for her just hurts me?

"It's not just me," she says through her tears. "My friends. My family. What if my mom doesn't let me see Emma anymore? What if they hate me?"

I hate how much her friends' opinions matter to her, but I can't blame her for her worry about her family. She knows them better than I do. And I know how much she loves Emma.

"This is just an endless circle," I tell her. "We get close. You freak out. You reject me. Then you miss me and come back. You want me, but you can't want me. I'm wrong, but we're right. None of this is making anything better. It just *hurts*."

"I don't want to hurt you," she says. "I don't want . . . oh God, I don't want to hurt anymore."

I wish I could be the person to make sure she doesn't hurt anymore. But I can't be, because she won't let me.

"Please don't give up on me," Sonya begs, her hands coming to grab mine.

I squeeze them back, wishing I could give her what she wants. But I'm not doing this anymore. Not if it hurts me while I do it. "I can't wait on anyone to live my life anymore," I say softly. "I can't do that to myself. I'm not going to waste my life being treated like shit. I'm not going to chase someone who's too scared to love me back."

Her fingers twist in mine like she knows I'm about to let go. Is this it? The last time we touch? I need to remember all of it.

"It's not that I'm scared to love you," she confesses. "It just scares me so much that I *do*."

If my heart weren't already broken, those are the words that would do it.

"I don't want to lose you," she says as I begin to pull away, my fingers trailing against her palm, reluctant to let go.

"Then don't," I say softly as the tips of our fingers skate across each other's, finally parting, bittersweet and sorrowful.

"I should go."

She straightens, clutching her arms to her body like she needs the comfort. "Wait, when will I see you again?"

"At school, I guess," I say.

"That's forever from now. There's nowhere else?" she asks, panicky.

I'm quiet, because I don't know. I don't know if I'm capable. If I'm able. If she is.

I tuck a strand of hair behind her ear, my finger tracing the shell of it until she shivers.

Last time, I tell myself as I lean forward.

Last time I press my lips to her forehead, my hands cradling her head.

Last time I walk away from her.

"Coley?"

I turn.

Last time she looks at me like this, like I'm the world and the moon and the entire universe she's losing.

"One day, I'll be as brave as you," she tells me.

Last time she shatters me with her words.

FORTY-ONE

On my day off from the restaurant, I go to the lake. It's not because I expect to see her there; I go early, hoping I beat her and her friends, if they do have plans to swim and tan on the shore.

I go because water isn't just about washing yourself clean. I don't need to cleanse myself of her. That would be thinking like her. Like the love we hold is dirty or wrong. I hated how she tripped into admitting that, not understanding she'd created a trap for herself. Not seeing she was hurting herself more than she was hurting me.

I go because water is about rebirth.

My toes slide in. It's morning chilly. No fog on the water, but almost mystical all the same, the trees and fluffy clouds reflecting across the lake. Water laps at my ankles, then my calves, my knees. I hesitate, my fingers swishing ripples in the ever-moving surface.

Am I brave enough for this?

To love myself?

To let her go and hope someday she finds her truth?

I take a deep breath.

There's only one way to find out.

I dive in.

I'm unlocking my bike from the rack in the far corner of the parking lot when I hear the sputter of an engine. It's like déjà vu, that minivan pulling up near the path toward the lake. Trenton and Alex pile out, followed by the girls. I look away as Sonya climbs out. Water drips down my back from my hair. I wind my chain around my bike. They go down the path, but she looks back and our eyes meet.

No hiding. No looking away.

Just her and me and what exists between us, burning bright. She smiles and I smile back, bittersweet.

Then I turn and I go. I don't look back. I can't bear to know if she's watching me go.

I'm out of the parking lot, across the street, and down it a good way when I hear the slap of flip-flops behind me.

"Coley, hey!"

I turn around to see SJ crossing the parking lot toward me.

"Hey. What's up?"

"I wanted to invite you to a party at my place tonight."

"SJ, you don't have to do that," I tell her.

"But I want to," she insists.

I can't help but look skeptical.

She takes a deep breath. "Look, I heard that it got around, your mom's—" She stops. "I'm sorry. Sonya told me about your mom because she was worried she hadn't handled it right. She was looking for my advice. Brooke overheard us. That's how it got blabbed all over. I want you to know that I wouldn't talk about it like it's gossip. The reason Sonya asked *me* was because I—" She licks her lips, looking down at her bejeweled flip-flops. "Because I've experienced something similar in my family."

My heart thumps as her voice lowers and slows, like she's picking each word carefully. This means something to her.

"My sister was really depressed a few years ago and she tried to end her life. My parents were able to get her the help she needed, and she has a diagnosis now and meds and a great therapist and is doing a lot better. But I'm so sorry about your mom and I'm so sorry about how this went down with everyone. If someone had gossiped about my sister, I'd want to tear their eyes out. I understand if you hate me. But I wanted you to know that Sonya wasn't trying to gossip. She was trying to understand how to help you best, and she came to me to make sure she wasn't fucking up. It's not an excuse—we should've closed the door so no one could've overheard us. But she—" SJ bites her lip. "Sonya's been home a week and she just seems so sad. Not like herself. I asked her about it, and she told me how she fucked up her friendship with you. So I thought, maybe if I explained—"

"I appreciate it," I interrupt her gently, trying to absorb it. Is it the truth? It has to be. SJ would have to be some kind of monster to lie about something like that.

"I live in the house stuck in the seventies on Luna Street," SJ says. "Come or don't. Totally up to you."

"We'll see."

"I hope I see you there. I know it'd make Sonya happy."

"And that's what you want?" I ask, curious despite myself. I wonder if she suspects. If she's read between the lines and looks and longing. Does she care? Does she approve? It doesn't matter to me, but I know it does to Sonya.

"She's my best friend," SJ says. "I love her. And you're the kind of girl who watches people's backs. That's a good person to have around."

"I'm glad she has you," is all I say. "Bye, SJ." I get on my bike and pedal away.

I'm not even home before I've decided: I'm going to go to the party. I want to prove to myself that I can do this. That I can handle being near her and not aching with each step and breath around her.

My way out of this is clear. But all paths should be tested.

All choices have what-ifs.

FORTY-TWO

When I get to SJ's street that afternoon, I'm already having to talk myself into it.

Maybe this isn't the greatest idea, but I'm on the street. I can see the '70s-looking house that has to be hers at the end of it, so I bike over and leave my bike leaning against the fountain in her driveway. Who the hell has a *fountain* in their driveway?

I can hear the thump of bass and the hum of voices all the way out here.

You can just make an appearance, I tell myself as I walk up the driveway. *See if you can talk to her. Then you can get out of here.*

I ring the doorbell and the door jerks open way too fast. I've got no time to prepare. And there she is. It's like light floods into Sonya's eyes that were only darkness before. "You came," she says as she breathes out. She leaps forward, going for a hug and then stopping, her arms half-outstretched for an awkward beat before she snatches them back.

"Yeah. Um. Thanks for inviting me."

"Everyone's in the living room," she tells me as I step inside.

It's a sweaty summer shit show of bodies and beer as we move toward the living room.

"Do you need a drink?" she asks.

I shake my head. "Not today."

She smiles. "I'm not really in the mood, either. Do you want to sit?"

I nod, sitting down next to her on the love seat with my knee up on the cushions, keeping as much space as I can between us. This isn't the right place to talk to her. We need to be somewhere quieter. The living room is full of people.

The music switches from thumping and fast to slow and languid, and the people who are dancing shuffle to change with it. Sonya giggles, nodding to the dancing couple closest to us.

"They've got nothing on us," she says.

I laugh. I can't help it. But it dies quick, because his voice booms out across the room, shattering the moment.

"Sonya! Babe, come on!"

Her face clouds instantly at Trenton's almost-order as he comes over to us, sitting down on the arm of the love seat, looming over her. He strokes his hand across her shoulder and she shakes him off.

"Come on," he says again, grabbing her hand and pulling her up against him.

"Trenton," she scolds. "You're drunk."

"You should be, too! C'mon. There's tequila." He drags her away as she protests.

I get up off the love seat, too. I refuse to let my heart sink as this plays out *again*. I'm not going to be part of this endless circle of shittiness. I tried to talk to her. It didn't work. That means it's time to go.

I slip out of the living room and into the hall, which is almost as crowded. I think about finding SJ and thanking her before I leave, but I decide it doesn't matter much. I'm out the front door and almost safe when:

"Hey!" someone calls behind me. I almost ignore it, and then: "Coley!"

I turn on the steps to see Alex closing the front door behind him and jogging down them to meet me. I wince as I remember the humiliating display in his driveway, and my cheeks turn red as I realize I know a lot more about Alex than he probably realizes.

"Hey," I say. "I was actually about to head out."

"So soon?"

I shrug, glancing at the ground. "Just not really into it, you know."

"I do," he says. "I just wanted—" He stops. "I know it's been like a month, but you looked really freaked that day Blake broke in to my place. I wanted to call you after, make sure you were okay, but I didn't have your number. I know things got intense—"

"That's an understatement," I say. "You came at me with a bat."

"I didn't know it was you," he says. "And Blake . . . she's gonna steal from the wrong person one of these days. And I don't want her to get hurt. She's got some stuff to figure out."

"Me too," I admit.

"Just . . . no more aiding and abetting, okay?"

"Never," I promise. "I'll see you at school?"

"Oh yeah, us non–silver spooners have to stick together," he says with a smile before ducking back into the house.

I make the mistake of looking to my right, toward the pool.

Sonya's sitting there, all alone, her feet dangling in the water. I should just go. But the opportunity I wanted is right there in front of me.

So I find myself walking back, through the house, through the hall and living room, pushing past people, until I get to the sliding doors that lead to the pool.

The music blasts as I step outside and then muffles as I close the door. She doesn't look over at me as I come to sit next to her, but she leans into me as soon as I do. Like she knew from the very first step it was me.

Her head falls into the crook of my shoulder, puzzle pieces fitting together, and I breathe the weight of her in, wishing it would never leave me.

"I'm so tired of living like this," she says softly. "Everything hurts when all I want to do is be with you. And all I do is run."

"You could stop."

The weight of her leaves me. My head tilts, meeting her gaze.

"You could stop," I say again. "You could be with me."

She is so close. A long line of heat against my thigh and arm, my hand not pressing into the concrete, aching to reach out.

"I could," she says and there's no question in her voice. "I want to," she whispers as she leans forward.

My eyes drift shut, anticipation buzzing through me. One second more and—

—Sonya screams my name. I blink, the back of my skull aching, and I blink again, my stunned brain trying to put it together—why does the back of my head hurt?

His fingers curl harder into my hair as Trenton jerks me up off the concrete only to throw me back as he yells.

Sweat trickles down my forehead as he lets me go, rounding on Sonya. "How could you do this to me?" he screams in Sonya's face. "With *her*? Is this some sort of sick joke?"

I touch the back of my head and my fingers are all stained with red. Huh. Not sweat. Shit.

Black spots dance along my vision, and for a second I think they're going to blot out everything. It'll just all go dark and it won't hurt anymore because *fuck* my head hurts.

But he's yelling, and my mind latches on to his words instead of slipping into the dark.

"Look at me! Don't look at her!" His fingers dig into her jaw and violently jerk her head toward his. She cries out in pain.

The sound is like a sharp hook in my belly. Everything goes red. And I'm up. Up and flying toward him, fists curled and ready. I've never punched anyone before, but it doesn't matter. I have love and rage on my side, and if he touches her again I'm going to kill him.

Three blows and he's down on the ground, but I don't stop. I pin him to the ground with my knees and I keep going. My knuckles might break, but it'll be worth it. So fucking worth it.

Someone grabs me from behind, pulling me back, lifting me off my feet, and I shriek, ready to fight back, until I see it's Alex. A crowd of people are hanging there on the porch, watching us.

"Coley!" Alex says, his eyes wide. "Your hands! You're bleeding."

"What the fuck?" Brooke comes running to Trenton, bending down to dab at his bleeding nose. "Oh my God! You psycho!"

"He hit her first," Sonya says softly, almost dazedly. "He

grabbed her. He just grabbed . . ." She sways, her eyes filling with tears.

"He hit her!?" SJ asks, her voice rising shrilly. "What the hell are you doing, hitting girls, Trenton?!" She whirls toward me, her eyes widening in concern. "Oh my God, Coley, your face."

"She attacked me!" Trenton moans. "I think that fucking bitch broke my nose!"

"You deserved it," I tell him. "You put your hands on Sonya again, and I'll do worse."

"What is she talking about?" SJ asks, her voice reaching glass-breaking levels. "Sonya, did he hurt you, too?!"

"You need to get out of here," Alex says to Trenton, his voice like ice. "This shit is not acceptable."

"Bro code, dude!" Trenton moans through the blood.

"*Fuck* that," Alex snarls.

"Oh my God, why are you believing these psychos?" Brooke whines, clutching Trenton protectively. "Trenton needs a doctor!"

I step away from their shouting, my face and hands throbbing as the adrenaline fades. The skin on one of my knuckles is split, and two more are turning purple. I keep backing up as Sonya's friends continue to square off, my feet hitting the driveway before anyone notices I'm gone.

I've done all I can. It's up to her now.

I pick up my bike, walking it into the street. I wince at how curling my hands around the handlebars hurts. When I lick my lips, all I taste is copper. I don't have a mirror, but I'm pretty sure Curtis's going to have a shit-fit when I get home and he sees me.

The house next door has its sprinklers on and I bend down, washing the blood from my knuckles, ignoring the sting of the spray against the wounds.

Battle scars. We all have them. These I'll wear proudly. A reminder.

I love her enough to fight for her. To protect her. To be her shelter, if she wants it.

I pick up my bike, about to get on it.

"Wait!"

Her voice breaks through, a spear to my heart. One that, once thrown, will always hit its target.

She's barefoot, running toward me, hair flying and tear-streaked. She pelts toward me at a sprint, breathless like she's afraid I'll be the one to run away this time.

But I don't.

I run toward her.

We collide, nearly tumbling into the wet grass. Her body against mine, her hands in my hair, her lips pressing into mine, copper tang mixing with strawberry gloss and the taste of both of our tears.

It's not like fireworks this time. It's like relief. My heart had been missing hers, and now, here she is, all of her, joyous in my arms. No mask. No pretense. No games.

Just *her*.

She only pulls away to gather me closer, her chin hooking gently over my shoulder as she holds me as tight as I hold her.

"I'll stop," she says fiercely in my ear. "I'll stop running. I want to be with you. I love you, Coley."

The huff of breath I let out against her neck makes her smile. I can feel it pressed against my hair, even if I can't see it.

"I love you, too," I whisper. "So much."

I kiss her this time, cradling her face gently, my thumb smoothing over the place Trenton grabbed her like I can erase the memory of it. Her fingers map my wounds, gentle against my hands and face, tucking my hair behind my ears before she runs her hands whisper-light through it.

The sprinklers turn off suddenly, startling us into pulling apart, just enough for our foreheads to press.

"Do you have to go?" she asks.

I run my hands up and down her arms. I don't want to. "We can't exactly keep making out here in the middle of the yard," I point out.

She sighs. "You promise you'll message me when you get home?" she asks. "You've got my screen name memorized at this point, right?"

"Right," I say, rolling my eyes as she beams.

"Okay, then I'll go," she says. "SJ will come looking for me in a second if I don't, anyway."

"She's a good friend," I say. "Are you going to be okay without me?"

She nods. "Brooke left with Trenton. It's just SJ and Alex now."

"It's going to be okay," I tell her.

"I know." She smiles, brilliant, beautiful. Fuck, I love her. "I have you."

I kiss her one more time. A sweet, simple kiss that we've never shared before. The kind of kiss you get to have when it's not sad or worried or weighted by anything bad. The kind of kiss that says *hi* and *I love you* and *I missed you* and *I'll always be next to you.*

I get on my bike, looking over my shoulder one more time at her. She's standing there, watching me like I'm a portrait in a museum—something priceless and rare to behold.

"You better not break your promise about messaging me," she warns. "I know where you live. I'll hunt you down."

Fuck, I love this wild, silly, and sometimes fearful girl.

"I'm counting on it," I say.

Her laughter is all I hear as I ride away.

ACKNOWLEDGMENTS

It never rains in Los Angeles but when it does it's pandemonium. Angelenos are running outside: "Look, rain!", "Look, look, there is water falling from the sky!" It becomes quite a chaotic scene.

But on this particular rainy day, instead of driving thirteen miles per hour on the freeway through sheets of downpour, I was in a recording studio.

Lily: "What is something you've never shared with anyone before?"

I paused.

Me: "Well I've never actually told any of my writing partners this but, I'm gay."

Lily: "What is something you've always wanted to write about?"

Me: "Being very gay."

That day we wrote a song called "Girls Like Girls."

I flew my friend James Flannigan from the UK to Los Angeles to produce the song in my parents' garage. I couldn't afford to get the song properly mixed, so James mixed the entire song on one of those iHome speakers where you plug in your iPod. They were terrible, but the song still sounded amazing so we went with it. I dreamed of doing a big narrative piece for the video but so many people were finding success having DJs do remixes. I took a chance and spent my last $5,000 on trying to make my dream video come true. We shot the music video for the song with massive help from my friends and Austin Winchell, my co-director. Every single person worked as a favor because they cared about the narrative.

The night before we posted the video I was terrified. Thinking of the countless nights feeling alone, missing hopeful queer content I desperately needed; we needed more representation. So on June 24, 2015, I released the music video on YouTube. I had about 9,000 subscribers. I was an unsigned artist just hoping the video would see the light of day.

Weeks went by: 400K views, 500K views, 1 million views. Then 2 million, then 3 million, then 4 million. I had no idea what was happening or where all of these people were coming from. Who was sharing the video? How did they find it? All I ever wanted was to find a community of belonging, to feel worthy and enough. All of a sudden, there they were, millions of people who reminded me I wasn't alone in my queerness. My fans, you.

Thank you, Owen Thomas and Lily May-Young, for creating a safe space to express my true self and co-writing the song "Girls Like Girls" with me. The start of something I could've never imagined. Thank you, James Flannigan, for producing the song and creating the iconic swell of bass synth that opens our music video. Thank you to my stars: Stefanie Scott, Kelsey Asbille, and Hayden Thompson, for your undeniable performances and bringing this story to life. You captured and healed the hearts of so many. Thank you to Austin Winchell, Chris Saul, and our entire cast and crew for believing in this narrative when it was just an idea. Thank you, Chris Brochu, for letting us film at your home.

Chloe Okuno and Stefanie Scott, thank you for being there from the beginning and helping me create the world of GLG.

To my former editor Sylvan Creekmore, your early support, extreme care, and thoughtfulness took this book to new heights.

To my editor Sara Goodman, thank you for always protecting the integrity and passion that is so deeply rooted in this project for me. I am grateful to you and my entire Wednesday Books/Macmillan team, who have worked so diligently and patiently to launch this book with me.

To my book agent Katelyn Dougherty, you have been my rock navigating this creative process and the ins and outs of the book publishing world. Thank you for championing my story and holding my hand through it all.

Virgilio Tzaj, thank you for introducing me to Cade Nelson, who created the perfect cover art. And Cade, thank you for honoring the world and my vision so flawlessly.

To my music manager Fabienne Leys, to think this all began with us having breakfast back in early 2015, trying to decide between shooting a music video for GLG or paying for an overpriced remix. Thank you for helping me build this world of GLG across so many mediums. To my literary manager Quincie Li, thank you for protecting and echoing my vision. Thank you, Ingrid Shaw, for being there throughout the highs and lows that only Hollywood can bring.

To Ghazi Shami at Empire, who believed in my solo artistry early on, and gave me the resources to create the music video that led to a bigger partnership with Atlantic Records. Thank you, Julie Greenwald and Craig Kallman, for seeing and investing in the vision all these years. Thank you, Brooks Roach, Chelsey Northern, and Andrew George for championing my voice and community so fearlessly.

Marla Vazquez, thank you for always reminding me to create art that feels like my most authentic self. To my band mates Lawrence William IV and Valerie Franco: playing "Girls Like Girls" with you on stage every night on tour continues to be one of the greatest honors of my life. My best friends Monica, Victoria, Arielle, and Gabby—thank you for bringing so much support and laughter into my life. Thank you to every friend, loved one, and colleague from my journey who has listened when times were hard, encouraged me to believe in myself, and said "you can do it."

Thank you, Mom and Dad, for allowing me to dream as far as I could see. Thank you to my brother Thatcher for always supporting me and my sister Alysse for leaving Post-It Notes all over my childhood bedroom: "You are enough. You are worthy." You were there for all of my heartbreaks and aches and I am beyond grateful for you.

To the love of my life, Becca, thank you for showing me what true love is. Love is deep-rooted, it is always patient. It shows up through adversity—it is magical beyond words.

And finally to my fans: the Kiyokians. Thank you for creating a space for me to belong and to truly celebrate myself. You've created a fandom that is so loving and supportive, it has kept me going. Your passion and heart have given me the opportunity to continue the story of "Girls Like Girls"; writing this book has been one of the most fulfilling experiences I've ever had. You make me feel free to be my authentic self and I will always be here to remind you to do the same. I love you so much. We keep climbing.

Some of the hardest years of my adolescence led me to finding strength, courage, a community, and self-worth. Whatever you are navigating in your life, I promise you it gets better.

You are capable.

You are worthy.

You deserve to find all things magic.

Enjoy a sneak peek from
Hayley Kiyoko's next novel

WHERE THERE'S ROOM FOR US

Available Now

My heart,

My life had been storm clouds, and then there was you. I will never forget that first sight of you across the ballroom. You were a spot of blue in a crowd of white and cream dresses, like a rare glimpse of the sky on a cloudy day. In that moment, my nerves at attending my first English ball bloomed into something different.

I could not look away. When you laughed with your sisters, I found myself wanting to cross that grand room to discover the joke. My feet were moving before I could stop them. It was like my body already knew it was yours as much as it was mine.

I had no intention of falling in love when I came to England. I'd done my fair share of chasing after girls, but I'd intended to apply that knowledge to help my brother find a bride. Help him adjust to your world of balls and titles and courting debutantes. . . . That was my aim. The flashy upstart full of opinions would not cause any trouble. I promised him! I was supposed to leave my reputation in America and behave myself. A rare thing, it's true.

We both know how that unfolded. The pull toward you was so strong. Neither of us could deny it, could we?

Some loves are so powerful they change worlds.

When our gazes met across the ballroom, you smiled, blue eyes so full of mischief. You were freer than a bird soaring across the sea. No one could look away from you.

It seemed so simple at the start. Before I knew your family. Before I knew your sisters and thought of them as my own.

But nothing is simple, is it, in love? It teaches you things you didn't even know about yourself. It asks you to choose things you never could've imagined, but cannot bear to lose or bury once they're discovered.

I'm afraid I get philosophical when I am far from you. *So serious*, you always say. *You carry the whole world on your shoulders, Ivy.*

But can you fault me for craving steadiness, when the story that lead to you and me has so many twists and turns?

After all, I wasn't at the ball to catch your eye.

I was there for your sister.

Yours always,
I

ABOUT THE AUTHOR

YK

HAYLEY KIYOKO is an award-winning American singer, director, actress, and author. Described by *Rolling Stone* as being "at the forefront of an unapologetically queer pop movement," Hayley is a passionate advocate for LGBTQIA+ rights. She is a *New York Times* bestselling author for her debut novel *Girls Like Girls,* based on her hit single and music video of the same name, and is set to make her feature film directing debut with Focus Features in 2026.